THE SLEEPLESS STARS

Fatal Insomnia, Book Three

CJ Lyons

THE
SLEEPLESS
STARS
Fatal Insomnia, Book Three

CJ Lyons

EDGY READS

"We are born in debt, owing the world a death."
~*David J. Morris*

Prologue

MY NAME IS Angela Rossi, and this is the story of how I die...

I once was a doctor, a wife, a daughter, a sister, a lover... Now I'm a fugitive, hiding from an enemy targeting everyone I hold dear.

This is a story of good and evil, of temptation and betrayal, of love and obsession.

I'm dying and alone, exiled from the people I love most, and this is the story of how I save the world.

At least I hope so.

Because, if I fail, you may be next...

Chapter 1

A TIGER RAGED inside Devon Price. Claws shredding, teeth gnashing, fighting to tear its way out. He desperately wanted to set it free, to give life to his fury and pain as he paced the makeshift dormitory twenty-one children now occupied, trapped below the streets of the city, their families gathered at their bedsides.

As Devon stalked the crowded space the size of a basketball court—best they could do on such short notice with only a few hours' warning to evacuate and hide twenty-one families from their enemies on the streets above—he tuned out the muffled weeping and anguished, hushed conversations echoing from the concrete walls.

The tunnels stank of damp and disuse. The constant gurgle of water streaming through the pipes overhead combined with the grumble of the air circulators to grate nerves raw, and the bunks and linens were military surplus, not designed for comfort. Yet, no one complained, not about their new accommodations in an underground bunker built to be the last resort in case of a nuclear emergency nor about being driven from their homes aboveground on Christmas Eve.

These families, all residents of the Kingston Tower, had spent their lives at the whim and mercy of gang wars, random and often conflicting government imperatives, and the hopeless grind that came with working as many hours as humanly possible and still being unable to provide for your family. Bunker mentality came naturally.

Devon himself had escaped the Tower a decade ago, fleeing to Philadelphia, where he'd clawed his way up the ranks of the Russian mob—a seemingly impossible feat for a mixed-race gangbanger, but he'd eventually earned their trust if not their respect. Last month he'd left Philly to return home to the daughter he'd never met...only to now be fighting to save her from a disease so rare most doctors had never heard of it.

This was not how his life was meant to be. Devon took care of himself, no one else. He was damn good at it—a trait inherited from his father, Daniel Kingston, even though Daniel had never acknowledged his bastard son.

Devon came to a stop at the bed in the far corner of the room. The one he'd been avoiding—despite wanting nothing more than to throw himself on the small form swaddled in sweat-stained sheets and cradle her in his arms, promise her everything would be all right, that her daddy would fix everything. Empty words from a man emptied of hope.

The overweight Labrador retriever nestled on top of Esme's covers looked up at Devon with mournful eyes.

"It'll be okay, boy," Devon promised the dog, Ozzie. More lies.

He looked down on the girl twitching in her fever-sleep. The nighttime low-level illumination shadowed her face in shades of red. Devon couldn't help himself as he crouched beside her and soothed her hair back from her brow. He caressed her cheekbones—so much like her mother's. Another loved one he'd failed.

This was what love did. Made you weak, exposed, left you

vulnerable in places you didn't even know existed.

"Esme," he whispered her name like a prayer. Her body calmed, her face relaxed. He couldn't help himself, couldn't stop from promising the impossible. "I'm going to get them, the men behind this. I'm going to make them give me the cure. I'm going to save you. I promise. Whatever it takes."

Then he stood, finishing his vow in silence: *And then I'm going to shred the flesh from their bodies as they scream for mercy.*

His fists clenched so tight his palms grew slick. He forced his hands open, surprised to find only sweat and that they weren't already stained with blood.

"Devon?" It was Flynn, beckoning him to the door. He joined her outside in the empty hallway where they could speak in private. She was dressed all in black, down to the formfitting lambskin gloves that covered her scarred hands. Her dark complexion made it difficult to see where the clothing ended and her flesh began.

"Where do we stand?" he asked, the weight of responsibility settling on him. Twenty-one children and their families to protect against an unknown force with massive resources. Fifty-four people total, most of them women, many elderly, caring for their grandchildren, the generation in between lost to drugs, prison, or worse. Their only advantage was this tunnel complex, and he intended to defend it with everything he had.

"I've added extra cameras at all the entrances. You can view the feeds on your phone. I selected a group of parents to monitor them on rotating shifts—they'll alert you if they see anything suspicious."

He nodded his approval. Who better to trust with their security than a girl tasked to circumvent the most sophisticated surveillance systems? Thanks to his father, Daniel Kingston, who had trained Flynn in the ways of corporate espionage.

Funny how every person Daniel touched became corrupted: Flynn was still a teenager, her youth twisted by Daniel as he forged her into the perfect weapon; Daniel's son and Devon's half-brother, Leo, a brilliant chemist turned sadistic serial killer; and Devon himself...

"Esme?" Flynn asked, interrupting his morbid thoughts. She was as devoted to Esme as he was—they would both die for Esme. Or kill. And they both had no doubt that it would come to that.

"Finally fell asleep." If you could call that restless twitching sleep. When Angela Rossi told him about her fatal insomnia, he'd studied the disease, fascinated by the bizarre symptoms leading to a horrific death. He'd hated the thought of a friend suffering that—had even once promised her that he'd help her end things if she wanted.

But he never in a million years dreamed he might be facing the prospect of his own child suffering such a cruel and relentless fate.

A shadow flitted across Flynn's usually neutral expression. "What's next?"

It took Devon a moment to lock away his anger and focus on logistics. "First, we find anything we can on Almanac Care." The corporation that had funded the creation of the artificial fatal insomnia. "What else have they been involved with? Any connection to the children and Angela."

"After losing contact with their lab, they'll come looking for answers."

"Let them." Devon had no remorse for killing the men in the Almanac lab—only that they'd gotten so little information before the building exploded. "When's Louise getting here? We need her to help Angela."

"Louise is on her way. Angela's up at St. Tim's."

He jerked to a stop. Angela, with her strange gift of communicating with people in comas, ripping their memories away, was their best weapon. "I told her not to leave the tunnels."

Flynn shrugged. "What do you want me to do, lock her up?"

"No. We need her cooperation. Keep an eye on her."

She hesitated, looking past him to the room where the children were.

"The best way to protect Esme is to find the men behind Almanac." Men like Dr. Tommaso Lazaretto, who'd pretended to be helping the children and Angela while secretly running a lab producing the very prions that had infected them. Tommaso was dead now, taking his secrets with him to the grave. Or wherever Flynn had disposed of his body. "You finished cleaning up?"

Flynn bared her teeth at that, revealing a hint of her own tiger yearning to be set loose. If she'd had her way, she would have tortured Tommaso for the information they needed—only the doctor had stolen her chance and committed suicide first.

"Time to see what secrets Daniel has been hiding." Their feeble plan to save the children, hell, save the whole damned world. Amazing the things you'd place your faith in when you ran out of options.

"I'll go get Angela."

"Don't let anyone see you."

She didn't bother to acknowledge his words, simply slipped into the shadows and vanished.

Chapter 2

I STOOD IN the bell tower of St. Timothy's Cathedral, watching Cambria City's faithful stream out after the final evening Mass on Christmas Day. I wasn't among them—I'd pretty much given up on religion twenty-two years ago when I was twelve and my dad died.

St. Tim's had thick stone walls and two square towers. The bells were long gone from both—although they were still rung via electronic recordings, calling the faithful to worship. The tower I was in was about fifteen feet square on the interior with a foot-wide, waist-high wall surrounding it. Twenty feet overhead, you could still see the massive iron grid that the bells had been suspended from, but the opening in the floor where their ropes had once dangled was now covered by thick particleboard.

The December-almost-January wind slid across the river to rustle my hair, sending dark curls cascading against my face. If I tried very hard, I could imagine Ryder's fingers doing the same. The thought made me shiver, an addict past due for a fix.

People will break your heart.

With their cruelty, their thoughtlessness, their narrow-minded blindness. When you're an ER doc, you're not surprised by this. But no amount of time can harden you against the most painful heartbreak. The heartbreak that comes from trying your best to save the people you love. And sometimes failing.

A shadow separated itself from the corner where the staircase opened onto the tower. Flynn stepped into the moonlight in that eerie, silent way she had.

"I don't understand why you torture yourself like this." Flynn craned her head out over the bell tower's ledge, appraising the lethal fall to the stone steps below. Her expression was clinical as she added the tower to her catalogue of potential kill sites.

Last night, I'd seen Flynn kill—in self-defense. She'd been efficient and merciless. Rumors were that Daniel Kingston had not only trained her in the arts of industrial espionage— surveillance, hacking, social engineering—but that he'd also turned her into an assassin. After last night, I was beginning to believe those rumors.

"Leaving Ryder was a sound strategic decision," Flynn continued. "He's not on their radar. Yet." She meant the mysterious, unknown people who'd created the fatal insomnia.

If you wanted to create a real-life zombie apocalypse, then prions—which also cause mad cow disease—are the way to go. Abnormal proteins, they can't be killed because they aren't alive to begin with. Unlike viruses, they can't even be sanitized. The only forces known to destroy them are extreme heat, the equivalent of what a crematorium produces, and caustic lye. Neither of which a human can survive.

"C'mon," Flynn said. "It's time."

"No. I just need—" Leaning over the railing, sandwiched between two weathered and pock-marked gargoyles grimacing at the worshippers below, I searched the crowd, scanning for one figure who stood out from the rest. I needed to see him, one last time. Know that he was all right. Then I could go, do what needed to be done.

We were at war. Me, Flynn, Devon Price, and my best friend, Louise Mehta, the closest thing to a medical genius I'd ever met.

Four of us up against an unseen, powerful enemy who had threatened the lives of everyone I cared about.

Including Ryder. As I looked down on the people weaving their way down the icy steps of St. Tim's, the white-gold light of the full moon seemed to favor one figure in particular. His stride appeared slower than I remembered but just as determined. As was his posture. A man who believed, yet who did not rely upon faith or miracles. Detective Matthew Ryder knew better than that. He depended on no one except himself to get the job done.

A lot like me that way—probably why we'd connected so quickly when we'd first met at Thanksgiving in my ER at Good Samaritan. Make that my former ER. Thanksgiving was when I'd held a dead nun's heart in my hand during a trauma resuscitation and heard her speak to me. Side effect of my fatal insomnia, this strange ability to talk to not-quite-dead-yet people, their memories emptying into my brain.

Now, as I watched Ryder walk down the steps, his overcoat flapping against his legs like a superhero's cape, I reached for the antique Pashtun pendant he'd given me. Inside a disk of amber as golden as sunshine was a silver tree of life. Touching it calmed me, centered me—but not as much as the man himself. When we were together, my symptoms improved. I could actually, finally sleep. I felt almost...human.

No more. We couldn't be together. Not when anyone close to me suddenly had a target on their back.

I needed answers. Fast. Before my mind and body deteriorated to the point where I was helpless, unable to care for myself or protect the children also infected with this ghastly man-made plague. Which was why I'd been hiding in the tunnels below the streets of Cambria City, preparing to ransack one more mind.

Daniel Kingston. Ruthless billionaire entrepreneur, father of the sadistic serial killer I killed last month, and, I hoped, the man with the answers I needed: Who created this new form of fatal insomnia and how did we stop them?

I couldn't save myself; I was too far gone, I knew. But I had to save the children. It was the only way I could atone for Jacob's death. I'd been powerless to save him. But no one else. That was my solemn vow. No one else would die fighting my battle.

"Ryder is more use to us without you around drawing attention to him," Flynn continued her dissection of my former love life. "He can go where we can't go, ask questions we can't ask, gain valuable intel. But he can't do any of that if Almanac realizes he's tied to you."

"I can't risk Ryder. It's got nothing to do with tactics. I can't lose him like I did Jacob."

Our enemy had tortured my ex-husband and then, as he lay dying, forced me to enter his mind in order to test my abilities. My stomach clenched, trying to control the nausea roiling through me at the memory. I'd lived through the pain and anguish Jacob had suffered on my behalf. I'd been inside him when he died.

What they'd done to a man I'd once loved—simply to test a theory? Never again.

I turned away from Flynn, my words more for myself and the night wind than for her. "The only way to keep Ryder safe is for me to leave his life. Forever. He can't be any part of this."

"Good luck with that." Flynn sniffed in derision. "Guy like Ryder, he's not going to give up so easy—not going to give you up. I've seen the way he looks at you. But he was a soldier, he'll understand the importance of a strategic retreat. Build some cover, create a little maneuvering distance, do what needs to be done, then maybe..."

I hated the spark of hope her "maybe" ignited. Hope was the enemy. I had to guard against it if I was going to find the strength to do what needed to be done. I drew my breath in, letting the frigid air singe away any thoughts of Ryder or a future.

Below me, Ryder reached the sidewalk. He stopped, the rest of the crowd flowing past him. He turned back and looked up. At me.

I held my breath and closed my eyes. Pressed myself deeper into the shadows of the archway, rough stone digging its fingers into my spine. There was no way he could see me. Yet, I was certain he did. That was Ryder's gift: He saw me, the real me, no matter how far apart we were, no matter how much I needed to hide.

He would always see me. Even if it might get him killed.

Chapter 3

RYDER NAVIGATED PAST the piles of freshly plowed snow heaped up against the curb at the bottom of the steps leading away from St. Tim's. He knew Rossi watched him from the tower, but as much as he wanted to rush to her side, he understood the danger.

She was safe for now, hiding out with Devon Price. But the faster he found the men behind all this, the faster she'd be back where she belonged: in Ryder's arms.

The night was cold, although during the day, the temperatures had risen above freezing, leaving the snow now contained beneath a crackling coat of ice. He'd sleepwalked through the holiday celebrations, smiling and nodding at his family gathered around the dinner table, shoveling food in his mouth that he didn't taste, tearing wrapping paper and beaming thanks for presents he now couldn't even remember.

All day long, he found himself making mental notes. Things he wanted to talk to Rossi about, stories he wanted to share, even how it'd felt to fire his weapon last night, take the kill shot. He'd been a soldier before he joined the force, had taken lives and never, ever talked about it, not with anyone...and yet, here he was, searching the holiday table for Rossi's face, anxious for a moment alone with her so he could spill his guts.

When had she become such an essential part of his life? How could he have been so careless, so reckless? To find her and then lose her so quickly?

Anyone who knew him would shake their head in disbelief. Not Ryder, they'd say. Not Mr. Detached, Mr. Cool Under Pressure. He'd never lose his head, much less his heart.

They'd be wrong.

He walked down the street, past the Kingston Tower housing complex, his coat hanging open despite the wind off the river. Instead of heading home, he continued down to the wharf, where there'd been an explosion and multiple fatalities last night.

One of the vehicles found at the scene was registered to a Dr. Tommaso Lazaretto. Who just happened to be the same doctor helping Louise Mehta care for Rossi's fatal insomnia, and who just happened to be the doctor on duty when Rossi's ex, Jacob, died, and who just happened to have left Good Samaritan in the middle of his shift before vanishing. Last person seen with him? Dr. Angela Rossi.

Rossi, one minute giddy with joy, telling Ryder she couldn't wait to move in with him, that they'd face her uncertain future together...and a few hours later, he comes home to find a Dear John letter?

The skin at the base of his skull drew taut—like it used to in Afghanistan when a sniper had his squad in their sights. Rossi had left to protect him. Which meant the threat against them was bigger than he'd imagined. He hoped to find some answers here at the scene of the crime, a thread to pull on, anything to begin to unravel whatever she'd become tangled up in.

Crime scene tape shredded by the wind tried and failed to cordon off the block surrounding the building's wreckage. The explosion and resulting fire had leveled the warehouse, leaving only the steel support beams and piles of brick in its wake. The stench was unlike anything Ryder had encountered before—acrid, but not like smoke from a typical fire. It burned his nostrils and mouth. He pulled his scarf up higher as he approached the scene. Any evidence that had survived the explosion was now covered in firefighting foam, rendering it useless as far as forensics.

No one challenged him. No one had been left to secure the scene. Which confirmed Devon Price's warning that Ryder's department had been compromised. Ryder wasn't surprised. Disappointed was more like it. Most of the men and women he worked with were honest, dedicated public servants. But the taint of corruption had invaded the ranks at every level, starting at the top. It was obvious Ryder could no longer trust in his own department—another reason why he missed Rossi. Despite her illness, she was as solid as any man he'd gone into battle with.

The street ended at the wharf—empty now except for a lone barge awaiting cargo. No signs of any activity until Ryder spotted a man leaving the relatively intact building still standing between the exploded warehouse and the water. That building was supposed to have been abandoned, slated for demolition when the city had funds, just like its neighbors.

Ryder picked his way through the rubbish—the fire department had done a good job of clearing it into piles that were easy to navigate around, despite the puddles of water beginning to freeze, but that would also play hell with any attempt at evidence collection—and approached the man where he stood on the building's front stoop. The man was Caucasian, mid-thirties, clean-cut, wearing a suit and coat that were almost mirror images of Ryder's own, although more expensive and better tailored.

"Cambria City Police," Ryder identified himself. "Can I see some ID?"

The man remained on the building's steps, placing him above Ryder, but given the black ice and firefighting foam slicking the concrete, he was at a tactical disadvantage. The fact didn't seem to bother him. He took his time assessing Ryder, not moving, keeping his hands in plain sight.

Law enforcement, was Ryder's own assessment. But no one he knew. Arson investigator, maybe? They were county. Or someone from the state, sent down from Harrisburg? But on Christmas Day?

"You realize this is a crime scene, right?" he continued, gesturing with a hand for the man's ID, keeping his other hand free and close to the pistol holstered on his belt.

The man smiled. It was a slow, contented creasing of his mouth that somehow put Ryder at ease. A feeling he immediately combated. Alone at a crime scene, this was not the time to relax his guard.

"Actually, Detective—"

"Ryder. Matthew Ryder."

"Detective Ryder," the stranger continued. His accent was from everywhere and nowhere at once, giving him an air of cultivation that went along with the expensive suit. "This is now my crime scene. Michael Grey, FBI. Okay if I reach into my coat for my credentials?"

Ryder nodded. The man slipped two fingers inside his coat and retrieved a slim leather wallet. He held it open for Ryder to read. Proper federal credentials, the photo was Grey, and the seal and other details were correct.

"What's your business here, Special Agent Grey?" Ryder asked. The man stepped down to join Ryder on the street.

Grey didn't answer Ryder's question right away, instead turned away from the crime scene to look out across the river. Without any boat traffic, it was a vast inky blackness stretching to the tree line on the opposite side where the mountain rose above the riverbank. Cambria Mountain was home to several abandoned coal mines, and most of the forest was off-limits because of the pollution they'd left behind.

"I could ask you the same thing. May I see your identification, Detective?"

Ryder reached for his wallet and held up his own credentials for Grey to scrutinize. "Want to call the station, verify that I am who I am?"

"No. But tell me why you're here, Detective Ryder. Your name doesn't appear on my list of investigators cleared to be on this scene. Interesting that you'd show up now, after everyone else has gone." Grey's tone centered the spotlight of suspicion on Ryder.

"You're right. It's not my case. But it's not every day that a building blows up under such suspicious circumstances."

"So you're spending your Christmas prowling around a crime scene because you're curious? Why do I suspect that there's something you're not telling me?"

"You still haven't told me why the FBI is involved."

"No, I haven't." Grey smiled, and Ryder thought he wouldn't answer. Feds were like that, loved hoarding their intel. But finally the agent relented. "Your people asked me to see if our Evidence Recovery Team could help." Grey gestured with one hand to the crime scene behind him.

"Pretty hopeless, if you ask me," Ryder said. Even though he hadn't spoken to Rossi about what had happened here, Devon Price had filled him in with enough details for him to know that the lack of evidence had little to do with the fire or the efforts to put it out and everything to do with the actors who had set it. They'd basically melted the building and everything—and everyone—inside it with lye.

Extreme tactics. From the same men who'd tried to kill Rossi. Leaving Ryder to play catch-up, trying to ferret what little info he could from the uncooperative fed.

"Ever seen anything like this?" he asked Grey.

"Using caustic lye to cover up your tracks? Definitely not your typical meth lab." The story the city had decided to go public with. "Or any other kind of drug-manufacturing process. But you already knew that, didn't you, Detective? That's why you're here."

"Like I said. Just curious, is all."

"Curious. Good word."

Cagey was one thing, especially as Grey was right—Ryder had no authorization to be at this crime scene. But still, Grey was beginning to annoy him. Ryder wanted to know more specifics— and then he'd see if the Fed's story held up. After all, if his own department could be bought, no reason why a federal agent couldn't. "Which field office are you from? Harrisburg?"

Grey shook his head, staring at the barge. "DC."

"WaFO?" Ryder used the shorthand for the FBI's Washington Field Office in charge of Quantico and the labs there—including the evidence response teams.

"No. Pennsylvania Avenue." The Hoover Building. Which meant administrators and special investigations. Like domestic terrorism. Grey extended a business card embossed with the FBI's seal. "Go ahead and call, if you like. The desk agent can verify my identity."

"Where's your partner?" In Ryder's experience, no Fed ever went anywhere alone—they were like women, even went to the bathroom in pairs. "Or your team?"

Grey turned to him, his smile widening to reveal more perfectly aligned teeth. "Just me. And I was never even here. If you get my drift."

Ryder narrowed his eyes. If he couldn't trust his own department, he was glad to have the Feds involved, but he hated cloak-and-dagger bullshit. Too easy to deny and walk away from—make that slither back into the shadows—after the shit hit the fan.

Which it always did.

What the hell had Rossi gotten involved in?

Chapter 4

FRANCESCA LAZARETTO'S PHONE rang. Ignoring her brother's withering glare from the head of the table, she left the annual Christmas gathering of the family's leadership and stepped outside to the Hotel Danieli's private terrace. The lights of San Giorgio reflected in the rippling black waters of Venice's Grand Canal. The city sparkled, jewel-toned holiday lights adding to its already magical ambience.

"Report."

"No sign of Tommaso," Tyrone told her. "But we're following several leads."

She frowned, although no creases marred her exquisitely maintained facial musculature. At fifty-seven, her skin was as flawless as any fashion model's. She insisted upon it. A perfect facade was necessary to disguise the ravages her flawed DNA wrought.

"His cohort is missing as well." Tommaso's cohort was in Cambria City, Pennsylvania, where he followed two dozen school-age children.

She glanced through the windows to the dining room, met Marco's knife-edged glare. Her brother. Younger than Francesca by two years, yet chosen to act as the family's leader after their father died last year. Not because she was a woman, but because she bore the family curse, while stupid, shortsighted, self-serving Marco's DNA was pure.

It should be her sitting at the head of the table, leading her family into the future, saving them from the Scourge. Tommaso's research cohort was her chance to usurp Marco, take her rightful place, save them all. "You lost track of two dozen families?"

"Not me. I was tying up the final loose ends on the subjects who escaped Roberto."

Beyond the terrace's stone balustrade, she looked past San Giorgio to where a cruise ship sailed out of port, its lights bright against the Lido shoreline. Roberto's body was at the bottom of that same shipping channel. What was left of him after he'd taken a shotgun to his own face. The price of failure, if you were a Lazaretto. "Yes. The Virginia subjects."

"West Virginia."

Below her on the promenade, crowds celebrating the holiday shot glowing neon plastic disks in the air. One whizzed overhead before falling back to land on the walkway alongside the canal. Almost as annoying as Tyrone's correction of her geography. Did she really care where a failed cohort was situated as long as nothing traced back to her? If Marco ever realized what she'd done, how far her research had progressed...

She couldn't risk Marco learning about the cohorts, especially not now when she was so close to success. All she needed was a little more time free of Marco's interference. As soon as she had Tommaso's research cohort, then another month, maybe two, and she'd be able to announce to the family that not only had she, Francesca Lazaretto, found a cure for the Scourge, she'd also cemented the family's place of power for future generations.

With one fell stroke, she would claim the Lazaretto legacy as her own. Poor Marco would be doomed to become a barely legible footnote in the centuries-old history of their family, while Francesca would be forever lauded as the family's savior.

"We need Tommaso's data—his was the only cohort producing favorable results."

"Or he was the only one smart enough to suggest that in his reports."

His snide tone surprised her. "You think he lied? To me?"

"You've set a high price for failure."

"Keep in mind that the punishment for deception is even worse." She left it to his imagination to fill in the details of a fate worse than death. From the moment of their carefully engineered conception, each of her children faced a death sentence far more horrible than most people could envision. Which meant her incentives tended to the extreme. What choice did she have, when she had the fate of the entire family in her hands?

"Orders?"

"Retrieve anything you can from Tommaso's lab. Find his cohort and keep them under scrutiny. Bring me Tommaso." She needed to debrief him face-to-face.

At first, she interpreted Tyrone's silence as hesitation. She was about to chide him then thought better of it. Of all her children, he was the one most like her. Not hesitation, then. Silence as a weapon, an attempt to force her to reveal her secrets.

She waited. Two could play that game.

"And Tommaso's other assignment?" he finally asked.

"What exactly do you think you know?"

"He had a patient. A doctor. Angela Rossi. She has the Scourge. Her medical record makes for..." He paused. "Fascinating reading. She may be of interest to you."

Time to end the charade. "Don't play the fool with me. You know very well who Angela Rossi is."

"She's missing as well. Last seen with Tommaso. Before

the laboratory explosion."

Damn. Was Tommaso attempting to outmaneuver her? Pursuing some misguided fantasy of playing the hero, returning home with the prize that would allow him to assume control of the family himself?

Or perhaps he'd already betrayed her? Gone to Marco with the research—her research, the result of decades of her work. No. If he had, she'd be dead already. Marco might be stupid, but he also had a distinct knack for self-preservation. If killing her became more advantageous than the money and power her scientific endeavors provided the family, he wouldn't hesitate to dispose of her.

One thing they shared: the Lazaretto pragmatism.

"Do whatever you need. But find them. Tommaso and Angela Rossi. Bring them to me. Alive."

"Yes, Mother."

Francesca returned to the opulent dining room and resumed her seat. Marco acknowledged her with a slight nod, then stood. "Thank you all for coming tonight," he began. "While it is traditional to look back upon our family's many accomplishments over the past year, I'd like to, instead, look forward to our future."

Usually, the holiday dinner was a long, dull night filled with reminiscing over past Lazaretto glories, but Marco's opening words signaled a departure from tradition. The dozen men and women seated at the table, all Lazarettos leading various family enterprises, stirred. The Vatican faction smirked, obviously in on his plans, while the financial managers checked their cuff links and creases, trying to hide their concern. The men and women whose job it was to gather intelligence and eliminate the family's competition kept their expressions blank.

Francesca took a cautious sip of her wine, certain that she

was not going to enjoy whatever Marco had planned for tonight's gathering.

"Ladies and gentlemen," Marco continued, "what I am proposing may seem radical, but I'm sure you'll agree that it is the best way to ensure our family's future." He raised his glass and nodded to Francesca. "While we are all indebted to my sister and her people for the sacrifices they have made for our family in generations past, it's become obvious to me that we no longer live in a world where that sacrifice is necessary. I propose to you that we end the Scourge once and for all."

A murmur spread around the table, but no one seemed genuinely surprised. Of course not. Marco would have tested the waters before making his proclamation. Francesca set her glass down and dropped her hand into her lap, the better to hide its uncontrollable trembling.

"We have always protected family members afflicted by the Scourge," she said, keeping her tone calm and unemotional.

Of all the family leaders, she was the only one suffering from fatal insomnia, the Lazaretto Scourge. The others led normal lives, free from fear, free from the excruciating knowledge of exactly how they would die. The price they paid for that freedom was to care for their brothers and sisters. For hundreds of years, countless generations, it had always been that way. What Marco was proposing would, in one fell swoop, erase an entire arm of the family.

"In return," she continued, "those of us afflicted have served the rest of the family well. Securing you wealth and power—"

"But it's been over two decades since the last Vessel appeared," a distant cousin dressed in the robes of a Vatican bishop protested.

"And with modern technology, we've been able to steal

what information we need without their use," Marco added.

"We've also created new revenue streams via our medical research," Francesca put in.

"Research that will be continued, of course. By talented, healthy Lazarettos with no fear of dying before the promise of their work can be fulfilled. You of all people should appreciate that, dear sister."

Francesca pushed to her feet, the edges of her vision blurring. She inhaled deeply, forcing her fugue aside. No, not now. If she lost this battle, if she showed any hint of weakness, she would lose everything. Time, she just needed a little more time. Then she'd hold the power. She could save everyone—both afflicted and healthy.

"There are eighty-one of us as of the last census, dear brother. What are you proposing? Mass murder? Or would you like me and my sons and daughters, our cousins and aunts and uncles to drink willingly from the cup of death you offer us?"

"Francesca, always one for the dramatic. I'm simply proposing that we put that science of yours to good use and make sure this is the last generation to carry the Scourge. When they die, the Scourge dies with them. Until then, you are all welcome to live out your days on the island. We will care for you as we always have."

Exile. He was proposing exile. Which would mean an end to all of her plans. It was bad enough he'd already shut down her financial resources, now he was going to imprison her and her people as well?

"Who are you to decide our fate?" she challenged him, hoping to rally the others to her side. "Are we not Lazarettos as well? Have we not served the family faithfully, without question? And have you all," she favored each of her relatives with a sharp-eyed glance in turn, "each of you, not benefitted from our suffering?"

Without waiting for her brother's answer, she swept her hand through the air, sending her wineglass crashing to the floor. She honestly had no idea if her action was the result of an impending fugue, a muscle tremor, or her fury. "Yes, we are dying. But no, we are not done living. And we will not go quietly. We will not go without a fight."

Marco merely smiled, waving a hand to the wait staff to clean up the mess she'd created, banishing any evidence of her rebellion. "Then, dear sister, you will lose." He turned to the others. "All in favor?"

Chapter 5

FROM THE BELL tower's shadows I stared long and hard at Ryder until he finally passed out of sight, leaving me alone beneath the golden moon, silver wisps of clouds racing across its surface. I shivered and wrapped my arms around my chest, noticing the cold for the first time.

"Were you able to make contact with Louise?" I asked Flynn.

"Devon's boys got a burner phone to her—smuggled it in inside a poinsettia. The cops watching her never had a clue." Since we couldn't trust the police, Devon had organized the former gangbangers he'd run with to be our eyes and ears on the street.

"Are Louise and her family safe?" Louise knew about my and the children's fatal insomnia. Which meant she was a valuable asset to us—and a loose end for the enemy.

"They are for now," Flynn answered. "Devon arranged for news of a family emergency in London as a cover story. Kingston Enterprises' corporate jet will fly her husband and daughter to the UK, and we're sneaking Louise into the tunnels."

"No. She should stay with her family."

In the dark, I couldn't see Flynn's eye roll, but I felt it in her posture and tone of voice. "Those kids need a doctor.

Someone besides you—you're barely functional. And you said yourself, Louise is the smartest doctor you know."

"It's too dangerous."

"It's her choice. You'll have to live with it."

Like I had to live with the echoes of Jacob's death spiraling through my vision each time I blinked? I hunched my shoulders against the wind that had shifted to turn against me and gave her a nod of resignation.

As Flynn led the way down the bell tower's spiral staircase and along the private passages that skirted St. Tim's main worship area, I hoped she hadn't noticed how distracted I was. It was becoming increasingly difficult to filter out the foreign memories invading my conscious awareness. In the space of a month, I now had the memories of five people swirling through my mind, bobbing to the surface randomly.

As I walked through the cathedral's stone arches, incense and the murmur of prayers filled my senses. Most from here and now, but a good portion contributed by Sister Patrice, the nun who'd started all this last month when she spoke to me while I held her heart in my hand. A cascade of memories layered on top of memories clouded my vision.

Was this door I passed the hand-carved solid oak of St. Tim's, or was it a blur of memory, another door in another house of worship from another time and another woman's life? I stopped, reached a hand out, hating my weakness, but I had to know.

Relief swept over me as my fingers connected with a solid, very real, very here, door.

I was well aware that I was losing my mind. I had the memories of a murdered nun, a young girl tortured to death, the sadistic serial killer who killed her, my loving ex-husband who'd died because of me, and an elderly Hungarian woman all percolating through my consciousness...

And now Flynn was taking me to steal the memories of one more person hovering on the brink of death: Daniel Kingston.

We traversed the steps leading below the cathedral, past Sister Patrice's illegal clinic, and down two more flights of stairs into the tunnels. The tunnels always reminded me of what it might feel like being trapped in a warehouse store during a blackout. Impenetrable darkness, sounds echoing from every stray corner, the dank stench, and lack of fresh air all combined to create a strange sensation of overwhelming claustrophobia, despite the cavernous space.

Bad things happened in these tunnels. I hated that we'd been forced to retreat to them like rats trapped on a submarine sinking into an abyss.

Flynn, however, was in her element. If she had her way, instead of following the slow and plodding maze of twisting corridors lined with metal vault-like doors leading into equally vault-like rooms, she'd be racing silent as the night over the catwalks and pipes suspended above us.

Right now, it was taking everything I had to stay upright. Ghosts of memories—mainly from Leo, who had used these tunnels as his private killing ground—called to me from the rooms we passed in the dark corridors lit only by red lights spaced at intervals. Shrieks of pain and screams of terror surrounded me, echoes of the not-so-distant past. Despite the fact that the tunnels stayed at a constant temperature, my skin crawled with sudden fever sweat.

I tried to drown out the sounds with memories of my music, my fingers forming chords as we walked. Alamea, the young girl whose memories I sheltered, one of Leo's victims and a gifted pianist, contributed music of her own, as did Jacob, creating a harmony of notes to drive back the horror.

"Remember," Flynn was saying when I finally tuned back in to reality, "we need the names of the people behind Almanac Care—not the shell companies it's hiding behind. Real names, real locations. I know Daniel—there is no way in hell he didn't know exactly who he was doing business with."

"It doesn't work that way. It's not like a search engine, where you just riffle through results."

Her glance filled with curiosity. "What's it like, then? Being in someone else's head?"

How to explain? "Like falling down a dark well, then a light shoots out of nowhere and illuminates a handhold. That handhold turns into a path, and the world dissolves until it's just the two of you."

"You can actually talk with Daniel? Have a conversation?"

"Maybe. But not words alone. It's difficult to tell what's real and what's my own mind trying to sort things out, make some kind of sense of the chaos. Sister Patrice showed me visions. With Alamea, we didn't use words but communicated through music."

"And Jacob?"

I flinched, the loss too fresh. "Music as well, but mostly words—always words with Jacob. The man could argue his way out of a locked room with no doors or windows."

"You don't keep their personalities, right? Just their memories?" She was thinking of Leo, her hand dropping to rest on the pistol holstered at her hip.

"Memories are colored by personalities." As if to prove my point, a stray scream ricocheted through the space—a combination of Leo's and Alamea's memories. Flynn frowned at my shudder. "But it's still me in charge."

"Except when you drift off into one of those freaky fugues

or start hallucinating..." She turned away before I could see her expression.

It was clear she'd rather be taking care of Esme than babysitting me but also very obvious that I needed watching. As our team's ace in the hole, top-secret weapon—hell, our only weapon—I pretty much sucked eggs. More liability than advantage, that much Flynn had made clear, but I was all we had.

We reached the exit closest to the Kingston family mansion. A narrow metal staircase led up to a maintenance shed in the park across the street from the sprawling brownstone. While Flynn checked for any unwelcome surveillance, I waited behind a false wall at the rear of the shed. The air was dusty with fertilizer and mulch, making my nose itch and eyes water.

Finally, Flynn released me, and I stepped out into the night air, inhaling in gratitude. Devon wanted me to stay in the tunnels where it was safe, but I couldn't stand being trapped below ground where the weight of memories was too much to bear.

We were surrounded by trees. The old, broken-down carousel was to our left, while across the street stood Millionaire's Row, where the original coal and steel barons had built their homes. Now, in Cambria City's current economic decline, they all stood empty or had been converted into multi-unit condos for the few who could afford the address. All except one: Kingston Manor.

Somehow the Kingston family had not only survived but thrived during the economic upheavals that colored the past decades. The family home, known affectionately as the Brownstone, sprawled like an English manor from a Jane Austen novel, including a Victorian-style greenhouse on the roof of one of the wings. Before his stroke, Daniel Kingston had made the Brownstone the hub of Cambria City's social life and business world—nothing happened in the city without Daniel's approval, involvement, and profit sharing.

Tonight no lights were visible in the Brownstone; even the outside holiday decorations were dark, as if the house stood in mourning, unable to celebrate while its master lay in a coma.

Flynn led me across the street, urging me to move faster, fearful we'd be spotted by some random vehicle. But there was no one. The entire block was silent, the only movement the wind rustling through the treetops in the park we'd left behind.

The gate guarding the drive swung open after Flynn entered the security code. We raced through it. On the other side, I pressed my back to the brick wall and froze.

Flynn continued several steps across the drive toward the house before she realized I wasn't with her and turned back in annoyance. "What's wrong?"

I shook my head, scrambling to catch a breath. I was hyperventilating, unable to speak, my hands and feet growing numb.

"Is it a fugue?" She pressed closer. I shook my head—my fugues left me unable to move, not even able to blink, so it was enough to answer her question. "Then what?"

It took me a moment to regain enough control to answer her. Breathe, just breathe, I ordered my rebellious lungs. Slow, slow, slow... "I can't do it."

"Do what? Talk with Daniel? Sure you can—"

I shook my head, closed my eyes against her logic. "No. You don't understand. Every person I've connected with, they've died after I left with their memories. It's worse than stealing—it's more like, like..." My eyes popped open, wide with horror. "It's a violation."

"It's mental rape," Flynn supplied in her usual blunt way. "And who deserves it more than Daniel? The man was my mentor, but after what he's done—what he had me do, what he did to Esme, his own flesh and blood—I owe him no loyalty. Hell, if I could, I'd do it myself. Go inside his head and rip out the information we need to save Esme and the other kids. Wouldn't have a second thought about it. Those kids are worth it. They don't deserve to die just so Daniel and whoever he's working with can make a profit."

It was the longest speech I'd ever heard her utter. But it didn't change the facts. It wouldn't be Flynn breaking every oath she'd ever made—as a physician, as a human being. My entire career, I'd worked as a victim's advocate; now I was being forced to become the predator.

Flynn's code of vigilante justice might work for her and Devon—they'd both do anything to save Esme—but it made me sick. If we hold one life to be sacred, shouldn't we hold them all? When is it okay to justify torture, stealing someone's entire life, all their private moments, secret hopes, and then leaving them to die?

In the ER, we're trained in triage. In the event of a mass casualty, some patients, despite arriving with hearts beating and lungs breathing, are deemed as "black tags," irredeemable, not without using up resources that could save other lives. They're left to die while our efforts are devoted to the patients most likely to survive.

The algorithms are heartless, using research and statistics to justify a few deaths in the name of saving many more.

I understood that. Understood what kind of man Daniel Kingston was—more monster than man by my observation. Even understood what was at stake: the lives of twenty-one kids and possibly many, many more.

But was I ready to condemn myself along with Daniel? Was I ready to become as much of a monster as he was?

Flynn surprised me by resting her palm on my arm and

squeezing gently. "Sometimes we all need to make sacrifices," she told me. "This one is yours. For Esme and the children. We need you, doc. No one else can get the job done."

I hauled in a breath, the cold air finally penetrating my frozen limbs. Couldn't meet Flynn's eyes but nodded. "For Esme and the children."

God help me, I followed her inside.

Chapter 6

AFTER RYDER CALLED FBI HQ and verified Grey's identity—although the desk agent refused to "confirm or deny" Grey's current assignment or whereabouts—Grey did the same. At least Ryder assumed he did, based on hearing half of a cryptic conversation. Then they continued their stroll around the crime scene, engaging in a verbal tug of war. "Caustic lye—you think they used it to cover their tracks or because it was part of whatever they were manufacturing?"

The FBI agent didn't answer right away—part of the power game, Ryder knew. Instead, Grey crouched, pretended to examine a shard of glass in the beam of his Maglite, nodded as if the mysteries of the universe had just been imparted to him, and finally stood. "They went to the trouble of converting the sprinkler system to use the lye, so what do you think?"

"Same thing I thought when I first heard: some sort of domestic terrorism. Which makes me wonder why there aren't more of your boys around."

"Who says there aren't?" Grey favored him with an inscrutable smile. "Maybe at this minute, my guys are pushing through paperwork that will allow them to transport all this evidence to a safe place where they can comb through it. Free from the prying eyes of a city whose mayor and DA's office were recently indicted on public corruption charges and whose police chief can't be far behind."

That would make sense, doing it on the sly, away from reporters and public panic. But still, something didn't feel quite right...

"Tell me about your officer-involved shooting last night, Detective," Grey continued amiably, although it was obvious he was trying to keep Ryder off-balance. "Your second in a month, correct?"

"At least I wasn't the one getting shot this time." Ryder wasn't impressed by the special agent's sudden omnipotent knowledge of his career—easily the work product of minions scurrying on the other end of a text message. "It was a good shoot." Bottom line for any police officer on the front lines.

"I'm sure it was."

Ryder could have done without the patronizing hint of condescension. "If this was an act of domestic terrorism, then what were they after? Nothing around here except closed-down steel mills and coal mines."

Grey stopped to think about that, his gaze scouring the waterfront as if expecting a flotilla of well-armed terrorists to appear in the night. "Exactly. Maybe that's the point? That if it can happen here, it can happen anywhere?"

"Or maybe this is merely their staging area? Safe, quiet, little in the way of prying eyes. A few hours from Philly, DC, Baltimore, Manhattan."

"In that case, we better hope that this," Grey indicated the wasteland of debris behind them, "is the end of it. But somehow I don't think it is." He lasered in on Ryder again. "Otherwise, why would a detective kicked off Major Cases and assigned to work at a victims' advocacy center be here, poking around on Christmas Day?"

"Routine curiosity. Heard it on the scanner, nothing better to do. Sad to say," Ryder added in a self-deprecating tone. It was all the truth but none of what actually mattered.

"So you keep saying."

It was clear Grey didn't buy Ryder's explanation. Tough. No way was Ryder giving the Fed more, not until he was certain that it wouldn't end up backfiring, placing Rossi in more danger.

Grey continued, "You don't think any of this could be connected to the doctor who got you shot last month? After all, it was her family's bar that you saved from being blown up last night."

Such a specific question gave away more than any answer Ryder could provide. So Grey not only knew about Rossi, he'd tied her to Ryder. Not difficult for anyone with the resources of a federal agent, but still, it made him uncomfortable.

"Right," he answered warily. "The perpetrator had a grudge against both Dr. Rossi and the police. The bar hosting a Christmas Eve celebration and filled with off-duty cops was the perfect target. But since we were there, there's no way we could have been here." He circled his finger around the crime scene perimeter, hoping Grey interpreted his royal "we" as meaning both him and Rossi.

Grey put his hands into the pockets of his expensive overcoat. "You know they pulled five bodies out of here, right?"

"I heard."

"Did you also hear there's a man missing? A Dr. Tommaso Lazaretto?"

"Are you thinking he's a victim or an actor?" Ryder asked, using law enforcement shorthand for a person responsible for a criminal act.

"Why don't you tell me? I'm guessing he's the reason you're here."

"Never met the man." Again, it was the truth. Tired of the cat and mouse and certain Grey wouldn't be dropping any more breadcrumbs, Ryder called his bluff and started to walk away.

Before he'd gone three steps, Grey's voice reached out from behind him. "I guess you don't know, then. Your Dr. Rossi also seems to have disappeared. Vanished from the face of the planet, best we can tell. Any thoughts on that, Detective?"

Ryder whirled. "Why are you really here, Grey? And don't give me any song and dance about evidence recovery."

Grey was silent for a long moment, his gaze narrowed as he scrutinized Ryder in the moonlight. "I'm here because I think you and your Dr. Rossi have gotten mixed up with a very dangerous man. A terrorist my team has been tracking."

"You think this," Ryder waved a hand at the debris surrounding them, "was the result of domestic terrorism?"

"I think this is just the tip of the iceberg. And a lot more people will die if you don't help me stop him."

Chapter 7

THE INTERIOR OF the Kingston mansion matched the exterior with its opulent indulgence. At least what little I could see in the dimly lit passages with their dark wood paneling. It wasn't until Flynn reached a room at the rear of the second floor and opened the door that I could make out much in the way of detail.

The room was brightly lit behind thick blackout curtains. The furniture was all heavy, expensive antiques that made the entire room feel as if there should be cobwebs hanging from every corner. Except for the medical equipment—enough to outfit a small ICU. That was brand new, the packaging piled against one wall below a frowning ancestor's portrait.

A massive king-size four-poster bed with a single occupant held the center of attention. Daniel Kingston, bedridden and in a persistent vegetative state ever since a stroke felled him at Thanksgiving. The man whose memories I was here to steal.

I ignored Daniel to focus on the room's other occupants. Devon Price, Daniel's illegitimate son, stood beside my best friend and neurologist, Louise Mehta. Relieved to see her, I rushed into her arms. "You made it!"

"Just call me Bond, Jane Bond," she replied with her meticulous British accent. But her clothing was rumpled and her earrings didn't match, so I knew it was all a show of bravado.

"Geoff and Tiffany?" Her husband and three-year-old daughter.

"Halfway to London," Devon answered. "No one is going to lay a hand on them, I promise."

Louise nodded, her eyes tightening as if to hold back tears. "I would love it if someone explained to me exactly what the hell is going and why my family was forced to leave their home, go into hiding. I trusted Tommaso—trusted him with my patients. But now he's part of some international conspiracy to create an artificial form of fatal insomnia? And he's threatening my family?"

I glanced at Flynn and Devon. Obviously, neither of them had told Louise that Tommaso was dead, no longer a threat— although the men he worked for still were. Before I could say anything, she continued her rant.

"All those children? He's behind their fatal insomnia?" Her voice rose in indignation. "Has he gone mad? Is he part of some bizarre cult or terrorist group? What could possibly have driven him to do this? Do you have any idea what that could do, infectious prions unleashed into the world?"

Of course I knew the danger, but Louise was a talker. Her way of handling stress, just as mine was to go silent and play my fiddle. I wished I'd brought it with me, had to settle for curving my fingers in the shape of chords pressed against my thigh, imagining an uplifting chorus of the Knocknagree polka. But that brought with it memories of Jacob—last time I'd performed that song, we'd played it together.

"That's why we're here," Devon said in a gentle tone that surprised me. "To find the answers. To help the children. Keep them and your family safe."

Louise's chest heaved as she swallowed one breath then another. Her cheeks were flushed, lips pressed together as if she was choking back another outburst. Finally, she nodded. First at Devon, then at me. Then once more, her gaze vacant as she stared past us to the heavily curtained windows. "Yes. All right, then. Let's get to work."

"I saw the video Devon took at the lab," she continued. "Not much that I can help with. Looked like protein sequences from a virus or bacterium. Geoff is going to have one of his friends who's an immunologist take a look. Have you talked to anyone at the CDC?"

Before I could answer, Devon said, "No. We can't risk it."

"We can't risk contagious prions getting out either," she snapped.

"I was hoping Geoff could run the epidemiologic data on the children," I said. Geoff was a biostatistician who consulted with the CDC as well as other global health organizations. If anyone could pinpoint exactly how the children were exposed to the fatal insomnia, it was him. "Anonymously."

"He's already working on it—you know Geoff and his obsession with puzzles." Her voice trailed off, and I noticed that she'd turned so that she didn't have to look at Daniel. She glanced around the room again, as if searching for an escape. I understood. What I was asking her to do was not that different from Tommaso's betrayal of his own physician's oath.

"Angela, we need to get started." Devon was impatient with Louise's stalling.

Louise shot him a glare that said, *Give me a minute.* I gripped both her arms. "If you're not up for this—"

"I'm not, but more importantly, neither are you." She stepped back from me, her gaze one of appraisal. "Look at you. I saw you not two days ago, and already you look like hell."

"We both know it's not going to get any better, not for me. But if I can help to save the children—"

"You're no good to anyone if you're dead," she snapped, all patience gone. She whirled on Devon, hands on her hips. "Do you have any idea how dangerous this is? What you're asking her to do?"

"She's done it before."

"And from what you told me, she's paid the price." She shook her head. "I still don't believe it's even possible, this psychic communication—"

"I've seen it." Flynn surprised me by speaking up from her position guarding the door. "It's real."

"Daniel is our last hope to get the information we need," I added.

Louise scowled at us each in turn. Finally, she relented. "If we're doing this, then we're doing it my way. I'll be monitoring both you and Mr. Kingston every second of the procedure. Did you get the equipment I requested?"

Devon nodded and stepped aside to reveal another stack of medical supplies. Among them, wireless EEG caps. "Daniel had it all, already stockpiled down in the tunnels. More reason to suspect he knew what Tommaso and Almanac were up to with their experiments."

Louise ignored him as she busied herself setting up the equipment that would allow her to monitor both mine and Daniel's vital signs and brain waves. She started with Daniel, stepping back to observe his brain activity for a long moment. "Not much there except erratic theta spindles."

"Theta spindles—those are what you found on Angela's EEG as well, right?" Devon leaned over his father's still body to watch. "They're also created by PXA. Should we give them each a dose? We have the reversal agent in case we need it."

He sounded so damned certain, gambling with my life. We'd found a possible PXA reversal agent at the Almanac lab

41

before it exploded. Untested—at least by us—unproven, and who knew how unstable it might be? He also didn't mention that one of the side effects of PXA was heightened pain sensation. So much so that Leo Kingston had used it to torture his victims before he killed them.

Louise frowned. "Daniel's much too weak to handle a dose of PXA. In his condition, it could kill him before Angela has a chance to—" She stopped abruptly, gave a swift laugh born more of fear than humor. "I don't even know what the hell to call it. Psychic communication? Telepathy? Vulcan mind meld?"

"I don't know either," I confessed. "But you should keep a close eye on Daniel. Every person I've touched like this, done this to, they've died."

Devon stepped forward as if trying to block my words, clearly unhappy I'd mentioned that unfortunate side effect. "But they were all dying anyway. You can't blame yourself."

Louise scowled at him for a long moment before turning to me, this time taking my hands. Hers felt cold. Or maybe it was mine that were frozen numb. "Angie, think. Are you really okay with this?"

"What if it was your daughter?" I asked Louise. "What if it was Tiffany they'd infected?"

Her grip tightened, and she grimaced, her expression morphing from objective clinician to protective mother. It was a long, long moment before she answered. "I'd cut the bastard's heart out."

"There's no other way. The lab is destroyed, all of Tommaso's research gone—"

"Leaving Daniel as our only lead." Devon nodded to his father's still form. "I'm not going to force anyone to do anything. But—"

"We can't fight them if we don't even know who they are

or what they want," I finished for him.

"Or how they did it. Making prions communicable?" Louise shuddered. She turned to me with one of the wireless EEG caps. "Okay. Okay." As she adjusted the cap over my hair, pulling the thick curls away from the electrodes and snugging it tight, she whispered in my ear, "If you do something stupid and die, I swear I'll kill you."

We both laughed at the ridiculous threat.

After swallowing a dose of PXA, I settled myself on the bed beside Daniel, taking care not to touch him. Louise fussed with the equipment, making certain it was recording. Back to the role of curious scientist.

I felt the drug course through my body on a seek-and-destroy mission, rattling through every one of my nerve endings like a machine gun. I'd taken it before. Each time was a little easier. At least this time, I wasn't screaming in agony or slobbering, helpless as the pain swamped me.

Thank God Ryder isn't here to see this, was my last thought before I reached out to take Daniel's hand in mine.

Then I fell, spiraling through a black void, no end, no beginning, barely able to hang on to the fact that I was me...

Chapter 8

RYDER LEFT GREY ferreting among the crime scene debris and stepped into an alley to call Devon Price. Rossi's cell had been taken when she'd been kidnapped by Tommaso Lazaretto last night—it might even be part of the wreckage from the explosion. Although Price had given her a new untraceable replacement, Ryder didn't want to chance calling her from his phone.

Any precaution to keep her safe. At least that's the excuse he told himself. In reality, it was just too painful to think of talking with her, knowing he couldn't see her, be with her. Here they were, each trying to protect the other, both suffering for their efforts.

Until they knew the full extent of the threat against her, it was the only way.

"Our mutual friend okay?" he asked Price as soon as the other man answered. Wasn't the greeting he'd planned on, but Price would understand.

"Just fine. Should be a quiet evening at home."

Whatever the hell that meant. "I'm at the crime scene with a Fed from DC headquarters."

"Got a name? I'll run him."

Price was taking operational security extremely seriously. Ryder liked that in a man who was protecting the lives of twenty-some families along with Rossi. "Grey. With an 'e.' Michael Grey."

"Got it."

"From what he's not saying, I'm guessing he's from some hush-hush counterterrorism unit. He knows about the lab—not sure exactly what. Mentioned that he was on the trail of a domestic terrorist, but that could be for show. I'm going to stick with him, see if he has any leads that might help us."

Price had told him about the Almanac Care Institute that had provided financial backing for Lazaretto's lab and thugs— including the ones who killed Jacob and kidnapped Rossi. If they weren't all dead already, Ryder would have loved to have a few minutes alone with them.

"Be careful," Price answered. "Most of what we have going for us is that Almanac has no idea we're on to them. If this Fed stirs up trouble—"

"They'll know we know." Ryder thought about that. "Grey wouldn't have gotten here so soon, especially with the drug lab explosion cover story the brass gave the media, if he didn't already suspect someone. Plus, he dropped Lazaretto's name, said he was missing, not among the dead found at the scene."

Price was silent, not admitting to anything over the phone, but they both knew Lazaretto was dead. Ryder still wasn't clear on the details; Price had assured him it was self-inflicted and that he'd "take care of things." Ryder hadn't asked for specifics— couldn't, not without being forced to make a decision about upholding the law versus protecting Rossi. Although he guessed that by refusing to make that choice, he'd already committed himself.

To Rossi rather than his job. Still, it felt right. As if protecting her was the best way to also serve and protect the civilians he'd sworn an oath to.

"How could Grey know Tommaso wasn't among the dead if no one's been identified yet?" Price asked.

"My point exactly. He knows more than he's saying."

"More than we've got, then. Okay, stay with him. See if he'll give you anything we can follow."

Meaning Ryder's job would be to keep the Fed company while Price and Rossi did the real work. Damn it, if he could just be there with her... "Who knows? Maybe this domestic terrorism lead is another Almanac front to cover their tracks. A good way to hide something—like blowing up your own lab to destroy evidence."

"Detective Ryder, when did you start concocting such devious and twisted plots?"

"Since I started hanging out with you," Ryder retorted.

"If Grey is on the trail of Almanac and thinks they're terrorists, then you need to be careful. If he thinks you're holding out on him—"

"What's he going to do, arrest me?"

"I'm just saying, terrorism is a hot button for these guys."

"I know, but I'm a cop, not one of your Russian mob friends."

"Keep me in the loop."

Ryder considered that. Trusting a civilian with definite organized crime connections more than his fellow law enforcement professionals? Talk about a world gone crazy. He glanced over his shoulder to where Grey was talking on his own phone—no doubt sounding just as paranoid about Ryder as Ryder sounded about him.

"Okay. But don't do anything drastic without talking to me. Last thing we need is to piss off the FBI."

"Right. Keep me updated." Price hung up.

Ryder stared at the phone for a long moment before

pocketing it once more. He slogged back through the muddy street—the firefighters' foam had turned into rainbow puddles covered with a slick of ice—and rejoined Grey. "My guys have nothing on any domestic terrorist cell. So why don't you tell me what you have? Something must have brought you up here on Christmas night. Something that couldn't wait until morning?"

Grey was crouched, the remnants of a biohazard warning dangling from a silver ballpoint pen. He dropped the bit of yellow plastic and stood to face Ryder. "I wanted to see the scene fresh, but thanks to your fire department, I doubt there's anything of interest left behind. Still, our guys will double-check, just to be certain."

Ryder waited, saying nothing, giving the Fed space. Grey pivoted, staring out over the river. Finally, he nodded to the mountain across the water. "Ever hear of the Sons of Adam?"

"Fringe militia cult. Tried to blow up a hospital in Pittsburgh a few years ago."

"Right. They're back. Under new leadership. More radical than ever. Basically, if you're not a white, Christian male, you're fair game."

"You think they're behind all this?"

"Their new leader calls himself Brother Tyrone. Real name unknown—that's how good he is at covering his tracks. I've been trailing him across the Midwest and up through Appalachia. He's a charismatic SOB, sets up shop in a blue-collar town, offers his followers thrills along with his own special form of social activism. Snake handling, fire walking... Hell, he's led sermons from deep down in abandoned coal mines to the middle of a lake during a thunderstorm with tornados and water spouts racing past."

"Must make quite an impression. What's he preach? This activism of his?" Could this Brother Tyrone be connected to

Lazaretto and Almanac Care? If so, maybe there were more people infected with fatal insomnia. Ryder was half-tempted to reciprocate and share his own intel with Grey but decided it was better to play it safe. At least for now.

"He calls it purifying, but it translates to vigilantism. Gets poor folks frustrated with the way things are in their communities all riled up and tells them they can stand up for what's right, make a change, even if the police and government can't. By the time he's done with them, they've torn down crack houses, rousted the homeless out of town, burned out sex offender encampments, even firebombed a mosque. Whatever needs purifying—in their eyes—he empowers them to purify."

"Including murder?"

Grey shook his head. "Not until now. Which is why I'm here. Because I have the feeling that this," he gestured to the debris surrounding them, "is just the beginning."

Chapter 9

EVERY OTHER TIME I'd touched someone's mind, I'd been consumed by darkness. More than black, less than emptiness. A void, infinite and ravenous.

Not this time. Daniel's mind was gray fog, swirling thick, so thick it was difficult to tell which side was up. This fog wasn't like the kind that moved in from the river, swamping the city in its moist tendrils, easily swept aside. This fog was alive, a million spider webs tangled and interwoven, grasping for prey.

It took all my strength to shuffle through it. Unseen fingers grabbed at my ankles, trying to pull me down. Finally, I resorted to parting the thick mist with my arms, swimming past its greedy wisps.

A man's laughter came from behind me. The sound dispersed the fog with the sudden ferocity of a thunderclap, leaving me standing in bright sunshine, arms waving through clear air.

Daniel lounged in a wicker chaise alongside a large oval swimming pool with a waterfall at one end. He sipped some tropical-looking concoction and waved me over with his drinking hand. "That was easier than I thought it would be."

I shook away his offer of a drink but did sit in the chair that appeared beside him. "I'm Angela—"

"I know who you are, Dr. Rossi. I've been expecting you."

"You have?"

"Aren't you doctors always telling families that patients in comas can hear everything?"

"Right. Of course." The chair was low and deep, and I kept sinking farther into it. I shoved my weight forward to perch on the edge. "Then you know why I'm here?"

"Yes." A twinkle entered his eye. He was having fun, making me work for what I needed. "But don't let that stop you from asking."

"Why?" I asked, already infuriated with his games. True, he was dying, and I was hastening things with my visit, but if he'd heard everything, then he knew children's lives were at risk—including Devon's child, Daniel's own granddaughter.

"Because I'm bored and lonely." He pouted. "Do a dying man a favor and allow him to enjoy one last conversation."

"Okay, then. Who did Leo create the PXA for? What do they want? How do we stop them?" Once the questions began, it was difficult to stop them from all flooding out, but I managed to hold back after those three. They were the most important, anyway.

Daniel's expression was one of smug amusement. Again, I had the awful feeling of being trapped in a spider's web, as if that gruesome fog still clung to my skin.

"Leo did not create PXA." He took another sip of his orange-red drink. The colors swirled but never mixed, a sunset trapped in a glass.

"No? He only developed it into the ultimate torture and interrogation drug." My voice rose, becoming sharp. I let it. "You knew there was a reversal agent, didn't you? Those women who died after Leo overdosed them on PXA—you could have saved them."

"To what end? To testify that my son was a sadistic killer?"

He waved a hand as if the murders of over a dozen women were of no consequence.

"Give me the formula for the reversal agent." We had a sample, but it would take time to synthesize the formula, so I thought the request was a good test of his intentions.

He considered that. "And what will you give me in return?"

"What do you want?"

"Nothing except your company." Suddenly, we were in a lush, well-manicured garden somewhere in the countryside. The green stretched as far as I could see in one direction, in the other was a thick forest, and behind us a mansion even larger than Daniel's brownstone. It was like something out of a movie. "Come. Walk with me."

He led me into the garden, the sweet perfume of flowers in bloom wafting in the gentle breeze.

"The PXA reversal?" I reminded him.

He nodded, and a chemical formula appeared in my mind, inked on a piece of parchment that flitted to the ground before me. I stooped, grabbed it, committed it to memory, then folded it into a square and pocketed it.

"Thank you."

"How could I resist? You look so much like her."

I frowned. He was confused—I should have expected as much, given the severity of his stroke. "Everyone says I look like my father."

His smile was indulgent. "I never met your father." We continued down the path. "No, you remind me of an old friend. When I was young, so much younger."

I looked down, and my clothing had changed to riding pants and a silk blouse. I'd never been on a horse, so this must be a wisp of Daniel's memory about his childhood friend. "Tell me about the people who created the PXA. Did you know they also found a way to create an artificial form of fatal insomnia? What do they want? How did they do that?"

How do we stop them? was what I really wanted to ask. But I knew better than to push him. I was more certain than ever that Daniel's company was involved—if not Daniel himself.

"Fatal insomnia? Never heard of it."

I didn't believe him. "But you know who's behind the PXA?"

"It's not a new drug. Goes back centuries. My company— well, one of our divisions—was hired to create a synthetic form that could easily be produced in mass quantities. Until now, they never needed large amounts, distilled it by hand."

"They? Who's they?"

We reached the end of the gardens. Beyond the eight-foot-tall boxwood hedge, two young boys waited with horses. Big, black horses, their coats brushed sleek, fine leather saddles molded to their backs.

"Ride with me, and I'll show you." Daniel suddenly appeared younger, in his thirties. He climbed onto his horse with the grace and ease of experience.

I stared up at my mount with terror. I'd never even been this close to a horse before. Knew nothing of how to get up there onto the saddle, or what to do once I did. The groom knelt and cupped his hands, waiting for me.

"Do you want answers or not?" Daniel asked.

I gathered my breath and stepped onto the boy's hands. He handled my weight effortlessly, lifting me up into the saddle. It was so high up, higher than I'd imagined. He backed away to adjust the stirrups. The other boy handed me the reins. The horse sniffed and tossed its head as I gripped the reins tight.

"Relax. The horse knows what to do. Give it its head." With that, Daniel galloped into the woods, disappearing from sight.

My horse bolted after him with me clinging to its back with everything I had.

Chapter 10

AFTER DEVON HUNG up with Ryder, he continued pacing his father's bedroom, a nervous energy making him feel as if he were caged. He should be out there, doing something, not sitting around here where he was...helpless.

He glanced at Angela, her face vacant as if she was simply gone. He hated this part of things, hated watching her when she was inside someone else. It was creepy, like what she'd look like when she really was dead.

Louise, however, was fascinated, dancing from monitor to monitor, making certain the video captured every minute. "Look at these theta spikes," she exclaimed in excitement. "See how they're synchronizing? Amazing."

Devon couldn't take it anymore. He strode to the door. "Flynn, you stand guard. No one comes in unless it's me or Ryder."

"What about Esme?" It was clear that if she had to watch over anyone, she'd prefer it to be Esme.

"I'm going to check on her and take care of some loose ends. Call me if anything happens."

Flynn nodded her understanding, and Devon left, a feeling of relief washing over him as soon as the door shut on the view of Angela and his father.

He trusted Angela; she'd do everything she could to save Esme. But Daniel? The man was the devil incarnate. He hated that their only plan depended on him.

Unless he could devise a plan B. He slipped through the tunnels quickly, skirting their familiar shadows until he arrived at the makeshift dormitory where the children and their families had cots set up. Ozzie looked up from Esme's cot, where he covered her small body like a blanket, thumped his tail, and blinked at Devon as if to say, "What took you so long?"

"Sorry, bud," Devon said, soothing Esme's hair and grimacing at the fever that burned through her. He couldn't deny himself a moment to lean down and plant a kiss on her forehead.

This was what he'd worked so hard to avoid his entire life. Ten years ago, when he left Esme and her mother to protect them from the gang who'd targeted him, he thought that was the hard part, the painful part that about tore his heart in half. It'd hurt, more than getting gunned down would have, but that's what a man did: he stood for what was his and protected them with everything he had.

But now that Jess was gone and Esme was back in his life...he raised his eyes heavenward, appreciating the cosmic irony. The man who'd built a life on having no ties, no soft spots enemies could exploit, now lived his life for the greatest vulnerability of all.

A tiny noise interrupted his reverie. A woman politely clearing her throat. Veronica Lee, the mother of the first patient Angela had diagnosed with the artificial fatal insomnia, Randolph Lee. "Mr. Price?"

"How's Randolph?" Devon asked the mother, following her gaze to where an older man and woman sat on a cot with their backs to the concrete wall and a small boy stretched out across their laps.

"Same as the others. We'll be lucky if they sleep more than an hour at a time." Veronica was in her mid-twenties, pretty despite the anguish that creased her face—if she'd smiled, she'd be beautiful. She turned her back on the sight of her son and parents to face Devon. "Who did this, Mr. Price? Why would they want to hurt our children? We have no money, we pose no threat. I cannot understand how any human can be so heartless."

Who says they're human, Devon thought. He didn't believe in spooks or supernatural creatures; his time spent with the Russians had shown him that he didn't need to. There were way too many men—and a few women—willing to sacrifice their humanity in the name of glory, power, vengeance, or even a quick fix.

"You will find them." Veronica made it a statement, not a question. She squeezed Devon's arm, her rhinestone-studded nails glittering in the dim light. "I know that. But," her hand fell away from his body, "I feel so helpless. We all do. How can we help? Please."

Devon glanced around the large space, realized that the eyes of most of the parents and grandparents were on him. They needed more than guidance, they needed a mission. Something to focus on besides their dying children.

"I need all my resources to find the men behind this." He raised his voice slightly so it would carry past Veronica. Resources? Who was he kidding? His resources included a middle-aged neurologist, a dying ER doctor, a teenage sociopath, a renegade cop, and a Labrador retriever. Still, the parents nodded, anxious to believe.

God help him, Devon fed that belief. He stood. "I need you to organize and prepare for a possible siege. We've plenty of food, but I need a list of other supplies that we'll need: clothing, that kind of thing."

He trailed off uncertainly—he had no idea what kids this age needed. He'd never been a parent before. But Veronica nodded. "Toys and books, maybe some music? We should organize cleaning, cooking, chores like that, as well."

"Exactly. Just remember, we only have this section of rooms secured. Don't try to go past the orange doors." They were locked, and only he, Flynn, and Angela had keys.

"Yes, of course." Then she frowned, lowered her voice as she leaned closer. "We are safe here, aren't we? They won't come after us, not down here. We won't need to fight."

He hoped not. Sent a prayer to any deity on duty to prevent that. "No," he said, injecting as much confidence as possible into his voice. "Don't you worry about that. That's my job."

Her nod was so forceful it almost turned into a bow. "Thank you, Mr. Price." And she left to return to the other parents.

Devon called Ozzie to him. The Lab lumbered off the bed, moving slowly and not disturbing Esme.

"It's going to be okay," Devon promised Esme. Because that's what a man did; he changed the world, fought the monsters, went to hell and back, if that's what it took to protect his own.

He and Ozzie left the dormitory. He wasn't sure why the lights in the hallway made his eyes water—they were the red ones to help you see in the dark, weren't bright at all. But still the tunnel around him blurred, and he had to rely on the dog to keep him upright until he blinked his vision clear again.

Did nothing for the barbwire garroting his heart, but he knew the only cure for that would be to see Esme safe and healthy.

"This way," he told the dog who followed at Devon's knee.

Ozzie was trained as a Seeing Eye dog but had also proven useful as a tracker. "You're not going to like it. There's a lot of blood."

They arrived at their destination: the small dental clinic where Dr. Tommaso Lazaretto had taken his own life rather than risk Angela touching his memories.

Flynn had disposed of the body in the Good Sam incinerator, but first she'd stripped Tommaso, in case his clothing offered any leads. Other than the label of a good tailor in Milan, it hadn't; the only useful items were Tommaso's hospital ID and a cell phone. The phone was encrypted, but Devon had couriered it to one of his old Russian mob contacts; it would take time to crack, though.

Time Devon didn't have. He needed to track Tommaso's movements. He already knew the doctor and his cohorts had been living in the warehouse lab that exploded, so that was out. But between Ozzie's nose and the hospital ID, he hoped to expand his knowledge of where else the not-so-good doctor had been and any other accomplices he might have encountered.

He didn't want to overwhelm Ozzie with the blood that still stenched the room, so he left the dog in the hallway and went inside to collect the doctor's clothing. Each of the tunnel's sections were designed like compartments on a submarine, with steel doors that were airtight and locked.

The underground shelter was large enough to house several hundred people and had been built during the Cold War as an evacuation point for the state government in case of nuclear disaster. Daniel had upgraded many of its functions, adding state-of-the-art air filtration and water reclamation, geothermal energy, modern medical supplies, food, and enough weapons and ammo to invade a third world country. More evidence that he'd known something bad was coming. Devon couldn't help but wonder who exactly Daniel would have invited to join him in his nuclear wonderland underground city.

Not Devon, that was certain.

Inside the dentistry clinic, he steered clear of the ribbons and puddles of congealing blood centered around the exam chair. Awful way to go, biting your own tongue off and drowning in your own blood. But no less awful than the fate Tommaso had planned for Angela and the children he'd infected with fatal insomnia. Devon's only regret was that the man had taken the coward's way out, killing himself before they could get the information they needed from him.

He gathered the pile of clothing Flynn had left on the counter and returned to Ozzie, sealing the door behind him. He held the clothing out to Ozzie, letting the dog nose it, soak in the scents.

Tommaso had had a job at Good Sam, pretending to assist Louise Mehta while actually there to keep an eye on the patients he'd infected. Even though the lab with Tommaso's extracurricular research was destroyed, there was a chance he'd kept notes while at work at Good Sam. If they weren't on his cell phone, maybe there was a copy somewhere else.

Devon clipped Tommaso's ID to his shirt, not that he looked anything like the Italian doctor, but that seldom mattered. All that counted was the appearance of fitting in. If people expected to see an ID, you wore one prominently displayed—few would look closer.

He attached Ozzie's harness with its service-dog label— another all-access pass, he'd found.

"Ready?" he asked the dog. Ozzie thumped his tail eagerly. "Okay, let's nail these bastards."

Chapter 11

DANIEL AND I rode deeper into the woods. I somehow managed to stay on the horse, although it was definitely taking more of my concentration than I expected. I wanted to get the answers I came for and leave again, but Daniel had no intention of making it easy.

"You need me to stay in control, coherent enough to answer your questions, don't you?" he asked in an almost musing tone. "If you could grab the answers yourself, you would have taken the PXA formula directly from Leo's memory."

"We already had it. I was simply verifying it," I answered. It was impossible to lie, not here, mind-to-mind, but I could hedge the truth.

Daniel saw right through me. "But not from Leo, right? What's stopping you, Dr. Rossi? If I had your power—" His smile was wolfish as his face lit up with the possibilities. "I'd mind-fuck every adversary I had."

I lowered my face, pretended to be adjusting the reins. None of the others had ever so fully comprehended the situation—they'd all been focused on one last dying thought or wish. Not Daniel. He'd known I was coming, had been ready and waiting for me—but to what end? Nothing I did here could help him, and as soon as I left, he'd be dead.

"That's what it is, right?" he persisted. "Mental rape and pillage. When you leave, you'll take my memories, just as you've taken Leo's."

"How do you know that?"

"I can see them—well, not really seeing, not hearing either... It's as if they're cobwebs brushing against me, here and gone again. But I know my own son. And now he's inside you."

Despite the sun streaming through the trees, I shivered. Did the fact that Daniel could sense Leo's memories in my consciousness mean my mind was breaking down? Maybe I soon would no longer be me at all, just a random hodgepodge of whoever's memory rose to the surface?

No. I could control it. I had to.

Daniel's laugh was cruel. "You really have no idea what you're doing, do you? Poor girl—too bad you didn't absorb any of Leo's strength of will. That boy never let anything stand in his way. But you, you're a blade of grass, waiting to be trampled and broken."

"Tell me what I need to know."

"Why should I? You'll just leave and I'll be alone again, waiting to die."

Maybe he didn't realize that my leaving would hasten his death. It gave me the slightest edge. "Then I'll leave now."

"No. I don't believe you will. You're obviously desperate—which means you're not here to save yourself, but others. It's started, hasn't it? Were the children the first? How many have died?"

"You knew?" Fury burned through me, and I jerked upright so fast the horse startled. I hauled the reins in before it could bolt then realized it was time for me to show Daniel who really had the power here. I closed my eyes for a moment and focused my will. When I opened them, both horses had vanished, leaving Daniel and me standing across from each other in a clearing in the woods.

"Nicely done," he said with a smirk. "My turn." He gave a lazy wave of his hand, and we were suddenly on a cliff overlooking a churning sapphire sea, waves taller than houses breaking on the rocks below.

"Tell me what you know," I demanded, squaring off against him. "Who's behind the fatal insomnia?"

"I don't need to tell you anything." He held up a hand as I began to protest. "But I will. If you stay here with me a while longer. A few minutes of your time in exchange for the answers you want."

Time inside someone's mind moved at a different pace than time in the world outside. With Jacob, it'd felt like we'd spent days together, but it had only been a few minutes. So, as much as I wanted to take what I needed and flee, I nodded my agreement.

"Very good, then." He took my arm in his and led me along a path following the cliff's edge. "I didn't know anything about fatal insomnia specifically, but when I saw what they wanted Leo to produce, I realized what their motives were. An excellent profit-generating scheme. At least, that's what I thought at the time."

"Profit? Children are dying. Including your own granddaughter, Esme. Now, tell me why."

"I told you why: profit."

I rolled my eyes. "Then tell me who and how."

"Not so fast. First, you tell me about your family."

"My family? Why do you want to know about them?"

"Let's start with your father. She said it started before puberty."

"Who said? I don't understand."

He waved away my questions. "You were twelve when your father had his car crash. You watched him die. Did you touch him? Of course you did—but did you touch him like you're touching me now? Are his memories alive inside you?"

"No. Of course not." I pulled away in horror at the thought.

"Are you sure? Really sure?" He arched a disbelieving eyebrow. "Walk me through it. Every second leading up to his death."

"I'm not going to do that. Why should I?" Now I saw where Leo had inherited his sadism. My father's death was the single most painful event of my life, and Daniel wanted me to relive it for his entertainment?

"Because it will help me give you the answers you seek. I have a theory, but I need more information. Tell me about your father's death."

I walked faster, moving ahead of him so he couldn't see my face. The breeze was scented with wildflowers that reminded me of the honeysuckle that grew wild outside the bedroom window of my childhood home. The only home I knew—until my father died and I lost it.

Everything changed when I lost him.

Blinking back tears at the memory, I brushed my hair back from my face and turned to Daniel. "What do you want to know?"

Chapter 12

"TELL ME MORE about this Brother Tyrone," Ryder asked Grey. "Would he have the resources to build a lab like this one? Does he have a background in science? He doesn't sound like your typical bioterrorist."

"That's the problem. What is a typical bioterrorist?" Grey's gaze remained locked on the expanse of dark forest across the water. "I sure as hell don't know, and I've been doing this for years." His phone rang. "Yeah? Where? Okay, I'm on my way. No, wait—I think I have a local who can help with that." He hung up and turned to Ryder. "My guys think they may have located them. I have to go."

"Where?"

Instead of answering, Grey spun to his left, heading away from the river and the crime scene toward a black Tahoe parked a block up. Ryder followed.

"If there's a terrorist threat in my city, you need to tell me. I can call for backup."

Grey's expression was one of dismissal. "Right. As if I'd trust your department for backup."

"You said you had a local who could help. What did you mean?"

They reached the driver's door. Grey paused, assessing

Ryder. "You were in the Army, right? Early days in Afghanistan?"

"Yeah." Easy enough for a Fed to access Ryder's military record.

"Back when everyone else was in Iraq, it was pretty much just you guys and the DEA chasing Bin Laden in and out of caves and dirt holes." Ryder remained silent. "I need a guy like that now. We've tracked Tyrone's men to an abandoned mine not far from here."

"Up Cambria Mountain?" It was the mountain across the river, home to several abandoned mining operations. Meant to be posted off-limits, but all the locals, including Ryder's family, hunted there.

"Yeah, that's the place. My guys are going to meet us there, do a little recon. Someone who knows the terrain might be helpful."

Ryder hesitated.

Grey opened his door. "If you want to walk away from this, cover your ass, that's fine with me. As far as I'm concerned, we never met."

Ryder knew he was being played. But he also wanted in on the Fed's operation. At the very least, he could learn more about what the Feds knew, see if this Brother Tyrone was behind the fatal insomnia, maybe get a lead that would help Rossi. Not like he had any other leads to follow. "I'm in."

As he climbed into the Tahoe's passenger seat, Ryder sent Price a text letting him know that he was with Grey and asking him to see if he could find out anything on this Brother Tyrone.

Grey must have studied a map, because while he didn't take the back roads that Ryder would have chosen, he also didn't need directions or his nav system to get them to the nearest bridge. Of course, it helped that nine twenty on Christmas night meant no traffic.

"Tell me more about Brother Tyrone," Ryder asked. "And this reincarnated Sons of Adam group. Why haven't they shown up on law enforcement's radar?"

"Tyrone's smart, cunning." Grey tapped the side of his head with his pointer finger. "Never been arrested. Not even charged. Usually, by the time anyone figures out the Sons of Adam might be involved in an event, they're in the wind."

"They're not taking public credit?" Unusual for a terrorist group—usually, it was all about public perception, instilling fear that anyone, anywhere was vulnerable and could be their next target. Of course, that same publicity was also often what got them caught.

"No. Makes them all the more insidious. Take their last target. Small coal town in West Virginia. Population ninety-one percent Caucasian, one hundred percent below the poverty line. People lost the land that had been in their families for generations to the mines and their mountaintop removal. Lost their health after the mining polluted the water—after all, where else you going to dump the top third of a mountain and all the pollution it takes to dig it apart? Lost everything. Least, that's what they thought. Until Brother Tyrone came to town and they lost their souls."

"What happened?" If nothing else, Grey was a good storyteller.

The metal grill of the bridge vibrated beneath their tires. "Property around town began to get bought up. A bunch of Somali refugees—a dozen or so families—pooled their resources, thought West Virginia would be a good place to start over, rebuild, enjoy their newfound freedom. And for a while everything was good. The Somalis reopened the local grocery so people didn't have to drive thirty miles over a mountain just to use their food stamps. Their women began a craft cooperative, selling handmade jewelry and whatnot on the Internet and invited local women to join in."

They reached the end of the bridge. Instead of continuing straight through the tunnel that ran beneath the mountain and headed south to the turnpike, Ryder pointed Grey to the off-ramp heading east and a township road that would take them up the backside of the mountain, where they were less likely to be spotted.

The road narrowed from four lanes to two almost immediately. To their left, a thick growth of trees obscured the view of the river. To the right, the road hugged the curves of the mountain jutting up above them.

"Then Tyrone and his people showed up," Grey continued his story. "Suddenly, folks were boycotting the Somali store, the craft cooperative's website was hacked, folks were disgruntled that foreigners were making money off their hard times. Talk of terrorists hiding out—where better than beautiful West Virginia with its hospitality and good-natured Christian folk, after all? Rumors that the Somalis were planning something, something big."

"Did they run them out of town?"

Grey glanced up. "You could say that. It started with little things. Vandalizing the store and the rooms above it that the Somalis used as their mosque. Catcalls and stalking the women if they went out without a man. Sabotaging vehicles. But then...then they targeted the children. Masked men stopped the school bus one morning, made the Somali children get off and the others watch as they tore the head scarves from the girls and made them all lie down in the dirt. Then the men urinated on them."

Ryder sat up so fast his seat belt ratcheted in protest. "What the hell were they thinking? To do that to children?"

"None older than twelve, mind you. These were families

working for the American dream. They'd lost everything back home and just wanted a chance to start over where they could live in peace. They weren't jihadists, they weren't extremist, they weren't fanatics. They were families."

"Why haven't I heard about this?" Hate crimes would be under federal jurisdiction. And he couldn't imagine the media not having a field day with a story like that.

"Are you kidding? *We* didn't even hear about it until later—that's how terrorized everyone was. Either they agreed with Tyrone and were complicit, or they were too damned scared to make themselves a target. We only learned about it after the Somalis gathered in their store for a meeting about what to do, and the good people of the town, those fine, upstanding churchgoing folks, decided to light the building on fire."

"Anyone hurt?"

"No. Thank God. Someone called in a warning, and everyone got out. The building was leveled, nothing salvageable. Sheriff's department wasn't even going to call us, but a state arson investigator who'd dealt with other church fires that were hate crimes did. By the time we got there, the Somalis were long gone. So was Tyrone. No one would even mention them—the families or the Sons. As if it never happened. As if it was a coincidence they started listening to Tyrone's preaching about standing up for what was theirs and how might makes right and whatever other bullshit rhetoric he used to ignite their rage."

"You think he did that here, that his followers blew up that lab?" Ryder wasn't sure the logic actually worked, but that might be because he knew more than Grey did about what really happened in the lab.

"Yes. And I think the Sons might have taken Lazaretto and Rossi."

"Why? If Tyrone's people were trying to stop a drug lab

and didn't care who they killed, why would they kidnap two doctors who had nothing to do with the lab?"

"What if destroying the lab was just to hide their tracks? What if Tyrone wanted the doctors all along—maybe this time he's trying his hand at something really big."

"Rossi wouldn't be of any use to him. She's an ER doctor, not a lab researcher."

"Maybe she's collateral damage. Maybe Tyrone will use her to get Lazaretto to do what he wants. My research says Lazaretto has worked on some pretty scary stuff—things that kill you in the worst way possible, something called prions. There's no cure, no treatment. Maybe Tyrone's decided it's time to up his game and go for a full-blown apocalypse? If God isn't bringing the End Times fast enough, maybe he's decided to speed things up a bit."

Ryder let that soak in. It might explain why Rossi and the kids had been targeted—some kind of trial run? A test to see if whatever Lazaretto had done to make the fatal insomnia contagious worked?

"What if," he said in a hushed voice, playing into Grey's conspiracy theory, "Lazaretto wasn't an unwilling victim? What if he's been working with Tyrone all along?"

Grey nodded, hunched over the steering wheel, chin jutting out. "Maybe. If you'd seen and heard how Tyrone twists minds— normal, ordinary people turned into rampaging vigilantes. If anyone could pull this off, it's him. He's a charismatic devil. Believe me."

"If you're right...we can't take any chances. Not with something like this."

"Exactly."

"Slow down," Ryder instructed. "There's a logging road we can use. Trees are dense enough, and the ridge line juts out so we won't be spotted."

He directed Grey onto a narrow gravel logging road heading up the mountain. There was a gate guarding it, but it was open—from the rust pattern and snow piled up against it, it'd been that way for some time.

"Who do you think Tyrone and the Sons of Adam are targeting? What's their plan?" Ryder continued his fishing expedition. All of the children infected with the fatal insomnia came from Kingston Tower, a low-income housing project. Other than that, he didn't think they had anything in common.

Grey shrugged. "Wish I knew. Like I said, they target anyone who they see as encroaching on their idea of what this country should be—as long as they're too weak to fight back. Way he operates, under the radar, I think the last thing Tyrone wants is open warfare."

"Hence the bioterrorism."

"Exactly. You asked before what a typical bioterrorist looked like. Fact is, they hide in the shadows. That's their strength, their way of maximizing the terror while minimizing their own risk. Think of the anthrax attacks after 9/11. Or that synagogue whose congregation was poisoned after someone coated their prayer books with a caustic chemical."

"Great. A passive-aggressive homespun terrorist who thinks he has God on his side." Ryder did not like the thought of dealing with that combination of smart and crazy. Bioterrorism made it too easy to kill from a distance—not to mention the collateral damage, like the mail clerks and secretaries who'd opened the anthrax letters.

The Tahoe bounced over ruts gouged into the snow and gravel—it wasn't the first vehicle up this road since the snow had stopped last night.

Ryder thought about what Devon had told him about the infected children. They'd all had symptoms for months, about as long as Rossi had. Which meant they were all infected around the same time, sometime over the summer had been Rossi's best guess. Which also meant that whoever was behind this was playing a very, very long game.

"What if they blew up their lab because they didn't need it any longer? What if the attack has already begun?"

Grey straightened at that. "Then I guess we better hope we find them and can get them to talk. Before it's too late."

Chapter 13

DANIEL'S FIRST QUESTION surprised me. "Tell me about your father's family. Did you ever meet them?"

The sea below us threw up more whitecaps, taller, faster as they stormed the rocks only to surrender and return back to where they came from. A never-ending circle of destruction, stunning in its ravenous energy.

"No. They died before I was born."

Why did my answer make his lips quirk as if suppressing a smile? "And your father? What was he like?"

My father was the sun and the moon and every star adorning the heavens. He taught me to laugh without fear, to always run as fast as I could, to be kind—even to my bratty little sister—to sing and dance and play my fiddle with not just my hands and feet but my heart and soul.

None of which I would share with Daniel. But he nodded as if somehow he already knew. "The day he died. Tell me about that day."

"And you'll tell me what you know about Almanac?"

"And I'll tell you what I know about Almanac Care." He said the name as if it was important not to shorten it.

I didn't have time to wonder about that as I tried to wring words from the heartache that was my father's death. "It was my fault. That's what you want to know, right?"

There, that was the hard part over with. At least I thought so until he said, "No. I want it all. Everything that happened. Don't leave a single second out."

Lightning flashed through the sky in the distance. I stared out to sea and saw a wall of churning black clouds dancing across the horizon. My doing or his? He was getting what he wanted; this sudden storm had to come from me. I drew in a breath, feeling as if that raging storm was trapped inside my chest, and began.

"The nuns gave me detention. Again. I don't even remember why—usually, it was for arguing with a teacher." I shrugged. Wind whipped my hair against my face. It stung, but nothing compared to the pain the memory brought. "When no one came to get me after school and detention ended, I decided to walk home alone."

"It was raining, a storm?"

Suddenly, the clouds overhead darkened and rumbled with thunder. Rain sluiced down, plastering me—although, not three feet away, Daniel stood in a patch of sunshine, warm and dry. He'd grown taller... No. I'd grown smaller, back to the skinny twelve-year-old I had been twenty-two years ago. I shivered with the wet and cold and hugged my arms around my chest.

"Yes. But I'd have been just as drenched waiting outside the school as on the road home, so I started to walk. Back then we lived outside of town, up the mountain, a few miles from school. I almost made it."

"In other words, you were a stubborn child. Why does that not surprise me?"

I ignored him, wanting to get this over with. "Patsy, my mom, was home with my little sister, and I thought I'd make it there before Dad got home from work. Had some childish fantasy of somehow proving I was right—as if walking home alone in the rain and dark would win an argument my mother wasn't even there for."

I shrugged, the memory of those childish feelings rankling inside me. Maybe because even twenty-two years later I still sometimes clung to them. "It's just how I felt back then. Like I had to prove myself to everyone."

"Including your father?"

"Everyone except him." I trailed off, hoping the admission would satisfy his appetite for pain.

"Go on. You were almost home. It was dark, storming. What happened next?"

"I was halfway up the mountain. It was a blind curve, steep. He didn't see me, not until it was too late. He hit his brakes, swerved, crashed through the guardrail and into a tree." The words caught in my throat. I couldn't even swallow around them.

"Did he go through the windshield? Was there blood? But he was still alive, still conscious, wasn't he?"

I shook my head violently, protesting his callous words as much as the memory that filled my every sense. The sound of the storm changed; the smell of sea air vanished along with the crash of breaking waves. It grew darker, trees suddenly crowded around me as I stood on the muddy berm at the side of a narrow blacktop road. Red taillights spiked through the night, canted at an unnatural angle, aimed high at the sky while the car they clung to faced down the side of the mountain.

It was silent. Even the raindrops thudding against the blacktop grew distant. The only noise I could hear was the drumming of my heart and the shriek of agony that tore my soul in half. Because I'd seen his face, in that instant before everything was too late, I'd seen him, blurred by rain and windshield wipers and headlights, but it was him.

"Daddy!" I blinked, and my hearing returned, everything too loud: the rain and wind and blare of a horn giving a single, never-ending bleat, the creak of the trees, the grind of metal.

The guardrail was twisted and torn. I grabbed on to it like a lifeline, my palms sliced bloody by the sharp metal, half climbed, half slipped through the mud and dead leaves and fallen tree branches to make it to the driver's side of the car.

The door was open, its chiming adding to the cacophony. The interior light made the blood appear black.

"No, he didn't go through the windshield," Daniel said, and I realized he was there with me, walking around the crash, observing it all with a clinical appraisal. "Had his seat belt on." He made a clucking noise with his tongue. "No air bags, though."

"His truck was too old," I answered in my grown-up voice, although I was somehow still trapped inside the body of twelve-year-old me, scared spitless, howling at her father to open his eyes. Please, Daddy, open your eyes...

And he did. Trapped with the steering wheel caving in his chest, face bloodied, skull already swelling where he'd cracked it on the dashboard, he opened his eyes. Saw me. And his face, his face—I'd never seen him look at anything, at anyone, at *me* like that before.

"Go away," he shouted, waving me off with his one good hand. "Don't come any closer."

How could I obey when he needed my help? I slid along the side of the truck, reached out to him. "Daddy—"

He cringed. Pulled back, tried to slam the door shut between me and him. It refused to move, but that was little comfort to me when his face filled with horror.

"Daddy!" I screamed into the night.

"Don't touch me!" He screamed back. "Don't you touch

me!"

The last words I ever heard from him.

"And you didn't touch him, did you?" Daniel prodded the psychic wounds I'd ripped open.

"No. I went to get help."

"He lived another three days. In a coma."

I nodded.

"But you never saw him again. Never touched him."

"They didn't let children into the ICU. And Patsy—"

"His wife. She didn't want you there, did she?"

"No. I went to live with my aunt and uncle after that. I looked too much like him. Every time she laid eyes on me, it was like seeing him die all over again."

"He knew," Daniel murmured. "I wonder if she did as well."

I barely heard him over the sounds of my memory. I drew in a deep breath and forced another memory to take its place: me and Daddy dancing, my feet on his, my mother laughing as she spun with my baby sister in her arms, happy, everyone so very happy...

The moment burst like a bubble spun on air and hope. We were back on the cliff, the sea roaring below us, the sky above cloudless. Daniel smirked, and I knew he'd brought us back here, yanking me away from my memory.

"Your father had fatal insomnia, right?"

"Yes. We didn't know it back then, of course. But Louise tested his DNA from a sample I gave her. It's autosomal dominant, so my sister and I each had a fifty-fifty chance of inheriting it. Guess who won that coin toss?" Actually, I was happy my little sister had been spared—despite the distance between my mother and me, I couldn't imagine her suffering the loss of both of us.

"I don't think your sister ever had a chance of inheriting your father's affliction. Just as I don't think you ever had a chance of not inheriting it."

I frowned at him. "What are you saying?"

"Your mother, Patsy, she told you that you look just like him, your father?"

"Yes."

"She's only half right. You look just like your mother. Your *real* mother."

Chapter 14

FRANCESCA HAD ORIGINALLY planned to spend the night at the Danieli but changed her mind once the vote didn't go her way. Or rather, Marco changed it for her. After the vote condemning her and her people to a life of exile on their island, she'd left the dining room and found a trio of armed men waiting for her.

Marco appeared behind her. The restaurant lobby was empty except for them, the hostess vanished, the wait staff behind mahogany doors that Francesca was certain would be locked if she tried them. She stood, ignoring the three men with their designer suit coats open to reveal the menacing pistols in their shoulder holsters, and focused on her brother.

"Is this how it begins, little brother?" she asked, ice in her voice. "With my murder? The first of many."

He shook his head sadly but didn't bother to hide his smirk. "I'm sorry, but the family has spoken. It's time for a new era. One without the encumbrance that you and the others pose. In these economic times, it's essential to prune away any non-profitable branches of the family tree. For the good of the family."

Francesca rarely indulged her emotions. Fifty-seven years of living with a death sentence threatening her every hope and dream had stripped her of sentimentality. She could be ruthless, heartless, even with the lives of her own children if they threatened her plans. But this... "It has nothing to do with economics or the good of the family," she spat at her brother. "This is about power. You are afraid of what you cannot control. Our power."

"It's been decades since you've wielded any power. When the last Vessel died, so did your last chance. It's only through Father's sentimentality that you've lived this long. But Father's gone, and the time has come, Francesca." He stretched his arms wide as if embracing the future. "And the family will live on, free of fear. Healthy and more powerful than ever."

"No, dear brother. It won't. You're making a mistake. The Lazaretto power comes not from the strength of our healthy members but rather from those of us with the Scourge. We decide each and every day to face our fears, to conquer them. We dare to live, knowing the horror that awaits us in death. That is true strength. Without us, the family will shrivel and wither away to nothing. Dust scattered in the wind. The Lazaretto name—your name—forgotten, forever."

"You always had such an imagination, Francesca. Must come of those fever-dreams your people suffer. What do you call them? Your fugues?" He shook his head as if scolding a toddler. "Fantasies wrought of brains deranged by the Scourge. No one is here to kill you. We're here to watch over and protect you. You will return to your island and recall your people so that they can join you."

He nodded to the men, and they surrounded Francesca, two taking her arms as if leading a doddering old woman who'd had too much to drink. "In a week's time, after the holiday, I'll send more men to dismantle your lab. All that fancy equipment, such an expense for the family. Hopefully, we'll recoup some of its value."

Worse than exile. Without the lab, she was helpless to finish her work. "No. Why? We can still contribute. My people are expert scientists. You won't find any more dedicated. You can't take their life's work from them like this."

"Not me. You, Francesca. Did you really think I wouldn't learn about those monstrosities you call your children, what they're doing? They're risking exposing the family. They're dangerous. Any of them who aren't safely locked away on the island by dawn of the New Year will be hunted down and killed." He waved a hand in dismissal, and the guards tugged her forward.

"You'll regret this, Marco," Francesca called over her shoulder.

His laughter accompanied her down the hallway, echoing from the marble floor and walls.

☽ ✴ ☾

I WONDERED IF I was wrong about lies being impossible when I met someone via their mind. Because what Daniel was saying about my parents—it could not be true.

"What do you mean, my 'real' mother? Do you think I don't know who my own mother is?" Maybe Patsy and I didn't always get along, but she was my mother, that much I was certain of.

Daniel merely shrugged. "Maybe all I meant was she could be your mother, you look so much alike."

"This woman, who is she?" None of this made any sense.

Then I relaxed. Of course none of it made sense. His mind had been damaged by the stroke—unlike the other people I'd visited, Daniel's brain was already ravaged, riddled with areas of dead tissue. I couldn't take anything he said or showed me literally. Yet, he seemed so deliberate. A form of confabulation?

Maybe, given his supersize ego and narcissism, he couldn't admit to himself that his mental functions were impaired?

"You're trying to sidetrack me," I told him. "You think that if you can distract me with innuendoes about my family, you can hide the truth from me."

He raised an eyebrow. "Is that what I'm doing? Or is this my way of unveiling the truth?"

"I told you about my father's death. Now tell me what I need to know to save the children Tommaso infected with fatal insomnia."

"Are you certain it was him? Maybe he stumbled onto this so-called epidemic of yours and was studying it." He began walking inland, away from the rocky coast. Trees and shrubs appeared, at first ragged and wild, then gradually becoming more cultivated.

"No. He and his men killed Jacob to test my abilities. They had an entire lab set up where they could study prions. A lab funded by Almanac Care and filled with equipment from Kingston Enterprises."

"We sell state-of-the-art medical equipment all over the world. Why do you expect me to remember one random client?"

"Not so random. Not when your son was also working for them. Tell me, did Leo create a way for them to infect us with the prions? Was it his doing?"

The more agitated I became, the calmer his demeanor. Infuriating. The boxwood hedges around us now stretched higher than my head, casting shadows on our path. They closed in, separated by a mere arm's width. Daniel had led me into a maze.

"Leo was a genius. But he wasn't the one who developed the artificial prions—that was another brilliant mind. One obsessed with fatal insomnia."

"You said you'd never heard of fatal insomnia."

"Maybe I didn't. At least not by that name. Not until I learned about it from your memories." He turned to grin at me. "After all, this is a meeting of the minds, Dr. Rossi. What you know, I know."

Except I wasn't learning what I needed from him. He'd hidden his truth under layers of misdirection—and I'd helped by playing his twisted game, telling him about my father's death.

In the distance, from beyond the maze, I heard a woman's laugh, followed by the sound of horses galloping.

"Who is this mysterious woman you keep mentioning? The one you say I look like. She's the brilliant mind you're talking about, right?"

"Her name would be meaningless to you."

"Then don't tell me her name. Tell me about her. Her work with fatal insomnia."

"Her name is Francesca," he answered, zigging to my zag, avoiding answering me with the information I needed. "And she was the love of my life."

Chapter 15

BACK WHEN HE worked for the Russians, Devon had learned the necessity of playing offense and defense simultaneously. You had to grow your turf while also protecting against encroachment from rivals.

But back then, he'd known the players and their playbook. They weren't nameless, faceless, ruthless Machiavellian assholes who targeted children. They didn't have a six-month head start—Angela's best guess as to when she and the children had been infected. And they single-mindedly pursued their goals, making it easy for Devon to play them against themselves.

These guys? Almanac? He didn't even know what the hell they wanted.

No matter. They'd made a lethal mistake, coming here, targeting his daughter. Bastards were already dead, they just didn't know it.

He led Ozzie through the tunnels to the entrance at Good Sam's basement. They took the stairs up to the ER, Ozzie's nails click-clacking against the linoleum floor.

The ER was its usual flavor of mayhem: raucous noise echoing through the halls, the stench of bleach and blood mingling to leave a metallic taste behind, the lights of an approaching ambulance washing the tile walls in neon.

He turned away from the cacophony and sidled down the back corridor to the doors of the Advocacy Center. The lights were off, which he took as a good sign that at least on Christmas night there was no need for the center's services to perform sexual assault or abuse examinations. Sad to say, he was certain that wouldn't be the case come tomorrow. Nature of the beast.

He and Ozzie continued through empty hallways to the main wing, where they took an elevator up to the third floor.

First stop, Louise's office and the lab she'd shared with Tommaso. She'd given Devon her keys and computer access codes so he could retrieve the children's medical records. Hopefully, there would be a link between them that would lead back to how they were all infected.

While the computer did its thing, dumping the information onto the thumb drive he'd brought as well as uploading it to the cloud so Louise's husband could also access it from London, he left Ozzie standing guard—okay, curled up on the floor in front of the office door, his bulk preventing any entrance—and prowled through Louise's office space. It was as meticulous and cheerful as its owner. In between the walnut-framed diplomas from Oxford, Penn, and Johns Hopkins were delightful watercolor and pencil sketches, the kind you'd find being sold by street artists in any major city, framed with as much loving care as the academic achievements.

Despite the world having long gone to computer databases, Louise still had floor-to-ceiling bookcases brimming with old, well-worn medical texts. He took one at random, *Robbins Basic Pathology*, and opened it to find notes in the margins in Louise's precise script.

The computer finished its work. He pocketed the thumb drive and moved into the lab next door. There was a desk in the corner—Tommaso's—but the laptop was gone, and other than leftover carryout napkins and condiments, there was nothing.

Of course not. He wouldn't leave his research—his real research, not the prion assay he'd been working on with Louise—out in the open. Still, just to be on the safe side, Devon took photos of the whiteboards with their chemical equations and every scrap of paper that had any writing on it. Then he shot a video of the lab setup in case Louise needed to replicate it.

There was a small glass-fronted refrigerator beside the lab bench. Inside were tiny plastic tubes labeled with patient names: Angela, Esme, and the other children. These were the tests Tommaso had run to diagnose their fatal insomnia. The tubes with their drops of pink fluid at the bottom looked too small to be carrying death sentences.

Of course, so did a bullet. Right before it blasted through someone's skull.

Devon debated taking the specimens but decided to wait. He could always send someone back for them with the proper equipment to keep them at the right temperature, and Louise hadn't said she needed them. Besides, there was one more key on Tommaso's key ring that he wanted to check out.

It was a hospital key, that much he recognized. Since last month when he took over the tunnels, he'd been collecting keys from Good Sam in order to access the rooms closest to the underground entrance—including the room that held the hospital's incinerator, which had come in handy. That key he'd taken from Leo's body. He'd also found a duplicate in Daniel's study, making him wonder how many generations of Kingstons had used Good Samaritan to dispose of unwanted bodies.

This key was old, the letters and numbers on it worn to the point where he could barely feel them. Using one of the magnifiers in the lab, he examined it more closely. SB24. Subbasement. Room twenty-four. Where the hell was that?

You could wander lost for days through the maze of rooms below Good Sam. Good thing he'd brought a canine GPS with him. "Let's go."

They retreated back down to the hospital's subbasement. Devon gave Ozzie his head to lead them through the labyrinth of forgotten storage areas and utility rooms.

As always, Devon found the dog to be a better companion than most humans. He wondered if Ozzie felt the same about him, decided that on a list of favorite humans, he fell far behind Esme but probably ahead of Flynn, with Angela and Ryder somewhere in between. For some reason, the thought made him smile.

Ozzie alerted, clearly scenting something more interesting than the stench of mold and decay that filled Devon's nostrils, his tail arching upright as he padded through the dimly lit concrete-walled corridors, turning without hesitation at intersections.

This part of the hospital was the original building, well over a hundred years old with faded brick peeking through cracked plaster and peeling paint. The overhead lights had been changed from incandescent bulbs—the abandoned housings still lined the ceiling, stark-white porcelain receptacles appearing naked and empty—to suspended fluorescent strips that flickered annoyingly.

Finally, they came to a stop in front of a solid door, dark wood streaked with peeling gray paint. Ozzie sat, tail thumping against the concrete floor, nose tilted to Devon as if waiting for a treat. Devon hadn't thought to bring any but did spare a moment to crouch down and rub the dog's head and belly. Ozzie bobbed his head, nodding his muzzle against Devon's palm.

Devon stood and scraped the small brass plate in the center of the door with his thumbnail. SB24. "Good dog."

He inserted Lazaretto's key in the old-fashioned lock. It turned easily—recently oiled, as were the hinges that swung the door open without protest.

Instead of the cobwebs and disuse that permeated the rest of the floor, when he clicked on the light switch, he saw a series of gleaming metal shelves stacked with white plastic jugs of chemicals. Not exactly the revelation he'd been hoping for, but he snapped photos of each label in the hopes that knowing what chemicals Tommaso had been working with might help Louise and Angela re-create his research.

He'd reached the rear of the room when he spotted a door painted to match the wall, hidden behind a final shelf. Curiosity piqued, he rolled the shelving unit aside—not only did it move easily on its casters, the containers stacked on it were empty. The door was locked, and none of the keys on Tommaso's ring fit.

Devon knelt to examine the lock. Brand new. A Schlage J Series. Tommaso might have gone one better and used a digital or electronic lock, but it would have been bulkier, made the door stand out.

He opened his wallet and slid free a narrow length of steel along with its companion, a stiff piece of wire, from their hiding place in the seams. Picking locks was one of Devon's natural talents—something he'd found to his advantage when he was a kid and the Royales gang had inducted him. He was the shrimp, the runt of the litter, no match for any of them in a fistfight, but he was smart, fast, and had nimble fingers that could sweet-talk any lock into giving up its secrets.

The Schlage was no exception. The lock clicked open, and he turned the knob. The room beyond was dark. He reached inside, felt for a light switch. Nothing.

Ozzie startled him, nudging the back of his knee and giving a low moan as if warning Devon that he wouldn't like what he found inside the cave of a room.

Devon ignored the dog's instincts—even though he was

certain Ozzie was right. He stepped into the room, using his cellphone as a flashlight. The bluish glare of the light revealed a woman's face, twisted and wrinkled, eyes cloudy, tongue protruding from a slack jaw.

He jerked away, hand brushing against an overhead chain. He pulled the chain, and the room was illuminated.

Not one face. A dozen or more. Staring at him from specimen jars where their decapitated heads floated.

Chapter 16

DANIEL WAS TRYING to divert me from the truth I needed, that much I was certain of. What was he hiding? More of Leo's crimes? But Leo was already dead, would never be punished for any of the murders he'd committed. Why was Daniel so interested in my family? And who was this Francesca he seemed to think I looked like? How could she possibly be my biological mother?

Focus, I reminded myself. I was here to get answers, not find more questions.

"Tell me about Francesca," I said. The boxwood walls of the maze crowded closer, forcing us to walk single file, me behind Daniel.

"I first met Francesca when I was young." His tone grew wistful. "My father still ran Kingston Enterprises, so I had more freedom. He'd taken me on a business trip to Europe, wanted to teach me the art of negotiation as he entered into a new partnership."

I stopped, not caring that we were still lost in the maze. I tried to curb my impatience—after all, if I left without answers, there was no coming back for a second attempt. Which meant Daniel could take all the time he wanted, and I had no choice but to let him. Still, it was so frustrating, knowing the price we paid for any delay. "I'm not interested in your father or Kingston

Enterprises. Tell me what I need to know."

He looked over his shoulder at me, a smug smile playing across his features. "I'm trying to. You need to learn to have more faith in people."

So said the father of a sadistic serial killer. But I held my tongue and nodded. "Go on. You met Francesca in Europe."

"My father preferred to do business with established, family-run companies similar to Kingston Enterprises. He hated the idea of allowing stockholders or government regulators to interfere with our business. Francesca's family is one of the oldest on the Continent. While our fathers met for their business discussions, Francesca and I shared more intimate negotiations."

I was about to make a snide remark about not caring about his sex life, but from his expression, I knew that was exactly what he wanted. "What was her family's business?"

That earned me another of his sly smiles. We turned a corner, and the maze walls changed from boxwood to holly with sharp-edged leaves and red and white berries. The sky overhead brightened, but the hedge that held us hostage was still tall enough to keep us in shadows.

"Almanac Care is only one of their many subsidiaries. Francesca's family deals in power. Over generations they have accumulated immense financial wealth, but more importantly, they hold influence with every major European government. My father wanted to expand Kingston Enterprises into Europe, and the Lazarettos—"

"Wait. Lazaretto? As in Dr. Tommaso Lazaretto?"

"Exactly. Tommaso is—was—Francesca's son."

"He killed himself rather than tell us the truth behind the fatal insomnia. But I'm sure he's the one who infected the children."

"Of course he was." He was agreeing to something that

not five minutes ago he'd argued against. I held my tongue, let him continue. "But that's not why he killed himself. He killed himself to protect his family and their secrets."

"What kind of secrets? Why would they do this? If they run a business, it makes no sense. Prion disease is much too rare to make a profit—" I stopped myself. He nodded encouragingly, which made me suspicious that he was leading me. But it did make sense in a Machiavellian, money-hungry way. "Unless you find a way to make a hard-to-spread, impossible-to-treat, rare disease common. Then it becomes a threat to everyone."

"And a potential profit-making engine." Daniel sounded as if he approved of the scheme. Of course he did. His own company had been accused of concealing early warning signs of the Ebola epidemic in order to increase their profit margin on the vaccine they developed.

I stopped. The hedgerow beside me thinned, leaving a gap wide enough for me to spy a gazebo covered in roses and dripping with wisteria on the other side of the maze. "If Francesca's family wants to spread prions, create an artificial epidemic of fatal insomnia, then that means they must have a cure. There's no money in it otherwise."

"It's how I would do it. *If* that's their objective."

Was he baiting me, trying to lead me away from questions about a cure? Or dangling a clue that there was more going on here? I wanted desperately to leave, to escape this ridiculous cat-and-mouse game Daniel had trapped me inside. Riddles inside riddles and not a straight answer in sight.

I grabbed his arm and pushed through the gap in the hedge, pulling him along with me to the gazebo. The holly scratched at me, but it parted miraculously for Daniel, leaving him unscathed. Of course. His mind, his rules.

We sat down on old-fashioned high-backed wicker chairs,

the breeze a relief after the claustrophobic air of the maze. "You are going to answer me. Is there a cure for fatal insomnia?"

A tea set appeared on the table between us. Daniel helped himself, carefully pouring tea into a delicate cup, then measuring sugar, prolonging my agony.

"I don't know," he finally answered.

"Why did Francesca's family hire Leo to refine the PXA formulation? What do they use it for?"

I knew what we were using it for—not just to help me slip inside minds, but also to alleviate some of my symptoms, make my fugues easier to manage. And Leo, well, he'd made his own special, highly concentrated form of PXA and used it to torture his victims before killing them. The pain created by Leo's PXA was so great, he could use it to convince his victims to do almost anything. But the doses required to achieve that level of control invariably left his victims dead or in an irreversible coma.

Daniel sipped at his tea, watching me. He knew exactly what I was thinking. "You have his memories. Why not search them?"

"Because it would mean reliving every murder he committed," I snapped. "Besides, maybe the Lazarettos didn't tell him what they wanted it for."

"Leo had vision. Understood the power behind possibilities."

"No more fortune-cookie truisms. Tell me."

"I'll do better than that. I'll show you."

☽ �*/☾

RYDER AND GREY drove slowly up the mountain. Ryder craned his head, looking up through the windshield. "Stop. I see lights above us. Could be Tyrone and his men."

92

Grey turned off the headlights and pulled over. He hopped out and headed to the SUV's rear. Ryder opened his door, ice-covered branches scraping against the metal, and stepped into a snowdrift. He barely noticed the snow slipping into the tops of his Rockports, he was so focused on the mission. First thing, they needed backup. Along with weapons and better outerwear. A little aerial recon might help as well.

He joined Grey at the back of the Tahoe. Grey had a Remington 870 and a box of slugs for it.

"How many men do you have?" Ryder asked as he pulled his gloves off so he could dial.

"Who are you calling?" Grey snapped, frowning at Ryder.

"The sheriff's department. It's their jurisdiction." Then he glanced at his cell. No service. Of course not, damn mountain. He'd forgotten how the iron ore interfered with what limited cell coverage there was on this side of the river.

"We can't call anyone, not yet."

"We sure as hell aren't going in there alone." Ryder glanced at Grey's fancy leather shoes.

"First of all, we don't even know where *there* is. Or who's waiting for us. Those lights could be some kids partying or hunters or some other civilians. And if it is Tyrone and the Sons, we can't risk spooking them."

"What's your plan?" Ryder asked, already certain he wouldn't like it.

"I put a tracker on Tyrone's vehicle. But I don't know if he's alone. And I've lost the signal." He reached into the Tahoe and pulled out a camouflage parka and a pair of boots. "We'll take a quick look—keep our distance, surveillance only. Got it? I don't want you playing hero. You're just here to observe and advise."

Grey stepped away from the car and exchanged his

overcoat for the parka. He was at the corner of the SUV, bent over to tie his boots, when the noise of ice cracking snapped through the air. Ryder spun, drawing his weapon, aiming into the darkness surrounding them.

"Drop the gun and keep your hands where I can see them," a man's voice came from the trees to his right.

Three men stepped out of the shadows, dressed in full winter camouflage down to the balaclavas covering their heads, each holding an assault rifle aimed at Grey and Ryder. Grey had been in the process of redressing, his SIG and shotgun behind them on the Tahoe's rear gate, out of reach. Leaving them only Ryder's pistol as a weapon.

The crunch of boots on the snow told Ryder that there were at least two more behind them as well. Grey raised his hands in surrender. The man nearest him grabbed him, aiming a pistol at Grey's head.

"Your turn," one of the men said. Ryder couldn't tell which one, since the voice had come from behind him.

Outgunned, surrounded, no backup, an FBI agent as a hostage. Ryder's lips twisted tight as he slowly lowered his weapon and set it on the Tahoe's rear bumper. Another masked man pulled him away from the vehicle, and frisked him, taking his cell phone and wallet.

Grey was receiving similar treatment a few yards away from Ryder. "Clear!" one of the men shouted.

A final man, this one dressed in regular civilian hiking clothing, his face uncovered, stepped forward. He was a little shorter than Ryder, with dark brown hair and an otherwise unremarkable face. Except for the gleam in his eyes when he caught sight of Grey.

"Special Agent Grey, so nice to finally meet you in person," the man—Brother Tyrone, Ryder assumed—drawled. He pulled a small black box, a vehicle tracker, from his pocket. "I believe this belongs to you?"

Chapter 17

OZZIE GAVE A single bark, then sank to his haunches and backed up until he was well outside the door to the room filled with decapitated heads.

"Good boy," Devon told him. "You're a damn sight smarter than me." He knew he was going to regret this, but he had to investigate. Not because of morbid curiosity, but because he thought he recognized one of those faces floating in a jar. Maybe more than one. "Stay."

Ozzie didn't argue the point as Devon stepped back inside the room. Closet was more like it, about ten feet square, three walls filled floor to ceiling with metal shelving. He counted fourteen heads. Beside each one was a large plastic tub the size of a dishpan, sealed with an airtight lid.

"I'm not going to like this, am I?" He reached for the nearest tub and snapped the lid off. Inside, arranged in sheets of plastic, resembling frozen hamburger patties sealed to stay fresh, were slices of brain. Except they didn't look right. Weird holes honeycombed through them.

Devon yanked his hand back and reached for his phone. "Louise? I could use a pair of expert eyes over here."

"All right, as soon as I'm done monitoring Angela. It's really quite fascinating—more than the theta spindles, the brain activity in the speech and auditory areas of the brain are synchronizing as if they're having an actual conversation. And your father's stroke destroyed most of that area, so—"

"Wait. Angela is still with Daniel?" He glanced at the time; it'd been over two hours.

"Yes. Why? Is that unusual?" She spoke as if he was some kind of expert. Guess since he was the only person who'd watched Angela enter a mind, he was.

"I'm not sure. When I saw her do it, it only lasted a few minutes. But the person she was inside was—"

"Dying. If their brain function deteriorated while they were communicating with Angela, perhaps that broke the bond. Which means she's wrong and it wasn't her reaching out to them that killed them."

"And so Daniel might not die after she leaves him?" Damn, he was rather looking forward to the old devil finally getting his due.

"Perhaps not. At any rate, both of their vitals are stable, no signs of any distress from either of them."

"Still. If it lasts much longer. or if you see any change at all, you might want to pull her out."

"What if that does more harm?"

He remembered when Angela entered his mother's mind. Her brain had been too damaged for even Angela to reach, and it had been difficult to wake Angela back up—but she'd also shown "distress," as Louise put it, enough so that even a layperson like Devon had known she was in trouble.

"No. She'll be fine," he reassured Louise, inserting a measure of confidence in his voice to hide the fact that he was half-ass guessing.

Speaking of freaky events... "Is there any chance Tommaso was working with Leo?"

"Leo Kingston? Your half-brother?"

"My half-brother, the sadistic serial killer, yeah."

"Whyever would you—"

"Because the police never found most of his victims. Before he died, Angela pulled their identities from his memories, and I've been using the Kingston money to help the families. Angela told me Leo burned their bodies in the hospital incinerator, so we had no hope of ever finding any proof."

"Devon. What did you find?"

"Their heads. Decapitated. Stored inside a special locked room at Good Sam's that Tommaso kept hidden. Each one had their brains dissected, all sealed up in little plastic-wrap pouches. All with holes like Angela's brain scan—but a lot more and bigger."

Her inhalation was sharp enough to echo over the phone. "Don't touch anything. Can you send me photos? But without—"

"Touching. Yeah, I got it." He'd already taken photos of the faces to compare with the ones on the missing-persons fliers. Now he shot more of the slices of brain in the open container. "Sending them to you now. Each head has a container filled like this one. These are just from one of the tubs."

"Yes, I see. Definite spongiform encephalopathy. And from the concentration in the thalamic area, probably the same disease Angela is suffering from."

Devon stepped farther back, away from the room. "So, prions? He has brains infected with prions just sitting around? Why didn't he keep them in the Almanac lab with all those special biohazard pods?"

"You mean the portable Level Three labs? That certainly would have been the proper procedure, at the very least. Technically, prions require Level Four containment protocols."

"What do we do? I can't just let these sit around for some clueless janitor to stumble on."

"Don't try to move them yourself. From the photos, it appears that Tommaso at least took some precautions. Still, it begs the question—"

"What the hell was he hiding from his own guys at Almanac?"

"Exactly. Otherwise, he would have been working in their lab with proper equipment."

"Wait. Maybe he was using proper equipment. Just not here at Good Sam's and not in the Almanac lab. Leo had several labs of his own set up in the tunnels. Where he perfected his PXA."

"And probably synthesized the reversal agent for Almanac Care."

"Exactly. Plus, Leo had access to any medical equipment he wanted. I'll bet somewhere down in those tunnels there's a Level Three biohazard lab set up, and that's where Tommaso was working."

"Until you and Angela discovered Leo and you took over the tunnels, cleared them out. Forcing Tommaso to move." She paused. "If that's the case, and he was hiding this second avenue of research from his partners at Almanac, then he would have kept a record of his findings. Probably video recordings as well as written notes."

"Separate from the laptop he used here for his legitimate research, I hope. Because there wasn't any in his lab near your office."

"Don't you think a phone would be more likely? One used only for this project? He couldn't risk his partners in crime learning he was pursuing another agenda separate from theirs."

"Maybe the same agenda." Hell of a euphemism for

infecting almost two dozen children with a lethal disease. "Only, Tommaso wanted to get there first." Why the hell would they be competing to be the first to perfect an artificially transmitted prion disease?

"It would help if we had an idea what their objective was."

"Is it safe for me to search the room if I don't disturb any of the brain tissue?" He wasn't actually asking for permission— he was going to find Tommaso's research notes and didn't care if in the process he exposed himself to the prions that were already killing Esme.

If he lost her, he lost everything.

Chapter 18

TYRONE'S MEN RESTRAINED Ryder and Grey, handcuffing their hands behind their backs. The cuffs appeared regulation, which gave Ryder hope. Ever since last month, when he'd been held by a serial killer, he'd resumed using an old patrol officer's trick of secreting an emergency handcuff key inside his rear belt loop. All he needed now was a little time and privacy.

They crowded into the Tahoe's rear seat, Tyrone in the front and one of his men driving, while another guarded Ryder and Grey.

"Who's your friend, Agent Grey?" Tyrone asked once they were under way. He twisted in his seat, holding Ryder's identification up and squinting as if doubting what he saw. "Detective Matthew Ryder. I know you. You got shot by that serial killer last month."

Leo Kingston. The twisted genius who'd created the perfect chemical to torture his victims with. Ryder blinked, kept his expression neutral as pieces snapped together in his brain. Leo was hired to work on the PXA drug compound...and one of the uses of PXA was to temper the effects of fatal insomnia. Couldn't be a coincidence.

Which meant these men knew Leo. Probably blamed Ryder for his death. Maybe Lazaretto and the others in the lab had been completing Leo's work? Only one way to find out. He just hoped that he lived long enough to pass on any intel he might gain. "I know about the PXA and Leo Kingston."

Grey jerked from where he sat on the other side of Ryder. Stared at him with a "What the hell are you thinking?" glare. But if Tyrone was working with Leo, then Ryder wasn't telling him anything he didn't already know. The potential to gain useful information far outweighed any risks.

Tyrone merely chuckled. "Oh, you do, do you?"

"He was working for you. Was he also involved in the fatal insomnia distribution mechanism? Research genius like that, must have set you back when he died."

"Maybe," Tyrone conceded. "But not for long."

Tyrone's driver followed the twisting lane as it switchbacked through the forest, taking a virtually invisible turn onto an even more rutted and narrow trail. A lonely beam of light from above them teased through the thick trees as they headed up the mountain.

"I'll give you this," Ryder continued, trying to maneuver Tyrone into divulging something useful. "You guys definitely know how to play the long game. You infected those kids when? June? July? What was it like, sitting and waiting for their symptoms to appear, not knowing if it worked or not?"

"Easier than you think. We had other business to occupy us."

"Pretty genius. A disease that works so slowly, you're long gone before anyone even thinks to consider a terrorist attack. Not to mention there's no known cure." He paused, wishing he could see Tyrone's face more clearly in the dim light. There was a spark of something there. He hoped. "At least not known publicly. But you have a cure, don't you? You must. You'd never risk releasing prions without one. Did Leo come up with it? Or are you working with someone else? Like Tommaso Lazaretto?"

Tyrone's mouth quirked, and Ryder was sure he was about to respond, but the SUV slipped and fishtailed. It was enough to divert his attention from Ryder to the driver. "Slow down, there's no rush," he snapped.

The driver nodded and obeyed. The trees thinned, and a clearing with several trucks and SUVs parked in it appeared. The lone light came from a lantern beyond them. The guard jumped out then hauled Ryder from the rear seat. While they waited for the others, Ryder had a chance to get his bearings. The mountain jutted up directly in front of him, a stone face broken by a squared-off opening bordered by heavy timbers and guarded by a chain-link fence. In the light of the lantern, he made out a sign above the entrance: NO. 7 CAMBRIA COAL.

A burning chill twisted through Ryder's gut. It wasn't panic. He was too disciplined to allow emotions to override his mission. More like dread. How many times in the early days of the war had he led his men into dark pits as they scoured the caves of Paktika for Bin Laden? Every single time, he'd been certain it would be his last.

He'd left part of his soul behind in those dark crevices that devoured all light and life. Had barely dragged himself and his squad home again.

Other men had nightmares filled with blood and bombs, shrapnel, limbs flying, innocents and friends alike shredded...not Ryder, although he'd seen his fair share. No, it wasn't the blood that haunted Ryder, even all these years later. It was the black, where the greatest enemy you faced was the fear you'd carried in with you.

His captor yanked him forward toward the dark, gaping mouth of the mine.

Into the black once again, he thought, the words accompanied by the trees sighing in the wind. He'd barely escaped the first time.

This time, would it finally kill him?

) 🌿 (

I OPENED MY eyes to bright sunlight streaming through a set of tall windows. Definitely not my apartment. I blinked, surprised I didn't have the scratchy dry eyes I usually had after a fugue. None of the cottonmouth or body aches either. In fact, I felt amazingly refreshed.

Then I realized. I was still in Daniel's room, on his bed. Had I been there all night? I turned my head. I was alone on the bed. Where had he gone? Maybe my brain was more blurry than I realized.

"Morning, doc." Flynn appeared at my side, dressed head to toe in black as always. "How are you feeling?"

"Fine. Good. What happened to Daniel?"

She frowned at my question. "Daniel?"

"Where is he?"

"He's in his room. Where else would he be?"

As I blinked, the light shifted and I realized the wallpaper wasn't the muted blue of Daniel's room, but rather a pale peach. And the bed that a moment ago had looked exactly like Daniel's was now a simple cherry—instead of heavy, dark oak—with elegant lines and Queen Anne-style curves.

"I could have sworn..."

"You gave us a scare, sleeping so long," Flynn continued, sounding happier than I'd ever heard her. "Dr. Louise said it was a good thing, though."

Why wasn't she interrogating me for answers? Demanding any information that might help Esme or the other children?

Unless... "Esme? The children?"

"Fine. They're all fine." A strange look crossed over her face. "Why are you asking?"

"I'm not sure—I can't remember," I stammered. "Daniel was about to give me..." My mind stuttered. The answers were right there, but I couldn't quite grasp them.

"You really don't remember?"

I tried to sit up but could barely support my weight on my hands to push myself upright. That's when I realized I couldn't feel my legs. Panic surged through me like an electrical shock.

Flynn reached around my torso and shifted my position with practiced movements. Then she pressed a button to raise the head of the bed. It wasn't a regular bed. It was a hospital bed with a special mattress designed to prevent stasis ulcers.

I fought to keep my terror from my voice. "What happened?"

"I'm going to call Dr. Louise." She turned to leave, but I grabbed her.

Or rather, I tried to grab her, wanted to grab her arm. Instead, my hand flapped across the space separating us, fingers clumsily closing around her wrist but without enough strength to actually hold her in place.

"No. Tell me."

"After you visited Daniel, while you were inside him, your blood pressure shot up—from the PXA, Dr. Louise said. You had a stroke. When you woke up, you were fine except you were paralyzed."

"That was last night?"

She shook her head, glancing at the windows. For the first time, I noticed they were open. The trees beyond were green, the air scented with lilacs. "No. That was four months ago."

"Then why can't I remember?" Had I had another stroke

while I slept? "Did I have trouble with my memory after the stroke?"

"No. Angie—" Her eyes went wide. "You did it. You brought back the cure. The kids are saved because of you."

I frowned so hard it strained my muscles. "No. Daniel never—" I shook my head in frustration. "I don't remember him giving me the cure. I don't remember leaving him, waking up." My voice rose, pitched up like a toddler throwing a tantrum. "I don't remember any of it."

She patted my arm. So unlike Flynn who was always ready with a weapon but never with reassurance or comfort. "I'll get Dr. Louise. She'll sort all this out for you."

I watched her leave, wondering where Devon and Ryder were. At work, I assumed. And if Esme was cured, she'd be back at school.

I focused on my feet, straining to move them, to get the slightest twitch. Nothing. That's when I noticed the wheelchair waiting beside the bed. It looked brand new, as if it'd never been used—not even a butt crease in the cushion. Had I been trapped here in a bed for four months?

My energy spent, I flopped back against the pillows and closed my eyes against the sunshine. What else had I lost while I slept? I wanted to laugh and cry at the same time. If it really was April, I should have been long dead, killed by my fatal insomnia.

Yet, here I was...but I had no idea what sort of life I'd woken to.

Chapter 19

TYRONE'S MEN HAULED open the metal gate guarding the entrance to the mine and escorted Ryder and Grey inside. Ryder scoured the area for weapons, cover, alternative exits. Anything to give them an advantage when they made their move.

The entrance was a wide cavern carved from the rock. Several more lanterns were arranged on makeshift sawhorse tables, illuminating the space in wide swaths of shadow and light. Pebbles of shale and coal crunched underfoot, echoing off the ragged rock face that made up the walls and ceiling. Water dripped and dribbled along the front wall in rusty-gray streaks, leaving puddles in its wake. The smell was a strange mixture of fresh water, moldy wood, and rusted metal, making Ryder's nose wrinkle.

The right-hand side of the antechamber was filled with the remnants of a structure built into the cavern wall and partially caved in by a rock fall. He made out a timber doorway, twisted beneath the weight of the collapse. On the opposite side of the cavern stood a similar, fairly intact structure—he wasn't sure if it qualified as a room or a building, since half its walls were the native rock, but it also had a roof and windows—with a sign over the door in faded stencil letters, reading: HOSPITAL. The rear section of the chamber was cloaked in darkness, but he made out the faint gleam of metal scaffolding extending overhead.

"Tyrone, Tyrone," Grey said in a disapproving tone, ignoring his guard to saunter over to the nearest table, peering down at the papers scattered over it. "Up until now you've been so careful. But killing a federal agent and a police detective? Reckless."

"Who said anything about killing anyone?" Tyrone answered. He moved to roll up the set of building plans and nodded to the guard to escort Grey away from the table.

Ryder stayed where he was, motionless, hoping his guard would ignore him and pay attention to the conversation between the others, give him time to formulate a plan. So far, what he saw wasn't giving him many ideas short of a suicide mission. Too soon to think that way.

Grey turned to face Tyrone. "Don't play coy with me. I know you too well."

"Then you know we do not kill randomly. That's not what we're about."

"What do you want with us?"

"Information. And time, that's all."

"If it's answers you're looking for, the first one I'll give you for free. Ask me how many men are closing in on you right now." Grey's chest puffed out with bravado. "Go ahead. Between the federal, county, and state SWAT teams, I think we were up to forty operators, weren't we, Detective?"

Ryder played along and nodded, plastering a smug smile on his face. "Forty-two, to be exact. Seven six-man teams. Not counting support units, of course."

"Right." Grey shrugged his shoulders, ignoring the restraints securing his hands behind his back. "So now's your chance. Surrender, cooperate. You have my personal guarantee that you'll get the best deal possible."

For a moment, Ryder actually thought Grey's bluff had worked. He had no idea how large Grey's team was, but sooner or later they'd track them here. Just a matter of buying time.

Tyrone glanced at each of his men in turn. Then he smiled. It was the kind of smile seldom glimpsed on a person. It reminded Ryder of the stained glass at St. Tim's, portraits of a benevolent martyr beaming down at the men preparing to kill him. A smile not shadowed by fear, but rather, illuminated by private, secret knowledge and unshaken faith.

"Nice try," Tyrone said. He took the GPS tracker from his pocket, held it up against the lantern light before dashing it to the ground at Grey's feet, where it bounced against the rocks and chips of coal. "Not exactly government issue. Which, I'm guessing, means no warrant or authorization."

Ryder clenched his jaw tight before he could show any dismay. If Tyrone was right, then Grey had played him—there was no backup on the way, no rescue coming. He focused on Grey, trying to read the agent.

Grey's lips thinned, but he kept silent. Tyrone didn't seem to be expecting an answer. He drummed the rolled-up papers against his thigh, pacing away from Grey as if thinking. After a few steps, he whirled back, paused for dramatic effect, conveniently situated so the harsh light from the lantern was at his back, creating a halo effect. Whatever Tyrone's background, it had definitely included acting experience, Ryder decided.

"But I don't need to guess. Because," he slid a phone from his pocket, waggled it before Grey before tossing it onto the nearest table, "we've heard everything."

Shit. Ryder hated when the bad guys used law enforcement tactics. Cloning a subject's phone and switching it out with one equipped with an omnidirectional microphone was a tried-and-true method of planting a bug while also collecting a phone's data.

"Which means you have nothing to bargain with, Special Agent. I already know all I need to know about you and the lack of trust your supervisors have placed in the case you've been trying to build against me. But, your friend here..." Tyrone approached Ryder, still drumming the papers in that nerve-racking rhythm. "You, sir, you interest me. I can't wait to get you talking."

TOMMASO LAZARETTO MIGHT have been a brilliant scientist, but his skills as a criminal were no match for Devon's. He ferreted out Tommaso's hiding place within minutes: one of the cartons of specimen jars had creases on the cardboard lid where it had been repeatedly folded open, but the top layer of jars was intact. Once Devon lifted them out, below the cardboard separator was a video camera, collapsible tripod, laptop, and cell phone.

He smiled as he repacked the box. "If he'd taken a few out of the top, I might have missed it," he told Ozzie as they retired with their bounty back through the maze of corridors.

Ozzie wagged his tail at Devon's genius. It was a tiny, insignificant triumph, nothing compared to the forces they faced, but Devon would take it. He tried to stay positive around the others, talking about defeating their enemy and taking the fight to them, never surrendering, but it was all bullshit—and he was pretty sure everyone else saw through it as well.

"Like Dmitry always said, it's not good intentions that pave the road to hell, but denial." Ozzie liked that one as well, nodding his head at Devon's borrowed wisdom. Of course, it sounded better in Dmitry's Russian and after several shots of vodka.

They passed the corridor leading to the hospital

incinerator, heat and the smell of burning oil wafting from behind the closed metal doors, and then finally moved back into the tunnels. Devon breathed easier once the doors locked behind him. He searched out the cameras Flynn had placed and waved so as to not alarm the parents she had set to watch them.

Another corridor, this one lined floor to ceiling with shelves on both sides, and then two sets of fire doors, both with new locks Devon had added to create an inner security perimeter. Now they entered the heart of the tunnel complex—room upon room that Devon hadn't had time to fully investigate.

When he took over the tunnels, he'd quickly realized that it would take months to fully map and inventory them all, so instead he'd created a rough map. He'd started with the rooms he'd already accessed and set up what he visualized as honeycombs: collections of rooms secured behind locked doors. The rooms created rings of self-contained inner defense areas, each with at least one main room that he'd equipped with basic supplies: food, water, weapons, medical supplies, communications equipment.

He'd thought his plan was original, only to find that apparently both the initial designers and, more recently, Daniel Kingston had thought along the same lines. When he began exploring each section of the tunnels, a slow and dangerous process, given the booby traps Leo and the drug dealers who'd used the tunnels in the past had left behind, he'd found several of these supply stations already in place. A few had been ransacked—mainly the ones nearest the Kingston Tower, where the Royales gang had its headquarters—but many stood intact.

Devon and Ozzie moved through the tunnels lit by their red light bulbs, the noise of their passing covered by the intermittent gurgle of the pipes overhead. He didn't mind the dank and the dark, but he was growing to hate the siege mentality. He may not have had a formal education, but he'd studied history, especially that of great generals and leaders. Once a battle turned into a siege, it pretty much had already been lost.

They needed to find a way to go on the offensive—with more than Angela's gift to rely on as a weapon. Maybe Tommaso's work would give him some clue as to what the enemy wanted. Then he could find a way to use that against them.

They reached the next group of rooms he'd cleared of booby traps and secured. He led Ozzie to the room he'd stocked, unlocked the vault-like metal door, and swung it silently on its well-oiled hinges, gesturing for Ozzie to enter before sealing it shut again behind them. Only then did he turn on the lights, blinking against the brightness after the dim red-lit tunnels they'd just traveled through.

After getting Ozzie some water, Devon set up Tommaso's laptop and began to transfer its files to his thumb drive. While he waited, he accessed the memory card from the video camera. At first there was only black, and he wondered if the card had been erased. But then a woman's scream shrieked through the air, making Devon jump. Ozzie came to attention, nose in the air, scenting the potential threat. He let loose a sharp bark of dismay when the scream was abruptly cut short.

"No, I don't need that," Tommaso said.

"Why not? It's all part of the scientific discovery," came a voice that Devon recognized. One he'd hoped to never hear again. Leo's.

"Yours, maybe." Tommaso's tone was one of derision. He obviously didn't take the pleasure Leo had in torture. "Get it over with so I can film the dissection."

The footage stopped, a second of static filling the frame. When it resumed, Devon was staring at the naked, mutilated corpse of a young woman. Tommaso moved into the frame, his face barely visible behind the helmet of the biohazard suit he wore. He raised a scalpel, its blade reflecting the harsh overhead light. Devon didn't recognize the room. It was a mirror image of the one he sat in now, except that Tommaso's had been readied to handle dangerous pathogens with the same equipment Devon had seen in the biolabs in the Almanac building last night.

The camera was jittery; Leo must have been holding it, a fact confirmed when it moved in to document Tommaso reflecting the girl's scalp from back to front so that it hung over her face. The bare skull was now exposed, pink and glistening from the blood and tissue left behind, small globules of fat sliding free, a few threads of blood adding more color.

Devon watched in horror and fascination as Tommaso removed the top of the skull before separating the brain from its underpinnings. Then he reached in with both gloved hands to pluck it free. Tommaso examined the brain carefully, directing Leo to zoom in as he described his findings in a clinical tone. The medical jargon was beyond Devon's grasp, but there was no mistaking the physician's excitement when he sliced the brain apart, revealing the gaping holes riddling its interior.

"It works," Tommaso told Leo, holding half of the brain aloft to the camera as if it was a trophy. "Patient Zero is the key to creating a transmissible form of the Scourge."

Easy enough to translate "scourge" into fatal insomnia or prion disease.

Angela had told him that Patient Zero was medical shorthand for the first person who showed symptoms of a disease epidemic. Devon squinted at the time stamp on the video. March. Months before Angela or any of the children began having symptoms.

Who was this Patient Zero? If they were the key to starting

the fatal insomnia epidemic, could they also be the key to stopping it?

Chapter 20

RYDER GAVE TYRONE his best eat-shit-and-die glare. "Too bad I have nothing to say."

What else was he supposed to say when threatened by some creep who'd obviously fallen in love with one too many James Bond villains? The whole thing felt so surreal—spooky abandoned mine where no one can hear you scream, Tyrone planning to kill Lord knew how many people with a disease straight out of a horror film, and Ryder didn't even know why. Not to mention that he obviously couldn't trust Grey's judgment. Not if the FBI agent had gone rogue, so obsessed with capturing Tyrone that he'd been willing to risk their lives.

If it wasn't for Rossi and the sick kids she was helping, he might have laughed in Tyrone's face. But he'd learned from experience to never, ever laugh around the truly psychotic ones. The not-so-crazy ones, like the druggies with half their brains fried, they still understood humor when things went bat shit. In fact, Ryder had used humor to defuse more than one tense situation that had escalated out of control.

But not when delusions and paranoia were thrown into the mix. Like now with Tyrone, who was clearly not only psychotic, but also smart and charismatic enough to convince his men to do anything he wanted. Including capturing and possibly torturing two law enforcement officers.

So Ryder simply stayed calm and held his ground. Tyrone frowned when he didn't react, slapping the roll of papers against his open palm while assessing Ryder, trying to find his vulnerabilities.

Ryder gritted his teeth and remained impassive. He remembered another rule, one that his training officer had taught him when he'd first gone on patrol: Never look a rabid dog in the eyes. Too late for that.

The impasse was broken when one of Tyrone's men rushed up to whisper something in his ear, his body language screaming, *urgent*. Ryder watched closely, trying to decide if whatever had developed was something he could use. But Tyrone had a good poker face. He simply nodded, handed the man the set of blueprints, and stepped back to consider both Ryder and Grey.

"Put them somewhere safe—the elevator. I'll deal with them later."

Ryder exchanged a glance with Grey, wondering about the source of their reprieve, but Grey merely shrugged. Their guards dragged them to the darkened area at the far end of the cavern, one of them grabbing a lantern to light their path.

The original mine shafts stood here. Thick timbers framed out suggestions of openings, but only one remained intact behind a modern steel gate with a padlock dangling from it. Behind the gate, chains and wires came down from a narrow overhead shaft where Ryder could make out rusted gears and pulleys anchored into the rock. He wished the light was brighter so he could see if the shaft went all the way up to the surface. Might be a way out, easier than fighting through to the front entrance.

Tyrone's men didn't give him time for more appraisal. One of them hauled the gate open, while another cranked a wheel.

The sound of metal protesting against age and disuse echoed through the shaft, never quite vanishing, instead simply dying as a low moan. It was a long, long way down.

A small metal cage suspended from the cables and chains appeared. A few more cranks and it was level with the cavern floor. Ryder looked at the cage in dismay. It swung in the shaft. The floor was made of metal grating, as were the walls. They came up to chest level, leaving a narrow gap between the top of the wall and the roof. The cage's roof was a sheet of corrugated metal with rusty rivets connecting it to the steel bars that gave the cage its structure.

He knew the elevator—about eight feet square—was designed to carry a dozen or more miners, but it appeared so ancient and flimsy that he began to mentally calculate his and Grey's combined weight.

"You heard the man. Inside." Tyrone's goons didn't give them much choice, pushing them into the metal box. It shuddered with their weight, scraping against the rock at the rear of the shaft. The men secured the gate, then, with jagged motions as they cranked the wheel, they lowered the elevator car.

As it moved down into darkness, the light from the lantern above dimmed, blocked out by the cage's roof. Ryder peered through the floor's metal grating, ignoring the unsettling feeling of being suspended over a bottomless pit, trying to orient himself before the light totally vanished.

The shaft itself was wide enough to hold several elevator cages. He spotted one parked below them on one side, its roof canted at an unsettling angle. The other side of their cage opened up onto darkness, so best guess was that that elevator car was either somewhere below them out of sight or had been destroyed. In front of them, once they passed below the floor of the main cavern, was featureless rock face. The rear wall was also solid rock.

Only way out was up.

The cage shuddered to a stop, swinging hard enough to scrape the roof of the second cage suspended beside them. The thinnest sliver of light remained between the sheet metal at the roof of the cage and the rock wall. Tyrone's men must have lowered them just far enough so the roof sat level with the main cavern's floor.

Then the light disappeared, leaving them in darkness so total and absolute that Ryder suddenly felt as if he was falling.

"Any ideas?" Grey's voice came from Ryder's right. The rear of the cage, he oriented himself. He also noted that the Fed offered no apology for getting them into this mess—probably for the best; Ryder wasn't exactly in the forgiving mood.

"You mean like waiting for your men to arrive?" Ryder said scornfully. "Just how far off the reservation are you?"

"It's not that bad."

Ryder rattled his handcuffs in answer.

"We do have a team investigating Tyrone. And others like him. My boss calls us the crackpot squad."

"I'm guessing you have to screw up pretty bad to get that assignment."

"Nah, it's easy. Just piss off the wrong supervisor. But here's the thing—they aren't all crackpots. Look at Tyrone. I was right about him, wasn't I? And you obviously know more than you told me. What the hell were you talking about, this Leo Kingston? And fatal insomnia? What's Lazaretto and Rossi got to do with any of it? I didn't see anywhere that Tyrone could be keeping them prisoner, except that hospital building at the front, did you?"

Ryder was more focused on escape than conversation. "Think a cell phone would work in here?" he asked as he sidled across the uneven grate that made up the floor until he ran into the rear metal mesh wall. "I couldn't get a signal earlier."

"I doubt it. Not with all the iron ore. Why? Do you have one?"

"No. I was wondering about that message the guy gave Tyrone. They must have a sat phone or radio, maybe Voice over Internet Protocol tech, some method of communication." Devon Price had faced the same problem with his underground bunker and had installed his own private Wi-Fi communications network using VoIP. It was actually more secure and less traceable than standard cellular networks.

"Which means they also have more men on the outside."

Ryder had counted seven so far, including Tyrone. He felt along the steel mesh wall with his hands at his back, edging toward Grey's voice. "Any idea what they're planning?"

"Caught a glimpse of those plans before Tyrone snatched them away. Something Samaritan. Maybe a church?"

"Good Samaritan Medical Center. Why would they target a hospital?"

"No idea. But trust me, Tyrone is a big thinker. The hospital might be his real target or a diversion or part of a bigger plan." Grey's voice dropped. "I know you think I'm an idiot, coming here alone. I admit, I got in over my head. But Tyrone fooled everyone. We have to find a way to stop him."

Ryder brushed Grey's arm with his. He knew he'd only covered a few feet, but in the dark, with every movement quaking their suspended cage, it'd felt like a mile. "Plus, warn the hospital, evacuate it."

"Gonna be hard to do from here."

"Sit down, put your back to mine. I have a plan."

119

I WAS HARD-PRESSED to find words to describe how I felt as I lay there waiting for Louise. My entire body felt disconnected from my brain—and my brain felt just as distant from my mind. I could feel a dozen emotions roiling through me, a spectrum of confusion and panic spiced by frustration, but I wasn't really feeling them at all. No hammering of my pulse, no knot in my stomach, no nervous sweat or anxious tremors.

As if I wasn't even here—or worse, I wasn't even me. But I was. I had to be.

I closed my eyes against another wave of disorientation. I'd watched videos of fatal insomnia patients in their final stages— wished I hadn't after, but who can deny the morbid fascination of watching and knowing exactly how you'll die one day soon?

They'd lay in their beds—just like I was now. They'd stare into space—just like I would be if I let myself. Their hands would occasionally twitch as they pantomimed acts of normal life, like combing their hair or feeding themselves. But they weren't actually combing their hair or eating. It was all a charade—their body acting out a poor performance of the life they lived solely within the confines of their prion-addled brains.

Could that be what was happening now? Because a "stroke" made no sense—not anatomically speaking. And if I was really here, if this was really my room after a medical catastrophe like that, then where was the medical paraphernalia? A lift trapeze over the bed? Monitors and weights and range-of-motion machines? Nothing. Not even a row of medicine bottles nearby. Only the wheelchair that looked brand new and never used.

I forced my eyes open to confirm my suspicions. The light from the window had faded as if the sun was already setting— hadn't it been bright morning just a few minutes ago?

Rolling my gaze up, I saw a trapeze bar hanging above me.

How had I missed that? But...my neuro deficits still made no anatomic sense. Then I glanced to my right. Just as I had imagined them, a row of pill bottles appeared, neatly arranged on the bedside table.

Before I could think more about the sudden changes in my environment—a product of my imagination or a result of my brain not attending to visual cues when I'd first awakened?—Louise entered, followed by Flynn close on her heels.

Louise appeared flustered, rushing to my side and raising my wrist to take my pulse. Usually, the worse a situation was, the calmer she got—although more talkative. Louise liked to talk things through. Today she was dressed in black except for her white lab coat. Which was strange on two counts: Louise never, ever wore black, and why would she be wearing a lab coat outside of the hospital?

"Tell me about the cure," I said, yanking my wrist away. Or trying to and failing. Funny, because a minute ago that arm had felt stronger.

She released my hand. It flopped against my chest.

Ryder's pendant. It was gone.

That's when I knew.

"What was the cure?" I persisted. I focused on Louise's brown complexion, her Indian heritage. When she turned her face toward me, I saw intricately fashioned earrings—her favorite ones. I could have sworn they weren't there when she came in. A strange mix of emotions stirred through me, but I kept concentrating.

"A modified form of gene therapy," she finally answered. Only, instead of her normal, Oxford-born and raised British tones, her accent was very much Indian.

I slumped back, closed my eyes, finally understanding.

"Angie!" one of them called. I wasn't sure if it was Louise

or Flynn—their voices blended together so I couldn't tell them apart. I didn't care. I was busy ignoring them, ignoring everything. Including my own panic.

Because I was still in Daniel's mind. And if I didn't find a way to escape his control, I might be trapped here forever.

Chapter 21

DEVON FAST-FORWARDED THROUGH most of the video on Tommaso's camera, skipping over the technical research and discussions with Leo on refining their PXA protocol. Tommaso continued to mention Patient Zero occasionally, but never by name.

Instead, he talked about the blood-brain barrier and DNA viruses that could cross it and gene-splicing. He insisted that Leo replicate their initial success with more research subjects—something Leo was only too happy to do since it gave him a chance to play with his PXA torture of innocent victims until Tommaso was ready to dissect their brains to see if the prions had taken hold.

More interesting than the medical research was the timing. The date stamps and time codes on the videos suggested that Tommaso had been working with Leo for at least a year, perfecting both their use of PXA and their method to transmit the fatal insomnia prions. Their first successful transmission of the disease was in March—before Angela had her first symptoms. And since it wasn't her brain Devon had watched dissected in living color, she couldn't be their first patient, this mysterious Patient Zero.

Worse, it seemed that Leo's victims were all simply precursors to using the prions on what Tommaso called his cohort. Devon quickly realized "cohort" was a euphemism for the children from the Tower, the ones Tommaso was meant to be saving, not condemning to death.

If the man hadn't been dead already... Devon pushed back from the desk abruptly, making Ozzie sit up and give an inquiring whine. God, how he would love to hit something, someone. He remembered the way Tommaso had died, killing himself by biting off his own tongue, drowning in his own blood.

Coward. He'd gotten off too easy. Devon should have given the doctor a taste of his own medicine. Used Leo's PXA torture and let Angela rummage through his brain, taking the knowledge they needed.

He slapped his hand against the concrete wall, the sting clearing his mind. Heaving in a breath, he turned back to the screen where Tommaso's handsome face was frozen in eternal excitement, flushed by success as he sliced into another victim's brain. Closing down the camera, Devon reached for Tommaso's phone.

No records of any calls made or received. But dozens of audio files. He opened the most recent, dated yesterday, only hours before Tommaso's death.

"I know I should tell her everything," the voice of a dead man came through the phone's speakers. "After the failure of the Atlanta cohort, mine is the last remaining. Everything rests on this. But I feel strongly that my approach is the better one, even if it means disobeying her orders. Therefore, I've decided to keep my data secret until I can report my final findings. If I'm successful, and thanks to Patient Zero, I believe I will be, then our family is saved."

Devon noted the hint of pride in Tommaso's voice. He understood about saving the ones you loved, protecting family. But at what cost? Over a dozen innocent women tortured and killed? Not to mention twenty-one children now facing horrible deaths?

He scanned through the earlier recordings—mainly Tommaso rambling, debating whether or not to report his full findings to "her," whoever she was, obviously Tommaso's boss. Interspersed with Tommaso's research findings on his experimental subjects—the kids in the Tower, Tommaso had been monitoring their symptoms for months—were occasional personal commentaries on ways to use Patient Zero to infect more cohorts.

Then Devon came to a recording that stopped him cold. It was dated October, a month after the children began showing symptoms. "No evidence yet that any of the cohort is a Vessel, but it's too early to be certain. Even if none of them exhibit the gift, the cohort is too small to declare this a failure. Rather, I believe we should expand our subject pool by tenfold, really test Patient Zero's unique mutation and ability to infect others. It would require a great deal more of the original genetic material—stem cells, preferably—and a large, self-contained cohort. Perhaps a private school that we could sequester? A missionary school in an isolated third world country would be ideal."

It took everything Devon had not to hurl the phone across the room. Tommaso was discussing kidnapping an entire school to use for his experiments? And there was still no reason why.

How did spreading fatal insomnia into a larger group of children "save" Tommaso's family? What could anyone gain by an epidemic of prion diseases?

The only answer Devon could come up with was the same

one he'd proposed to Angela earlier: profiting from an artificial epidemic by controlling the cure.

But Tommaso had yet to mention any cure—or any treatment at all, for that matter. He seemed solely focused on creating and spreading the disease. Perhaps his mysterious boss had another group developing the treatment? Devon kept listening.

"With a larger study group, we could do more extensive refinement of the PXA protocols, see if we can manufacture Vessels independent of the family's genome. My goal is to not only be able to provide a pool of Vessels for the family's use for generations to come, but also to increase their effectiveness so that they can be used more than once before they expire. Leo Kingston's PXA compound is a good start, but further testing is required."

Tommaso paused, then his voice returned, less clinical, more curious, as if exploring an exciting area of potential research. "Even better would be the use of the subjects who show no indication of being Vessels as test subjects for a possible cure. Within two generations, we could not only rid the family of the Scourge, we could also use our new, artificial Scourge as a weapon against any population we wish to target. Infect their children and hold them hostage, ransom them for the cure."

Devon shook his head, not all that surprised that all this pain and death was driven by greed. It'd been the same with the Russian mob, the street gang he'd been jumped into as a boy, even Kingston Enterprises. Nothing trumped money and power. Not even the lives of innocent children.

"However," Tommaso continued, "before we could implement this new profit stream, we would need to complete development of my proposed cure. And for that, I'm afraid, we will definitely need Patient Zero. They're the key not only to the prion dispersal and creation of a new generation of Vessels, but also to the cure."

Devon froze, staring at the screen. He hit pause, then rewound, repeated that last part. The part where Tommaso said that there was a possible cure. If he could find and deliver Patient Zero.

Chapter 22

THE ELEVATOR CAGE swung, banging against the rear wall as Ryder and Grey crouched down. It wasn't easy with their hands cuffed behind their backs, but finally they were braced back to back against the cage's wire mesh rear wall.

"Hold my coat up," Ryder told Grey.

The special agent complied, bunching up wads of fabric. "You have a spare key, don't you?"

Ryder strained to stretch his arms far enough to give Grey room to pull the bulky fabric of his overcoat up and through the cuffs. "Patrolman's trick. Something they don't teach Feds, I'm guessing."

"Hate to break this to you, but we don't even carry our own cuffs. We leave that kind of thing to the locals." Grey leaned forward, holding the coat out of the way as Ryder bent his arms into his waist so he could retrieve the small plastic key clipped to a button behind his belt loop. "Don't suppose you have a spare weapon as well?"

Ryder knew a few especially paranoid types who carried small knives hidden inside their belt buckles, but he wasn't one of them. At least not before tonight. "No, sorry."

The air inside the mine was warmer than outside, but still cold enough to numb Ryder's fingers. He almost fumbled the key as he tugged it free. But he held on. "Got it."

Grey shoved the fabric of the coat back through Ryder's cuffs. Then he raised his own cuffed wrists as high as possible, bracing them on his back, so Ryder could work the key. "They didn't double-lock them, so that helps."

Ryder grunted. This was a lot easier when he could see what he was doing. "Hold still."

"Any ideas on getting out of this pendulum of doom? Or past Tyrone's men once we do? I counted seven of them."

"We don't need to get past the guards. All we need is to get access to a radio or phone."

"Still means getting out of this cage." Both men were silent as the key slipped free from the lock, forcing Ryder to reposition himself to get a better angle and start over. "What does Tyrone think you know, anyway? Didn't act like he was on a fishing expedition."

Ryder focused on the key, holding it in his numb fingers and relocating the proper hole on Grey's cuffs. There. "Don't move."

"I'm not."

The key was in the lock. Now he just had to turn it without dropping it. Easier said than done.

"Think it's a coincidence that both Rossi and Lazaretto worked at Good Samaritan and they both went missing after Tyrone's lab blew up?"

"Of course not," Ryder snapped as he strained to torque his arms. "Almost there."

"Maybe Tyrone has those plans not because he's going to blow up the hospital. Maybe the hospital is Ground Zero of a biothreat. Two doctors—that equals a lot of patients they could infect if they're working with Tyrone."

The lock clicked open. Grey ratcheted one cuff free. Then

Ryder felt Grey's hands connect with his.

"Got it?" he asked before releasing the precious handcuff key. Even with Grey's hands free, they were still working in total darkness, by feel alone.

"Got it." Grey slid the key from Ryder's numb fingers and removed the remaining cuff from his other wrist.

Ryder relaxed, leaned forward to let the other man reach his cuffs. "Rossi's not working with Tyrone, I can promise you that. Besides, she's sick herself."

"Sick? How? Could Tyrone have infected her?"

"I don't know. But you were right. It's a prion disease. Fatal insomnia."

"That's what Lazaretto works with. Maybe he's the one working for Tyrone. Where's Rossi now? I should put her into protective custody, interview her."

"She's safe," Ryder answered. "What's taking so long back there?"

"Idiots put your cuffs on inside out." Meaning instead of the locking mechanisms facing out where Grey could easily access them, Tyrone's men had put the cuffs on so the lock holes faced Ryder. Grey had to not only unlock them in the dark, blind, but also do it by reversing the usual motions and while working between Ryder's back and the cuffs.

Ryder leaned forward and raised his arms as high as possible to give Grey more room to work.

Grey's hand pressed against Ryder's back, steadying him. "Fatal insomnia? That doesn't sound good. Not if it's like other prion diseases like mad cow. Have to admit, they're the perfect bioweapon. I mean, the public would go nuts if they thought a disease like that was set loose."

"Rossi says it's not contagious—at least not through the air, like the flu or a cold."

"Yeah, but it wouldn't have to be. Not to cause a panic, I mean. All you'd need is a few cases that the government and medical community couldn't explain, some bad publicity, a viral video—hell, with that, my twelve-year-old nephew could whip up enough Internet frenzy to bring down the nation."

Grey paused for a moment. "Actually, it's amazing how little it really would take to create a fake epidemic. I'm surprised no one has done it before now." He swore. "Damn plastic key. I think you bent it. It doesn't want to fit."

The button-sized keys were meant for only one-time use. "Keep trying."

"All right, but hold still."

"It might be too late to stop Tyrone. Rossi said there were some sick kids as well. All with fatal insomnia."

Grey's hands paused for a moment as he considered the ramifications. "Shit. You're right, Tyrone's way ahead of us. How'd they get it? The insomnia, I mean."

"She didn't know. But Lazaretto was their doctor as well."

"We need to find that guy. And Rossi. They're the key."

"Speaking of which?"

"I'm trying. Wait. Got it. Hold still while I—"

The sound of plastic snapping cracked through the darkness.

"Damn it. It broke when I was turning it."

"Is there enough left that you can—"

"No. It broke flush with the lock." Which meant even a regular key wouldn't work—not until they pried the broken one out. "Sorry."

So was Ryder. But there was no time to waste on failed plans. "Guess I get to wait here while you get the cavalry."

Alone in the dark. Helpless. Worse, unable to do anything to warn Rossi.

Chapter 23

MY STOMACH LURCHED as I fell, my body spinning out of control. I kept my eyes closed, resisting any temptation to open them—whatever I saw would be the product of Daniel's manipulation. No. I would not open them again until I regained control. If not of my environment—after all, I was trespassing inside his mind—then at least of my body.

Of course, my body did not actually exist here. But it was a starting point. Something I could focus on.

Still, I kept falling. My limbs flailed in every direction as I struggled to take control. Slowly, the fall became a leap as I imagined my arms and legs pumping, coordinated. Instead of hurtling through the air, I envisioned hurtling across a field. I re-created the feel of a footfall, pushing off spongy grass, launching my weight forward into a sprint. And I ran and ran. I didn't stop, kept going until I felt Ryder's pendant bouncing with each stride.

I clutched at it, fingers curving around its polished surface. It felt warm. Real. Instinctively, I realized it was my key to escape, a lifeline back to reality.

Finally, my body mine again, I opened my eyes.

I stood in an office. Across from me, sitting behind an impressive mahogany desk, was Daniel. He tipped his expensive-appearing chair back and stared at me, clearly unhappy.

"Tell me what I need to know," I said, returning his stare without flinching.

There were no chairs on this side of the desk, despite the fact that the office spread out behind me with the expanse of a throne room. Exactly the effect he was going for. I reached into my mind for my favorite chair—an overstuffed, well-loved, plaid chair from Ryder's living room that had become "my" chair to curl up in—and suddenly I was sitting in it.

I couldn't see Daniel beyond the desk looming over me—but neither could he see me. The desk vanished, and he stood over me, a glower coloring his features. The windows behind him were suddenly slashed by rain and sleet.

"I need you to stay," he said. I said nothing. "Stay, and I'll tell you everything."

Was that a hint of desperation in his voice?

"I can't. You know that." I stood, twisting my hand, and the chair spun away, erased from existence. "I'm sorry." It was the truth. Because of my fugues and what I'd seen in the minds of the others, I understood what he faced better than anyone. Then I realized. "You saw. What's coming—what the others went through before they died."

"That's not going to happen," he thundered. "Not to me." Lightning crashed against the window behind him, but it barely shook. As if Daniel's power was spent. "I'm in control. It's my life. I decide—" His voice faded.

I glanced behind me and realized what had stopped him. A void blacker than black, devouring all light and life.

"We don't have much time. Tell me. I can't save you, but I can save your granddaughter."

I remembered the Latin phrase carved into his headboard—or rather, I didn't remember it, he did.

Omnes nominis defendere. "Above all, defend the family," I translated.

"She's not a Kingston," he protested. "Now that Leo's gone, I'm the only true Kingston left."

"Devon is your son. Esme is your granddaughter. Someone targeted her. Are you really going to let them get away with that? An attack on your family, on your flesh and blood?"

That caught his attention. Finally, I'd found the right tactic. Not his prestige or power, but rather, his pride. And there was nothing Daniel Kingston was more proud of than his family's honor—despite the way he and Leo had tarnished it.

"Help me save Esme."

The darkness crept closer, waves of roiling, inky blackness, dark tendrils swirling out, tasting, testing...

Daniel nodded.

The setting changed. We were on a grassy meadow at the edge of the forest. The darkness oozed from between the trees and bushes but held its distance.

The sun was shining. A few yards in front of us, a man and woman walked their horses. The young Daniel Kingston and the woman he loved, Francesca Lazaretto. I started to ask a question, but Daniel waved me to silence. To my surprise, sadness clouded his expression—the first true emotion, other than anger, I'd seen from him.

"I just asked her to marry me," he said as the young couple left the horses to graze and sat down in the grass. "She's telling me no."

"What's that have to do with me?"

"This is where you were conceived," he snapped.

I turned to him in horror.

"No, not that. You're no blood of mine. Where the idea of you was conceived. Francesca was only nineteen but already a talented researcher. She was desperate to save her family, so she decided to use her eggs to create a new generation of Lazarettos."

"Wait. Are you saying I'm the product of some lab experiment designed to eliminate the fatal insomnia genes?" The thought, as shocking as it was, made a kind of warped sense. Except for the fact that it had obviously failed terribly.

"You don't understand. The Scourge—what the Lazarettos have called their fatal insomnia going back centuries—is their family's greatest gift, the source of their power. But in the last generation, they had begun to see fewer affected children."

I didn't understand how a disease like fatal insomnia could ever be seen as a gift. "That's a good thing, right? Natural selection is designed to eventually breed out harmful genes."

He shook his head, obviously impatient with me. The black tendrils seeped through the grass, on a search-and-destroy mission. Behind us, the forest had vanished, replaced by ribbons of black tossed about by an unfelt wind.

"The Lazarettos have used the Scourge since the time of the Black Plague. Then, their mutant DNA protected them from certain diseases, like the plague, and allowed them to rise in Venetian society. But most of their power came from an unexpected gift from the disease. Usually, the Scourge didn't show up until adulthood, often after the afflicted already had children and had already passed the gene on. But occasionally, a handful of each generation would show symptoms at a young age—before adolescence. In them the disease moved faster, but it also left them with the ability to capture someone's memories under the right circumstances."

"Like what I can do."

"No." He shook his head. "What you can do is...enhanced. These children could take one person's memories, especially after the family learned to use various venoms to create a special form of coma—"

Venom would stimulate the same pain-response neurons as PXA. "Leo took their venom compound and used it to create PXA."

"Yes, basically. The point is, they use these children—Vessels, the family calls them—to steal the secrets of the most powerful men in the world."

"Children as spies? That's—" I didn't even have words for it.

"In the Lazaretto family, every member is treasured as long as they contribute. These children were revered, well taken care of before their deaths. Just as the adults suffering from the Scourge are—they're all tested for prion disease at a young age, their education accelerated so they can make real contributions before symptoms set in. While the healthy members of the family run the long-term business side of things, the members with the Scourge are trained in functions suitable to their shortened life-spans. Some are educated in science—to study their disease, find ways to increase the number of Vessels, better ways to induce coma in their targets, ways to prolong the productive life-span of the ones with fatal insomnia who aren't Vessels. If they aren't scientifically inclined, then they're set to work as assassins—well, in the old days, now I'm pretty sure they're just corporate spies—or placed in positions where they can help the family get close to their targets. Priests sent to the Vatican, executive assistants sent to seduce CEOs and marry politicians."

"I get the idea. This Lazaretto family has evolved like the Mafia—no scruples about what they do as long as it serves the family. You're not saying I'm one of them? Or my father?"

"Yes. Your father was assigned to join the priesthood. They wanted him to infiltrate the Opus Dei—the family's sworn enemy and most fierce competitor going back centuries. But first, Francesca used him as one of many donors to artificially inseminate her eggs. No member of the family with the Scourge is meant to ever have children, not the natural way. They only act as egg and sperm donors for their scientists to combine. Angelo learned of Francesca's research, recombining the family's mutant DNA in new ways in the hope of creating more powerful Vessels for the family to use."

"But the Vessels die after the family uses them. So she was basically genetically modifying her own children so that they would grow up to die?"

"Yes, but the family would survive. That's all that mattered. And if she knew the secret to creating future Vessels, Francesca could solidify her own position, maybe even lead the family. It almost worked. Except your father found you—I'm not sure how— rebelled against the family, and fled here with you when you were only an infant."

The encroaching darkness made my hair stand on end as it slithered toward us. We didn't have much time. "No. I don't believe it. Besides, what does it matter? Why are the Lazarettos here now? Why did they infect those children with fatal insomnia? And how?"

"It matters because the family needs more Vessels. That's why they infected the children. If they can create and control Vessels who aren't of the family, then they can let their own disease die out. The family will be cured of the Scourge, even as they inflict it upon others."

I wanted to slap the proud smirk from his face as he looked fondly across the field to where young Daniel and young Francesca spoke earnestly, their heads so close they almost touched. He nodded to the couple. "She's explaining the science and her idea. No one in her family took her seriously—not until much later. A decade later. But I did. I believed in her. That's why she trusted me to help."

"You helped her infect those children?" I demanded. The darkness surrounded us, swallowing his memories of his younger self and Francesca in a whirling vortex. It was still silent—making it all the more terrifying, but I was so enraged, I almost didn't care.

Daniel shook his head. "No. Not me. You did. You're Patient Zero. Not because you were the first patient with symptoms, but because you're the person who infected them. The fatal insomnia in the children came from you, Angela."

Chapter 24

MARCO'S MEN DELIVERED Francesca across the waters back to the Lazaretto family island that had been a safe haven for those afflicted with the Scourge for centuries. It was the middle of the night, those dark hours when the only lights visible on the nearby islands of Murano and San Michele came from the lamps guarding their docks. Then they turned toward Francesca's island. There, even still a mile out at sea, the horizon filled with glimmering golden willow wisps. Some would go out, but others would take their place, a constant dance of lights.

Legend had it that the island was haunted, and the lights were lamps carried by the dead who were forbidden entrance to heaven or hell, doomed to wander the earth. Yet another layer of protection for her people—no one set foot on their "cursed" land except her family. No one dared.

Tonight, the ancient monastery with its watchtower glittered with light, as did the modern glass and steel laboratory. Not for any holiday celebration. Every night was like this on the island where sleep never visited.

They pulled up to the dock, a concrete pier that broke the line of the centuries-old, fifteen-foot-high wall surrounding the island. The iron spikes jutting out from on top of the brick were invisible in the dark but no less deadly. Not that the island had needed any defense—it had been hundreds of years since anyone tried to attack the Lazarettos where they appeared to be vulnerable. The bodies of those who had tried had hung from the spikes near the massive iron gate, a warning heeded by all, even the most vicious and greedy of pirates.

Of course today, the spikes were only for show. A part of their history, like the monastery that ran the width of the island—the original hermitage where her people had come to die centuries ago, tended by monks who were also Lazarettos. There were no guards here today—there was no need. The Lazaretto name was protection enough from modern-day thieves.

Until tonight. Only, the thieves who brought Francesca home were worse. Sent by her own brother. Lazaretto turned against Lazaretto. Betraying the afflicted, the people who had built their family. Anger seared through her, although she kept her face a mask as she took the hand of one of Marco's men and allowed him to help her out of the launch and onto the dock.

"The six of us will secure the dock," he told her as his men leapt from the boat. They stood huddled on the suddenly crowded jetty before the wrought-iron gates. The men were armed with machine pistols similar to the ones the soldiers who patrolled the streets of Venice carried. "Tell your people to open the gates."

As a defense, the gates weren't much—but then, they hadn't had to do any actual work other than serve as an ornamental barricade to the occasional lost tourist in a rented boat who wandered on shore thinking the island was open to the public. They were controlled by electronics housed in the monastery and manned by her people. Tonight, it was a teenage boy who left the security office to press his face against the wrought iron as if he didn't believe what he'd seen on his monitor. "Francesca?"

"It's all right, Enrico. You can open the gate." No need to risk bloodshed. Not here, not tonight. She smiled at Enrico and, ignoring her armed escort, strode forward just as the gates swung open, welcoming her home. "These men will be taking over guard duty. I'll find you a new assignment."

The boy looked flustered—the afflicted took care of themselves, those with few symptoms caring for those at the end of their days. Laundry, cooking, cleaning, monitoring the sick, working in the lab, each was assigned a job according to their abilities. Francesca's people. Her true family. Each would do her bidding until they died.

Each would kill for her if she asked.

Out of sight of Marco's men, she allowed herself to finally smile. Poor Marco. His men were as good as dead already. They simply didn't know it yet.

☽ ☀ ☾

RYDER REMAINED ON the floor of their cage while Grey examined their prison more closely—well, at least as best he could in the dark.

"I was thinking you could climb out between the top of the wall and the ceiling, shimmy up onto the chains and out over the gate at the top of the shaft," Ryder told the other man, not even sure if he was aiming his voice in the right direction, the darkness was that complete.

The sound of metal being shaken combined with the motion of the cage to let him know Grey had heard and was testing his theory. "I think it will work, if you don't mind me using you as a step stool—I want as much height as I can get before I have to trust a blind climb."

"No problem. It's a long way down if we don't get this

right the first time."

"The chains are anchored to each corner, so I'll go up the front right corner."

"You can brace yourself against the wall." Keeping his balance in the disorienting pitch black would be the trickiest part.

The cage swayed as Grey returned and crouched beside Ryder. "Do you know where Rossi is? I really should send some guys for her, get her into protective custody."

"I don't know exactly where she is, but Devon Price will." Ryder debated whether to tell Grey everything, but he couldn't risk it. If the Fed escaped, a call to Price wouldn't compromise Rossi's safety or the children's. And Price could take care of himself. Funny how he'd come to trust the former criminal more than fellow law enforcement officers. Proof of just how crazy his world had become.

"Price? Why do I know that name? Wait, he was there when you were shot and Leo Kingston was killed. What's Price got to do with Rossi?"

"Call him. He'll know how to get word to Rossi."

"Interesting group you hang out with."

"So says the man following the trail of a madman." Ryder accepted Grey's help up. "I wouldn't wait for the FBI, the Staties can get here quicker with their Special Response Team."

"You think I'd risk your life to get some credit from my bosses?" Grey's tone was wry. "Seriously, Ryder, I'm not obsessed or crazy. Just decided to follow a lead on my own time, see if it led to any solid evidence before I risked taking it up the chain of command. Don't tell me you've never done the same."

Ryder never broke the law doing it—like planting an illegal tracking device on a suspect. And he certainly never endangered anyone else's life. But he said nothing; he needed Grey focused on bringing back help, not playing the hero.

They moved to the front corner of the car, the floor swaying beneath them with each step. Between the total darkness and the unreliable spatial cues from the cage's constant swinging, Ryder counted himself lucky he didn't suffer from motion sickness. Although his hands were now almost totally numb, and sooner or later, hypothermia would do him in—if Tyrone's goons didn't take care of matters before that.

"Good luck," Ryder whispered to Grey. He knelt down, head pressed to his knees, while Grey climbed onto his back. The cage shook, then Grey's weight vanished. Ryder scooted back in case the other man fell, but a thud sounded from the metal ceiling, telling him Grey had made it that far.

Ryder visualized Grey's progress in his imagination, translating each shudder of the cage. That quaking was Grey clinging to the chain, reaching for the barrier gate at the top of the shaft. The sudden push back was Grey jumping onto the gate. The rattle of metal was his climbing over.

Then there was nothing. The cage slowly came to a stop—other than the occasional shiver from the air currents in the shaft. The darkness remained, but that was no surprise—Tyrone's men would have taken the lantern with them back to the mine's entrance and their main work area.

The absolute silence was the most difficult part for Ryder as he sat shivering. He could project anything onto that silence, from miraculous success to catastrophic failure.

Neither helped. Nothing he could do now except wait. He focused on contracting his core muscles, performing awkward squats and lunges in the confined space, trying to keep warm and alert for what came next.

The sudden sound of gunfire made him jump. He strained to listen as men shouted, their words obscured by the way noise ricocheted from the stone walls surrounding him. Grey, had they caught him? Had he been able to call for backup first?

Silence reigned once more. Ryder stared up at the exit Grey had escaped through, despite the fact that he knew he'd never be able to see anything.

He strained to listen as the sound of men's voices and a shuffling noise came closer. Was that the faintest sliver of light forming along the edge of the ceiling?

Before he could decide if he was imagining things, the anguished cry of a wounded animal shrieked through the air.

Not an animal, Ryder realized with a sinking feeling. Grey. Being tortured.

Chapter 25

I WAS DROWNING in black, a silence that swallowed all light, stole all thought and sound. Floating, no up or down, no arms or legs, no me...

A bright light skewered one eye and then the other. I blinked. The light pulled back to reveal Louise, holding an ophthalmoscope.

"Angie, are you okay?" Louise asked, her voice filled with concern. Her features were cloudy from the artificial tear gel she'd put into my eyes to keep them from drying out during my fugue, but a few more blinks and my vision cleared.

Wish I could say the same for my brain. I nodded in answer to her question—didn't have the strength for words yet. She checked my pulse, nodded, patted my hand, and then moved away from me. I closed my eyes—it was too much work to keep them open.

Usually after a fugue, I was exhausted, but there was also a weird energy. And my other fugues had ended with cascades of music and light and sensory experiences that, while frightening, were also stimulating. This one hadn't been like any of the others—I felt drained, as if I was the one who'd been sucked dry of every memory.

Maybe it was because with the other fugues the people had

had a final thought, one last wish, if you will, that they wanted passed on? Patrice had wanted me to save Esme. All of her focus had been directing me there. Alamea had wanted forgiveness from her family—not that she needed it. She hadn't done anything wrong, but she'd felt guilty for the pain her family had gone through because of her. Leo, the man who kidnapped and tortured her, hadn't wanted forgiveness. He'd wanted to be remembered for his crimes. In a warped way, he'd been proud of them, wanted his fame to continue beyond his death.

And Jacob? Other than the message Tommaso had forced him to give me, all Jacob had wanted was to tell me he loved me...and that he forgave me. Even in death, he was a better person than I'd ever be.

Feeling slowly returned to the rest of my body. I raised my hand and sought out Ryder's pendant. Still there—somehow I knew that meant I really was back.

A tear escaped my closed eyes. I was back. And without the cure. Without anything that might help save the children. Except Daniel's accusation that I was the reason why they were dying.

Opening my eyes, I looked around. Definitely Daniel's room and Daniel's bed, but I was no longer touching him. Even so, I squirmed as far away as I could from where he lay beside me. I couldn't see the monitors, but his chest was still rising, although his breathing was slower than normal.

"Drink this," Flynn said, approaching me with a glass and a straw. "Did you get anything out of him?" she asked without waiting for me to finish.

My throat was too parched for me to talk yet. Definitely my Flynn, the real Flynn, with her abrupt, to-the-point manners. As I sipped the electrolyte cocktail, I raised my free hand to my head, felt the EEG monitor pinching my scalp like a tight-fitting swim cap. Louise should have gotten some great readings, given what Daniel had put me through. I blinked the rest of the eye gel clear and scanned the room for a clock—I'd been gone for almost three hours.

I'd had longer fugues—almost died from one a few days ago that lasted over a day—but had never been inside someone for that long. No wonder my brain felt as if it'd gone through an industrial-sized shredder.

Flynn steadied the glass for me as tremors shook my body. "You okay, doc?"

I nodded, let her take the glass away before I dropped it. "C-cold."

She felt my forehead in a most uncharacteristic maternal fashion. "You're burning up. Louise, she's burning up."

Louise was already coming around the bed, leaving Daniel's side where she'd been monitoring him. "Does this usually happen?" she asked.

My teeth were chattering too hard for me to form words, so I nodded. It usually wasn't this bad, but we could argue semantics later. She checked my vitals, popped a few pills into my mouth, held the glass as I drank and swallowed. Flynn hovered, watching closely. Sometimes I had the feeling that if Flynn was a normal girl who'd lived a normal life, she could have been anything she wanted—her powers of observation were so finely honed that she quickly learned almost any task.

Like now, handing Louise a small handheld testing unit without Louise asking. "Checking your electrolytes, see if I need to start an IV to rehydrate you faster."

As if I didn't know that already. See how quickly you can go from being in charge of an entire emergency department to being a helpless patient? Already feeling better, I rolled my eyes. "I'm fine."

She ignored me, poking my finger and letting the blood

drip onto the testing strip. I yanked my hand away, a drop of blood staining Daniel's silk coverlet. Flynn was right there with a bandage and another glass of electrolytes.

I drained it even faster than the first, my hands steadying, the chills fading. The fog clouding my brain also receded. I tried to sit up, wanting to get off the bed and farther away from Daniel. I didn't make it very far, the room swimming around me. But Flynn anticipated my needs and helped me move from the bed to a chair near the fire. A fireplace in a bedroom—such extravagance only punctuated just how out of place I was here in Daniel's house, fighting a family who, according to him, had even more money and power than the Kingstons.

"I need a pad and pen."

Flynn rummaged in the bedside table and handed both to me. The paper wasn't the recycled hospital scratch pad I was used to. Instead, it was heavy, with a cloth-like texture. And the pen was an old-fashioned fountain pen. As I sketched the formula for the PXA reversal agent, I imagined Daniel sitting here, jotting down late-night notes to sack the economy or pillage a competitor. My eyes barely open, I dumped everything I could remember onto the paper, then handed it to Louise.

"What's this?"

"Daniel gave me the PXA reversal agent."

Her eyebrows raised as she scrutinized my notes. "This is...astounding. Your EEG while you were writing it just now—it wasn't what I would expect from someone copying from rote memory. More like the pattern of someone reliving an experience."

"You said the fatal insomnia affects my thalamus. That's the area where sensory and somatic nerve tracts are concentrated. Muscle memory," I explained to Flynn. "Why did you pull me out?" I asked them both. "I didn't get much more than this formula."

They exchanged a look. "The readings—" Louise started, then stopped. I didn't blame her. Fatal insomnia required a whole new vocabulary beyond typical medical jargon.

"Was Daniel starting to die?"

She shook her head. "No."

"It was you," Flynn said in her usual blunt way. "You died."

"Not really," Louise rushed to explain before I could register the shock. "But for a minute—less than a minute, a few seconds at most—your EEG went flat. I've never seen anything like it. I was certain it was equipment failure, except at the same time Daniel's EEG suddenly lit up. As if he were somehow waking up from his coma."

My mouth went dry as I processed that. It must have been when Daniel had tried to imprison me in his false reality.

Could he really somehow have used my own memories to jump-start his brain? No. I could explain a lot of what was happening to me—hell, medical science had already demonstrated the ability to transfer memories from one rat to another, so why not a human under the right circumstances?—but I could not fathom a reality where one person could take over another's consciousness.

"It was only for a few seconds," Louise repeated, trying to be reassuring despite the puzzled expression on her face. "Then Daniel's EEG went almost totally flat, while yours went back to normal. But your blood pressure and pulse were increasing, so I pulled you out."

"It was too soon. He was getting ready to show me—" I stared at Louise, not sure what to do with the anger that suddenly swamped me as I remembered what Daniel had shown me there at the end. "You knew, didn't you?"

She jerked at my tone of accusation, while Flynn braced herself as if facing an unexpected danger.

"When you confirmed that I had the fatal insomnia gene, you tested my DNA along with Patsy's. You knew she wasn't my biological mother. Why didn't you tell me?"

Louise's features tightened into a frown, then her gaze shifted to Daniel's still form, then back to me again, morphing into curiosity. "He told you that?"

"Yes."

"How could he know Patsy wasn't your real mother?" Louise asked, still hovering between me and Daniel.

"He knew my real mother. Was in love with her, asked her to marry him. But she said no, because she had a grand plan to save her family." It was all coming back in a confused rush. From the looks on their faces, I wasn't making much sense. I kept talking in the hopes of untangling the threads Daniel had woven through his memories. Memories that I now carried like a remnant of frayed cloth. "Her name was Francesca. Francesca Lazaretto."

"Wait," Louise said. "Lazaretto? She was related to Tommaso?"

I nodded slowly. "She was his mother. And mine."

Chapter 26

TYRONE AND HIS men must have dragged Grey back to the top of the elevator shaft. Of course they did—they didn't want Ryder to miss a single second of Grey's torture. Muffled thuds followed by cries of pain echoed from the rock walls surrounding Ryder's cage.

Anguish sliced through him, but there was nothing he could do, not trapped down here. He couldn't shut his hearing off, but he could focus on escaping, anything that might help him save Grey. Contorting his arms as best he could, Ryder felt along the surface of the handcuffs to where the key was broken off in the lock. Grey was right, the flimsy plastic key had snapped flush with the metal—except for a tiny shard that poked into Ryder's numb fingers.

He tried to grasp it and failed. No way would he be able to use the jagged sliver to turn the key that was stuck fast in the lock.

As he sagged against the metal wall of the cage, another scream pierced the blackness. The idea of giving up never occurred to Ryder. Instead, he quickly devised a plan B based on the variety of ways felons used to escape their restraints.

He wasn't flexible enough to pull his cuffed wrists to the front of his body, but if he could fashion a shim, he could slip a cuff open. One cuff open was all he needed. But first, he needed a thin sliver of metal, long enough to slip past the ratcheted edge of the cuff's jaws. If Rossi was here, he could use one of her barrette clips. Not that he wanted her anywhere near this hellhole.

He paced his cage in frustration, awkwardly skimming his hands along the metal supports and places where the wire mesh walls connected, searching for any hint of a metal spur he could break off. Nothing except a few useless flakes of rust. Despite its age, the cage was well constructed.

A sudden silence descended from above him. No more sounds of protests or cries of pain. Had they taken Grey away? Or worse?

The cage creaked and swung as it was raised. Ryder blinked to force his vision to adjust as light spilled down from above. The elevator stopped a few inches shy of the main floor. Before he could attempt to mount any resistance, two of Tyrone's men hauled him out.

The first thing Ryder saw was Grey's body, crumpled on the floor, dark blood slicking the rock wall above him. He wasn't moving, except for the heaving of his chest as he took one wheezy gasp after another.

The second thing Ryder saw was Tyrone's smiling face. Ryder focused on Tyrone.

"What do you want?" Ryder stalled for time as he scanned the area. They'd brought more lanterns, allowing him, for the first time, to make out details of his surroundings. A tarpaulin-covered stack of crates stood against the wall near where Grey was. Another of the makeshift tables had been placed a few feet in front of it. On it were more papers, pens and highlighters, rulers and staplers, the detritus of planning an op.

Including paper clips. Several sizes of the wire kind—one of those might be useful to pick a lock, but wouldn't work to shim one. Difficult, but maybe doable. Then he spotted the laminating machine and stack of fake IDs alongside a small pile of plastic shavings. And the slim box cutter used to trim them. Its thin metal blade would work as a shim—and then as a weapon.

Plan beginning to form, he stumbled toward Grey as if he'd just spotted the federal agent. "You killed him!"

Tyrone's men lunged for him, but he moved a fraction faster, spinning to the side. Just far enough to stagger into the table, brushing his coat sleeve over it, sending the pile of IDs spinning into space. While one of the men bent to pick up the scattered IDs—all from Good Samaritan, Ryder noted in dismay—Ryder palmed the box cutter and slid it up his sleeve. The other man pulled him back to face Tyrone.

"Idiot thought he could escape," Tyrone said, wiping his hands on a rag as if Grey's blood and sweat had contaminated him. "I'm sure you're smarter than he was, right, Detective?"

"I don't know anything."

Tyrone nodded to the man nearest Grey. The man yanked Grey up by the hair with one sharp, vicious movement that made Ryder wince. Then he drew a semiautomatic pistol and held it at Grey's temple. "Certain about that? Enough to bet your friend's life?"

Ryder steadied himself. He couldn't shim his cuffs, not without attracting attention with his movements, and the box cutter wasn't much use as a weapon, not while his hands were cuffed behind his back. All he could do was try to stall until they gave him a few moments of privacy.

Grey's eyes rolled toward Ryder as if he couldn't focus. The blood and coal dust coating his face weren't helping. His gasps grew louder, and one arm drooped—dislocated or broken, Ryder couldn't tell.

"Don't," Grey managed to get out before the man holding

him kneed him in the kidneys. He crumpled to the ground. The man yanked him back upright, again placed the pistol to his temple.

Ryder scrambled for something that might convince Tyrone to release Grey. "I'm sure if Special Agent Grey told you anything, he told you I have nothing to do with the warehouse explosion investigation. I wasn't even on scene last night when it happened."

Tyrone narrowed his eyes. "But he said you know Dr. Rossi."

Easy enough for Tyrone to find with a quick Google search, so Grey had done no harm. "I do. What's she to do with you?"

"I'm asking the questions. Where is she?"

"I don't know. I haven't seen her since yesterday morning." It was the truth, but Ryder still sold it with everything he had, keeping his voice level, his gaze focused on Tyrone, his breathing steady.

Tyrone jerked his chin at the man with the pistol. Ryder tried to ignore the muzzle digging into the flesh beside Grey's eye. But he couldn't avoid Grey's sharp cry of pain, despite Grey's efforts to squelch it.

"Where. Is. Dr. Rossi?" Tyrone asked, making it clear it would be the final time.

Ryder didn't flinch, kept his entire body still. He wouldn't betray Rossi. Couldn't condemn Grey by not answering. Either way, Tyrone would kill them both.

"I don't know. Killing us won't change that. Neither will anything else." Like torture, he didn't add—not wanting to put any ideas in the heads of men willing to murder a federal agent. He kept his gaze locked on Tyrone's, the rest of the cavern blurring around the other man's face.

Tyrone stepped toward Ryder, blocking his view of Grey. Tyrone's scowl cleared, and he jerked his chin to his man holding the pistol. Ryder relaxed and dared a breath—Tyrone believed him.

The crack of a gunshot split the silence.

Tyrone stepped aside, giving Ryder a clear view of Grey's body as it slumped to the floor, the side of his head covered in blood. Ryder's breath caught, but then his training took over, and he forced himself to exhale slowly and breathe in again.

No one in the cavern moved or said anything—not even the other men gathered in the shadows at the front. All eyes were on Tyrone, including Ryder's.

"That was Grey's last chance. Now it's yours." Across the cavern, the man with the pistol stepped away from Grey's body and aimed his weapon at Ryder. "Where is she?"

Ryder ignored the man with the gun to stare at Tyrone. "I don't know."

Tyrone pursed his lips. The man with the pistol waited, his face expressionless. Ryder felt strangely calm—maybe because he was certain that even if he did know where Rossi was, he would never tell them. Not because he was any kind of hero, not even because of his military training, but because she meant that much to him. He only wished he'd had a chance to let her know exactly how much.

Finally, Tyrone smiled and patted Ryder's cheek with a move straight from *The Godfather*.

"Good for you, brother?" Tyrone called over his shoulder.

Ryder watched in amazement as Grey climbed to his feet and walked into the light. He knifed the side of one hand against his head, slaking blood, mud, and coal dust from his miraculously uninjured face. One of the men handed him a wad of napkins to finish the job. "Took you long enough."

"Had to make sure he wouldn't give us anything else of value."

"Told you I already got everything. But, as usual, I do all the hard work so you can have your fun and games."

Grey smeared one of his "wounds" with the back of his hand across his mouth and licked his lips. "Ketchup and barbecue sauce. Nice combo."

The two men now stood side by side. Same deep-set eyes, same mouth. Literal brothers?

"Who are you?" Ryder asked. He would have preferred to remain silent, less risk of further betrayal, however good intentioned, that way. But he needed to stall them, give him time to come up with a plan to stop them before they could go after Rossi and the children. Thank God, Grey didn't know more than Price's name—something he would have found anyway as soon as he looked deeper into Rossi's history.

Pretending to be an ally, gaining your confidence, faked torture and execution—it was a manipulation that went back to the ancient Greeks, had been finely honed by the Gestapo, and yet still he'd fallen for it. He'd been so desperate for any chance to save Rossi.

This was exactly why she'd left. To protect them both. And still, he'd betrayed her.

"Kill him now?" Tyrone asked, raising his own pistol.

"No. Wait, you imbecile. He'll make a useful hostage to compel Rossi."

Tyrone looked disappointed as he holstered his weapon.

"Why do you want Rossi? What do you want? Why target her and the children?" Ryder peppered them with questions. If they stopped to answer even one, it would buy him time. Not that he was going to break free any time soon, but maybe, if he could get one of them close enough to use the box cutter...even with his hands restrained behind his back, he could swipe at their groin or femoral artery.

Tyrone tossed Grey the phone he'd taken from Ryder. "He got a text verifying Grey's ID. I couldn't trace the number, but it's probably Price's."

"Of course you couldn't trace it. Let me." Grey removed a tarp from a stack of crates. A laptop waited for him. While he worked, Tyrone paced in front of Ryder, a smirk filling his face.

"It's all a lie?" Ryder asked. Not because he cared about the answer, but because he needed to keep them talking, engage them while he figured out a new way out of here. Now that he knew they wanted Rossi, he had to make it out alive in order to warn her. The only thing he'd given Grey was Devon Price's name, and Price was smart, could take care of himself—and he'd never give up Rossi, not with his own daughter's life on the line.

"No," Tyrone answered. "Special Agent Michael Grey is real enough. Assigned to a secret task force overseas in the Philippines, so it was easy enough to assume his identity here in the States."

"That story about the Somalis, West Virginia?"

"Oh, West Virginia was also real. One of our brothers managed to lose part of his cohort in Atlanta. We," he gestured to Grey, "tracked them to West Virginia. But there was no church burning, nothing like that. Mother prefers us to operate under the radar, so to speak."

"West Virginia," Grey grinned as he typed, "best place in the entire country for body disposal."

"I disagree," Tyrone countered. "Everglades."

"No, no. Some buffoon kills the wrong alligator and finds body parts inside? But that slurry pond at the mine in West Virginia? We didn't even need to weigh them down, sucked them right in like quicksand. Acid had them dissolved to nothing before we made it out of the state."

"Why kill them at all?" Ryder asked.

"We have to," Tyrone said in a tone that sounded as if Ryder was the one being unreasonable. What did he expect from two homicidal psychopaths? "Can you imagine the risk if they died under uncontrolled circumstances and some hillbilly doctor did the autopsy? Even if the experiment failed, those brains in the wrong hands—"

"Because of the prions, right? That's how it spreads, through brain tissue. Like mad cow disease."

"Or by being born into the right family." He and Grey exchanged a glance at that. "Our job is to prevent any prions from escaping our control."

"Who are you, the prion police? Do you know who infected the children with fatal insomnia?"

Neither man answered Ryder. Instead, Tyrone moved to peer over Grey's shoulder at the computer. "Any luck tracking Devon Price?"

"Not yet. Number's a burner, untraceable. Ideas?"

Ryder needed to distract them. If they found Price, they'd find Rossi, and it was clear that was their true agenda. He wished he understood why. "Tommaso Lazaretto? He was working with you? Or against you?" More silence. "What if I told you where to find him?"

That got their attention, Grey's more than Tyrone's. "What do you know?"

Ryder stuck to the truth—or rather, a well-educated guess. He wasn't certain of the reality. Devon Price never told him everything. Best way to preserve their quasi-friendship. "He's at Good Samaritan Medical Center."

He left out the small part where Lazaretto was already dead.

Chapter 27

FLYNN AND LOUISE both stared at me. Flynn was the first to react, no surprise. "What did you say her name was? Francesca Lazaretto? Let me see what I can find out." And she was gone.

I climbed to my feet, more than weary or exhausted, feeling as if my limbs were ready to dissolve into puddles, taking me down with them.

"I'm going to clean up," I told Louise, heading for the bathroom.

"Leave the cap on. I want to keep monitoring your EEG, especially if you have another fugue."

The wireless brain readings would go directly to her tablet, but I hated the thought of wearing the cap. It was tight and tugged at my hair and itched. My expression must have said it all, because Louise sighed with one of her "you're acting like my toddler" sighs and grabbed a knit cap from the sleeve of a parka draped on one of the chairs.

It was black and bore the Steelers' logo. "Devon's idea of a disguise when he snuck me into his car," she said, gesturing to the oversize parka.

"Wish I had a picture to send Geoff and Tiffi," I said, a smile forcing its way past my exhaustion.

Louise shuddered. "Don't you dare." And she wondered

where little Tiffany got her fashionista attitude.

I pulled the cap over the wireless EEG monitor. "How's it look?" I turned to the mirror to answer my own question. The cap actually covered the ugly electrodes and their wire mesh filaments. Made me look normal—except for the purple bruises sagging beneath my eyes and my pale, cavernous cheeks. Too bad it wasn't Halloween, I could easily have passed as undead.

I washed my face and patted the sweat from my body using one of Daniel's ultra-fluffy towels. Poor Patsy. All those years, the distance between us...now I understood. How agonizing it must have been, losing the love of her life, raising his child by another woman, always fearful that her real mother would someday come steal her away.

It explained so much. But none of it was helpful. I still needed more answers. Answers Daniel didn't have—but Leo might.

When I emerged from the bathroom, Louise was turning off Daniel's monitors. "He's gone." She gently folded his hands together. We stared down at the man. He looked more peaceful in death than he ever had in life.

"It wasn't your fault," she said, touching my arm. "He was almost gone even before you—"

"I know." I spun away and headed to the door. Louise followed.

Flynn waited for us downstairs in the study where she was attacking a laptop and talking on the phone with at least one other person. "Let me know when you find anything," she said when she caught sight of us, and hung up. "You sure this woman is your mother?"

"That's what Daniel said." I hung on to the rest of what he'd said—about me being the source of the infectious fatal insomnia. It made no sense, and I needed time to process.

Flynn frowned. "I found Francesca Lazaretto. Age fifty-seven. Vice president of research and development at Almanac Care."

"Then she's our woman," Louise said, her voice jumping with excitement.

"Only problem is I can't find any record of her ever giving birth. Not to Tommaso. And certainly not to you."

"Why would Daniel lie about something like that?" Louise asked.

"He wouldn't," I answered, a few of Daniel's veiled hints becoming clear. "The Lazarettos like to keep their private business private. Especially if they're conducting unauthorized human genetic research."

"Or research on biothreats like prions," Flynn added. "What else did Daniel say?"

I was silent until we left the house and were crossing through the gate leading to the street. "He said my father was also a member of the Lazaretto family."

Louise made a face at that. "Seriously? As in your biological parents were related?"

I told them what little Daniel had told me about the strange clan and their centuries-old history with prion disease. "He said Francesca was a scientist, determined to take control of the Scourge—their name for fatal insomnia. She harvested and artificially inseminated her own eggs, combining them with sperm from other members of the family with specific genetic mutations. He made it sound like the family used anyone with the fatal insomnia gene as test subjects. Said both she and my father had fatal insomnia, and when my father heard what she'd done, that he had a child, he rebelled and stole me from the family."

We crossed into the park. The streetlights were spaced so far apart that we moved in virtual darkness—not that there was anyone around to see us. Flynn laughed as she unlocked the shed that camouflaged the tunnel entrance. "Sounds like a telenovela, not reality. Maybe Daniel's brain was more damaged than we realized."

"No," Louise said. "Actually, it makes sense. If their form of fatal insomnia produced individuals with the same..." She hesitated, searching for the right word.

"Gift," I supplied. "Daniel said they called the children who can access memories like I do Vessels. Treated them like they were royalty."

"That I get," Flynn said. "Since they're the way the family built its wealth and power. So, they started experimenting on their own family, inbreeding and crossbreeding, trying to create more of these Vessels?"

"Such a waste." Louise's disapproval was clear from her tone. We moved down the narrow staircase into the tunnels, Flynn locking the doors behind us. "They could have easily eradicated the fatal insomnia gene from their family generations ago."

"They didn't want to," I said. "To them it was their ultimate secret weapon. Until Francesca came along and decided to do nature one better by creating a form of fatal insomnia they could use to infect people outside of their family and harvest more of these Vessels to use to do their dirty work."

I sucked in my breath, hating the metallic taste of the tunnel's recycled air. We hadn't spent more than five minutes below the surface and already I was starving for fresh air. "And now they've hit the jackpot."

"That's why they want you. To be their new Vessel." Louise's voice was grave, and she reached for my hand, giving it a comforting squeeze.

"But if Angie inherited her fatal insomnia, how did the kids get it?" Flynn, as always, cut to the heart of the matter. "We need to know how it spreads before we can stop it."

I had no answer for her, but Louise did. "While you were inside Daniel, Devon called. He found some of Tommaso's research that indicated he was working with Leo not just on the PXA but also on infecting Leo's victims with prion disease. Sounds like their research had been going on for a year or more."

Research? The kidnapping and torture of innocent women? But it explained what had happened to Leo's earliest victims—the ones who'd never been found.

"Even a year is still too little time," I argued. "Prion diseases take much longer to develop before symptoms start." The children and I had only had symptoms for a few months, although our symptoms were progressing much faster than they should.

"We've only been working on this for less than a day," Louise said. "You can't expect us to have the answers so quickly."

"Those kids need answers. Now," Flynn put in.

I stopped. The others turned to me. I had to tell them the truth. "Daniel said I'm the one who gave the kids fatal insomnia."

Saying the words made me feel clammy and chilled—more than fear, guilt. The knowledge that I'd somehow been the cause of so much pain and was helpless to do anything about it.

Flynn was the first to recover from the shock of my words. "How? Not like you'd ever met any of these kids before they had symptoms, right, doc? Just like you never met Leo or Tommaso before they began infecting Leo's victims."

"I don't know. But how can I face them?" I asked, despair darkening my tone. "Knowing I'm the reason why they're sick?"

Neither of them had an answer. We trudged on through the dark tunnel, each step weighing on me like a shroud. I thought back through everything Daniel had told me—and realized what was more important than his ambiguous words with their slippery meanings was the way he'd been able to access specific memories.

The PXA reversal formula. Daniel wasn't a chemist. He'd never have known the exact formula. He must have retrieved it from Leo's memories—buried inside the jumble inside my head. And he'd been able to do it almost effortlessly. Why? How?

Because he wasn't the coward I was, refusing to face the truth.

It wasn't Daniel's memories I needed to steal: It was Leo's. Which meant I had to break past the fear of living through the horrors he'd performed and learn how to take the knowledge I needed to save the kids. The irony was not lost on me: In many ways, that was exactly what Leo had done with the victims he'd tortured.

Despite the fact that I was trying to help save lives, not take them, I really wasn't any better than he was. Not the way I'd trespassed into Daniel's mind, not the way I was willing to play voyeur to a sadistic killer in order to dig out the memories that would help me.

"I know what I need to do," I told them, trying and failing to keep my fear from squeaking through my voice. "I need to access Leo's memories. Learn exactly what he was doing with Tommaso."

"How are you going to do that?" Flynn asked.

"A dose of PXA. High enough to induce a fugue."

"No," Louise said. "You're not strong enough. Besides, you have no control over when your fugues hit."

"I read a case study of a man with fatal insomnia using a sensory-deprivation tank to induce a fugue state without the physiological side effects."

She shook her head. "Too risky. Besides, where are we going to find a sensory-deprivation tank on Christmas night?"

"We have four of them already," Flynn answered. "I found them when I found the EEG sensors and the other medical equipment."

Louise and I exchanged glances. "Daniel," I answered her unspoken question. "He was preparing in case the prions got loose. Or in case Francesca double-crossed him and tried to use them against him."

"Doesn't matter." Louise was adamant. "You're in no state—"

"Neither are those kids," I told her.

"Angie, it's too dangerous."

I stalked down the dark tunnel, leaving them a few steps behind. Finally, my anger trumped my fear. It felt good—like when dealing with a trauma in the ER and I transformed my natural flight-or-fight adrenaline rush into pure focus. "Louise, go check on the kids. Flynn, take me to the tanks. We're getting answers."

Even if it killed me.

Chapter 28

THERE HAD BEEN many times in his life when Devon had felt fear. He wasn't ashamed of the fact. His fear was a weapon, gave him an edge. Fear allowed him to focus on what was essential, without worrying about cost or consequences.

Fear had kept him alive.

But now, Tommaso's words echoing through his mind, he wasn't only afraid; for the first time that he could remember, he was truly frightened.

Definitely not as useful as fear. Too vague, amorphous, too many possible worst-case outcomes...including Esme dying.

Devon did not like this new feeling. It didn't give him direction, a path to victory that no one else dared to follow. Instead, it left him feeling queasy and anxious and uncertain. More emotions he was unfamiliar with.

His fingers mechanically finished uploading all of Tommaso's files to the secure cloud account he'd set up for himself, Louise, and Angela. Once the machine had done its work, he gathered all of Tommaso's materials back into the box, called to Ozzie, and left. He was torn between wanting to take his new information to Louise and needing to see Esme.

He gave in to need.

Usually, when Devon prowled his newly inherited underground complex, he made mental notes of locations, strategic improvements, repairs calling for attention. Not this trip. This time he found himself jogging, an unseen specter at his back urging him on. Ozzie felt it as well, springing ahead, pulling his lead taut, the low-level red lighting and hollow echoes of their footsteps enhancing the feeling of dread.

When they arrived at the makeshift dormitory, Devon had hoped to find Esme still asleep—right now, sleep was the best medicine Louise had to offer her and the other children. But to his dismay, Esme and most of the others were awake, despite the fact that their parents were all nodding off, exhausted.

He bent and removed Ozzie's lead. The children had gathered in a corner of the room and cheered when they spotted the dog. Veronica had done a good job of creating a play area. Someone had set up a computer, and an animated film was playing, keeping the majority of the group occupied. Others colored or read books, a few bobbed their heads in time to music, several were playing jacks, but a few simply stared into space, eyes vacant and unblinking.

Fugue states. Devon recognized them from his experience with Angela. The adults watching over the children hovered, despair at their helplessness evident on their faces as they watched the children simply vanish into their own minds, prisoners of their catatonic bodies.

Even more heartbreaking was how the children took it all in stride. When one girl abruptly froze in place, another simply eased the ball from her lifeless fingers and took her turn. A boy watching the movie shook himself free of a fugue, and the others paused the film, catching him up on what he missed before resuming it.

As if this was all normal. Living like rats below ground, not sleeping, their bodies betraying them as their minds slowly surrendered to the prions attacking them.

Devon wanted to scream in frustration. From the looks on the other adults' faces, he wasn't the only one.

Maybe, finally, thanks to Tommaso, they could do something about saving their children.

All he needed was to find Patient Zero and trade him for the cure.

"Sir, sir." Esme ran up to him and tapped his arm before politely taking a step back. He'd been out of her life for so many years that neither of them knew what tone to take with the other. Esme had chosen distant respect for an elder mixed with informal acceptance and affection.

Still, it broke Devon's heart every time she didn't call him Daddy. He hid his pain by swooping her up into his arms, releasing a gleeful giggle from her. "What can I do for you? Do you need your socks braided? Your fingernails nibbled?"

"No, silly." She was ten. Desperate to regain lost years, he treated her as if she was younger, but she was a good sport, going along with his masquerade of parental intimacy. "You don't braid socks, you braid hair. And I like my fingernails unnibbled, thank you very much."

"Okay, then." He set her feet on the ground and crouched down so their eyes were level. "What do you need?"

She shuffled her feet and looked down at them, frowning as if worried she might be in trouble. "It's Randolph. He won't wake up to play with us and," she glanced over both shoulders and lowered her voice, "he wet his pants."

Damn fugue. God, how he hated that word, so foreign to him until recently. More than a seizure, a fugue froze the body while it sped up the body's metabolism as well as all brain functions. When Angela had her fugues, her senses became almost superhuman, as did her memory and ability to process information. Of course, the fugues had also almost killed her several times—from dehydration, heat stroke, and the sheer vulnerability of being frozen and powerless to protect herself.

"That's okay," he assured Esme, taking her hand. "Let's get him all cleaned up and back to bed."

She led him back to the corner the children had appropriated. Randolph stood at the foot of a chalked hopscotch game, legs planted as if ready to jump, arms outstretched. Tremors shook his strained muscles as he stared, unblinking, not reacting to the wet spot spreading over his corduroy pants.

Devon ignored the urine—he'd dealt with much worse than a little piss in his time—and gently lifted the boy. He was burning up. And his lips and tongue were dry, but he wasn't sweating at all.

Early signs of heat stroke. "Esme." He forced himself to keep his voice calm as the other children watched with a strange mixture of curiosity and feigned indifference. "Go get Randolph's mom or grandparents. Ask them to meet me in the exam room across the hall, please."

She bobbed her head and sped away. Devon sighed, shifting Randolph's weight in his arms, and carried the boy away from the crowd of worried parents to the room they'd set up with medical equipment from Daniel's stockpile.

As he settled the six-year-old onto the bed and arranged a cooling blanket over him, Devon wondered yet again at Daniel's prescience. How much did he know about the potential for a prion-induced plague? Or had it been simple global paranoia that had led Daniel to hoard state-of-the-art medical equipment?

He was applying the monitor leads to Randolph when the door flew open and Veronica ran in, an older couple on her heels.

"Randolph," she cried out, rushing to his bedside and throwing her arms around him. "Wake up, sweetie. Come back to Momma." She turned her face to Devon. "He's burning up." Her tone was accusatory, as if it was Devon's fault that invisible proteins had chewed apart Randolph's thermoregulatory system.

"I started cooling him, but I think he'll need an IV," Devon said. He had no idea how to start an IV, and from the terrified look on her face, neither did Randolph's mother. Why should she? Before yesterday she'd been a waitress at her parents' restaurant, serving tea and dumplings.

The patter of feet distracted him. Esme breezed in, tugging Louise behind her. "I found Dr. Louise!"

"Good girl," Devon said. "How about if you take Randolph's grandparents out so Dr. Louise has room to work?"

Esme nodded and reached a hand to each of the older couple who had remained shock-still at the doorway since their arrival. Randolph's mother nodded her agreement, and they allowed Esme to lead them from the room. Louise moved past Devon to examine her patient while Devon closed the door and leaned against it.

Louise managed somehow to be both efficient and reassuring as she separated Randolph from his mother, finished undressing the boy, began an IV—Veronica gasped at the needle, but to Devon's relief didn't faint or scream—and arranged a wireless EEG cap over Randolph's head. Finally, she turned to the monitor, nodding at what she saw in the neon tracings. "Everything looks good," she told the mother. "I think with a little fluid, he'll be fine."

"When will he wake up?" she asked, stroking Randolph's arm.

"In his own good time. But with this," Louise gestured to the monitors measuring the boy's vital signs in brilliant neon, "we can make sure he doesn't get into any more difficulty."

Devon pushed a stool over to Veronica, who sank onto it, bowing her head over her son's still body. He gestured to Louise, and she joined him outside in the empty hallway, leaving the door open so she could keep an eye on her patient.

"I think we should have all the children wearing wireless EEG monitors," she said. "I can track them from my tablet, see if there's a way to warn when they're going into a fugue."

"We've got plenty of them. Daniel saw to that," Devon replied. "Speaking of Daniel—"

"I'm sorry. He died shortly after—" Her tone softened as if trying to ease the blow, but as far as Devon was concerned, Daniel's death was one less complication in his life. As long as they'd gotten what they needed from the bastard.

"What did Angela learn? Did he tell her about the cure?"

"No. He gave her the formula for the PXA reversal agent and showed her the woman behind the fatal insomnia. Francesca Lazaretto."

"Lazaretto?"

She frowned. "You don't sound surprised."

"I'm not." He explained about Tommaso's research, the experiments he had kept hidden from Francesca. "He said the key to spreading the prions came from Patient Zero. And that Francesca has a potential cure but needs Patient Zero to implement it."

He placed his palms on Louise's shoulders and lowered his voice, not wanting to risk his words carrying to Randolph's mother. He couldn't give these people false hope, not after everything they'd been through. "Don't you see, Louise? All we need to do is find this Patient Zero and trade him to the Lazarettos for the cure. We can save the children—Angela, too."

To his surprise, Louise's face filled with dismay. "No, Devon. We can't do that."

"Why the hell not?"

"Because Angie is Patient Zero."

Chapter 29

AFTER RYDER'S PRONOUNCEMENT of where they could find Lazaretto, Grey and Tyrone exchanged glances. Then both men burst out laughing. "He's desperate," Tyrone said. "Trying to deflect us."

"You really think we don't know Tommaso is dead?" Grey told Ryder. "We don't care where his body is. It's his research we want."

"Not the research he was doing with Dr. Mehta at Good Samaritan," Tyrone added as Ryder opened his mouth, ready to bait them with another red herring. He turned back to Grey. "Devon Price. That's the name he gave up to you. He's Leo Kingston's half-brother."

Grey nodded at that, moved away from the computer to the worktable where he unrolled the set of plans Tyrone had had earlier. They didn't try to hide it from Ryder. They were that confident he wouldn't survive to warn anyone. Grey leafed through the schematics of Good Samaritan's various wings, finally finding what he wanted: the map of the underground tunnels nearest the hospital.

"Leo Kingston used the tunnels to hide his killing spree. If Tommaso was working with him, hiding his extracurricular research from Mother, he probably continued his work down there." Grey drummed his fingers against the map. "But where?"

"More important," Tyrone said, leaning his back against the table to scrutinize Ryder while Grey poured over the schematics, "is that it's also the perfect place to hide our stolen cohort. Price must be involved."

Ryder kept his face blank, not totally following their conversation but also understanding that any questions he asked might reveal more than he wanted.

"When we'd learned Tommaso had gone radio silent, our first priority was to secure his cohort, like we did in West Virginia," Tyrone continued.

Cohort. He meant the kids infected with the prions, Ryder realized.

"Taking out the housing project where they all lived would have been easy," Tyrone said. "A gas leak, a spark, a few fire exits barricaded, problem solved."

"Almost a thousand people live in the Kingston Tower," Ryder protested.

Grey chuckled, still peering at the map, while Tyrone shrugged his indifference. "But when we arrived last night, we found someone had already created a disaster there. Place was evacuated. And our cohort mysteriously vanished. Not among the people sheltering at St. Timothy's or at the hospital or the school. Just," he snapped his fingers, "gone. How do you think that could happen, Detective?"

"Stop playing with him," Grey said. "Devon Price is the key. He controls the tunnels—they were built as an emergency evacuation for the state government. Hiding twenty-some families down there would be easy."

"That's the problem. It'll be just as easy for him to know we're coming." Tyrone frowned, then thought for a moment, his gaze locked on Ryder. "Why is Price involved, anyway? How did he know about the cohort? Why is he working with Angela Rossi?"

"She's the one who killed Leo," Grey answered. "With Price's help. They must be friends."

More to it than that, Ryder thought, keeping his face as neutral as possible. It was clear they didn't know that one of the children in their cohort was Price's daughter. Good thing Esme had her mother's last name.

Tyrone's frown deepened. "What was Tommaso thinking, trying to circumvent Mother's orders, doing his own research? He must have tipped Rossi somehow."

"Price is a criminal. Perhaps when regular law enforcement," Grey smirked at Ryder, "couldn't help, she turned to him?"

"Maybe." Tyrone didn't sound satisfied, but he nodded. "Maybe. In any case, seems like we have all we need from the good detective." He jerked his chin at the man guarding Ryder. "Put him back in the cage."

"Wait," Ryder called, trying to stall for time. "What are you going to do with Rossi?"

Tyrone favored him with a smug half smile. "Don't worry. Your doctor friend is very precious to us. In fact, she's the only reason why you're still alive."

※

DEVON STARED AT Louise in dismay. "Rossi? No. She can't be Patient Zero. Tommaso and Leo were infecting women and killing them with the prions months before Rossi had any symptoms."

"I know. She wasn't the first patient to show any symptoms. Which means—"

"She's the cause of the disease. Somehow they used her to create it?" He looked past her through the open doorway to Randolph's still form. "How? I mean—she didn't, she couldn't have known."

"Of course she didn't. And we're still not sure. But while I was busy here, Geoff started correlating all the patient data you uploaded. He thinks the children were infected during a public health lead screening. One of the few commonalities of all of their patient histories is that their parents reported that they were told that they had above-average lead levels, and they received a dose of chelation from a public health nurse making home visits."

"Chelation?"

"A treatment for lead poisoning. But outpatient treatment takes the form of an oral medication. Not an injection. And not by a public health nurse."

"And, I'm guessing, there's no home visit program?"

"None that I could find a record of. Whatever those kids received in that shot, good bet it was Tommaso's prion inoculation. What I can't figure is what he did to actually make it so easily transmissible. Usually, prions require direct contact with brain tissue. And it takes years before any symptoms show up."

"His research mentioned something about using a virus to pass the blood-brain barrier. And DNA splicing?"

"Damn CRISPR-Cas9. Despite all the good it can do, that's one genie that maybe should have stayed locked in a bottle."

"Right, the gene-editing stuff that's been in the news. I thought we were years away from using it on humans."

"Any legitimate research lab is. Clearly, Almanac doesn't mind rushing to human trials."

Devon remembered Tommaso's revenue-generating idea of infecting an entire school to harvest more genetic material and create more Vessels. "How do we stop it? If it's not the hereditary fatal insomnia and the kids have this artificial DNA they've been infected with, we can make antibodies or a vaccine or something, right?"

She frowned. "There are a number of techniques that might be used—including using a variation on the CRISPR-Cas9 itself. But a vaccine would be able to only prevent the original prion infection. Once they're already infected, the damage is done."

"It's irreversible?" No. He couldn't accept that. There had to be a way to fight this. Just because Almanac and Tommaso's people had the science and the wealth and the resources to create this monster and set it loose on the world, that didn't mean he was ever going to give up. Not on Angela. Not on Esme. Not on any of the children.

In the past, he'd always fought his own battles. Often as not, he'd found success in walking away, letting the other guy think he'd won. Never realizing that true victory came in living longer and better.

At least that's what he used to think. But this fight? He didn't have the luxury of walking away.

Randolph's mother looked up at him from across the hall. Too many people had placed their trust in him. He couldn't give up. This fight was to the death.

One way or the other. Only question was: whose?

Chapter 30

FRANCESCA SPENT THE rest of the night preparing to defend her people. Marco, poor, small-minded Marco, with his profit/loss statements and misguided belief that money could buy him power. He had no clue.

True power, real power, lasting power came not from money but from loyalty. And her people were more than loyal, they were devoted.

She started with the lab, the one building on the island with any real security. It wasn't designed to defend against armed attackers, rather to protect their work and keep it contained. But, if need be, she could turn its defenses into offensive weapons, use the lab as a trap, not unlike the pits her ancestors used to dig and line with poison-tipped pikes.

Poison. Yes, the perfect way to dispatch Marco's men. After all, now that they were here on her island, they would need to eat her food. She stopped by the kitchen and had a quick word with the cook. It had been decades since the family had to make use of homespun poisons, but the cook had been trained in more than simple culinary skills. Like everyone on the island, the elders passed their knowledge down to the youngest, their apprenticeships beginning as soon as they were able to walk and talk.

With such shortened life-spans, they had no choice but to accelerate each subsequent generation's education. Francesca herself had begun the tedious work of sequencing DNA when she was only nine. She knew little of art or literature or anything except the magical mysteries of the body's building blocks, but before most "normal" children were ready for college, she was already performing intricate experiments far beyond all but the most advanced leaders in her field. No publications or degrees, not for a Lazaretto. No, their reward was in advancing the family, creating new and novel ways to use their gifts and cement the family's power.

She left the kitchen and walked along the worn, stone corridor of the monastery that served as living quarters for the afflicted, ranging from four years old to sixty-three, all suffering the ravages of the Scourge. Once she dealt with Marco's initial squadron of muscle, he would no doubt retaliate. And the island had no conventional weapons. They would need to be secured from the outside world. In the meantime, once Marco's men were dead, she could make use of their guns to arm her own men.

Then she realized. She had a far superior weapon at her disposal: family.

Each of Marco's guards would have relatives here. If she could persuade them to side with her...maybe she wouldn't kill them. Not just yet.

She climbed the tower steps to her office at the top and called Tyrone. "Have you completed your work?"

His hesitation was answer enough. "No, but soon. We haven't found Angela yet but have a strong lead."

"Tommaso's research?" Defeating Marco was impossible until she completed Tommaso's work. Without it, she'd never convince the other family leaders to follow her instead of Marco.

"I think we will retrieve them both together."

"Time is of the essence." She told him about Marco and his deadline. "We'll need reinforcements, weapons." Luckily, Michael and Tyrone were worth at least a dozen of Marco's men. Although neither son had any affinity for the sciences, not like their brother Tommaso, they had definitely inherited Francesca's cunning.

Tyrone thought for a moment. "We have a man who can lead us to both Angela and Tommaso's research, given the right incentive. If things go as planned, we'll be headed home by morning."

She calculated the time difference—they were six hours behind—and the travel time necessary for a surreptitious return to the island. "Which means you'll be here by the twenty-eighth." She'd allow Marco's men to live until then, lull him into thinking he'd won. Perfect. "Yes, that will be acceptable. But do not fail me, Tyrone. Everything depends on this."

"On my life, Mother. We will prevail."

☽ ❦ ☾

FLYNN LED ME through the maze of tunnels. "Can't take the straight path, because it leads through the section where the Royales left booby traps to guard their drug stash," she told me as we zigzagged through the corridors. "Unless you want to climb up to the catwalks?" Her voice upticked as she glanced into the shadows above us where pipes gurgled. "Those can get us there faster."

I knew the catwalks were Flynn's preferred method of traversing the tunnels. "You can go anywhere on them?"

"Pretty much. Each of the various sections of rooms is self-contained, but you still need some way to not only reach the pipes and electrical conduits and all but also to reach an area if it's

179

sealed off, like if there's a fire or something."

"Wait. How does that work?" I hadn't spotted any hatches in the ceilings of the vault-like rooms in the modular sections.

"Guys who designed this were pretty slick. There are crawl spaces between some of the walls for the plumbing and electricity and air handlers. I checked a few of those, and there's access panels into rooms, usually hidden behind the backs of cabinets and vanities."

"Like a plumbing chase in a regular building."

"Right."

I stopped and craned my neck to search the darkness above us. "If someone finds us down here, how do we protect from an attack from above?"

To my surprise, she smiled. "My thoughts exactly. Don't worry, doc. No one can get up there except me. Not without getting themselves killed for their trouble."

"You booby-trapped access to the catwalks?" Not for the first time, I realized that Flynn, in her own warped way, was a kind of genius. I was glad she was on our side.

We reached another of Devon's safe zones and stopped while Flynn unlocked the doors. This one must not have been monitored, because she didn't wave to anyone before we crossed inside and locked the door behind us. I hated the way all the doors in this place closed with such definitive thuds—not unlike I imagined the door of a prison cell would.

I looked around. The doors in this section were painted green. I shuddered as I realized where we were: the medical ward. The same section where Tommaso had killed himself while we were questioning him last night. I was surprised the walls and floor weren't covered in his blood—silly, since all the blood had been contained to the dentistry room where his body had been strapped to an exam chair. Still, the air felt sticky, and I wrinkled my nose against a coppery scent.

"You know the air down here is filtered and recirculated like a thousand times a day, right?" Flynn asked as she noticed my reaction. Clearly, being so close to the scene of our crime didn't bother her in the slightest. "We moved most of the medical gear to the section where the kids are, but no way could we move these." She opened a door and switched the lights on inside a room the size of a college dorm room. Only, instead of beds, there were two large containers shaped like eggs resting on their sides. "They kind of look like space pods or something, don't they?"

I walked around one. It was a little more than ten feet long and four feet across with a curved hatch at the front. The roof of the tank was just below my eye line, and the base was angled to make it easy to climb in and out without any of the super-salinated water leaking out from the inside. Flynn went to the rear and adjusted some controls. "Doesn't take long to heat up. Both the air and water will be the same as your body temperature. Did you know there's more salt in there than in the water in the Dead Sea? You can't sink, no matter how much you weigh."

"Did you read the instructions?" I was surprised; Flynn wasn't a by-the-book type.

She grinned, giving me a fleeting glimpse of the schoolgirl she might have been if her life had turned out differently. "I Googled it. An hour in there is like four hours of sleep, and with everything going on right now, I don't have time to sleep, so I tried it this morning. It really worked. Can't remember feeling so relaxed."

Clearly, she hadn't used the sensory-deprivation experience to delve into a sadistic serial killer's memories.

Flynn realized that and immediately sobered. "What do you need from me? Should I be monitoring some vital signs or that

EEG thing? Louise showed me some of what she was watching for."

"No. I should be fine." It was a lie—I had no idea what to expect. I wasn't even sure if the EEG monitor was safe in the water, so I used that as an excuse to take it off. My hair was clammy and stiff with sweat, but soon it'd be coated with the salt water. I slid my pill case from my pocket. It was a palm-sized octagon designed to hold a week's worth of meds, but I was lucky if the pills I shoved inside its compartments lasted a day. In addition to the pharmaceutical-grade PXA, I was balancing my symptoms with a cocktail of a variety of amphetamines, mega-doses of vitamins, melatonin, doxycycline, quinacrine, and anything else Louise and I could find in the literature that had shown to be of any help.

Flynn handed me a bottle of water, and I swallowed the meds. "There's an intercom," she pointed to the speaker grill on the side of the module. "I'm leaving it on in case you need anything."

Except I'd be in a fugue, frozen, unable to speak. I didn't bother correcting her—not as if anyone could have anticipated my particular needs when they designed their new-age flotation tank. I stripped naked and climbed inside, sliding my body into the warm water. As soon as I sat down, my legs tried to float, the rest of my body as well, but I held on to the safety bar beside the door as I acclimated myself.

There was a soft blue light inside the tank. I tapped the light switch beside the door, turning it off. Flynn leaned in, one hand on the hatch. "Sure you don't need anything?"

I shook my head, the meds rushing through my system. I now understood why addicts called it a "buzz." A million wasps vibrated beneath my skin, threatening to separate it from the rest of my skeleton. The floaty feeling of the tank only heightened the sensation.

"Hey, Angie," Flynn said as she lowered the hatch. "Kick Leo's ass. Don't let him get away with it."

She spoke as if I was about to confront Leo the killer rather than the wispy remnants of his memories. But I understood the sentiment. I knew, logically, that there was no way Leo the person, not his mind nor his personality, could be resurrected simply because I held his memories.

Somehow, that did nothing to squelch the terror spiking my heart rate so high my pulse beat inside my throat, throttling me as if Leo's hands were tightening around my neck. Helpless, I slid the rest of the way into the tank, the hatch shutting behind me, leaving me in total, absolute silence and darkness.

I wanted to shout, protest, bang on the hatch, beg to be released back into the light, but as the fugue overtook my body, my scream died, silent.

Thunder and drums and crashing cars and whirling neon music filled my awareness. My body was gone, left far, far behind as I swept through the dark alleys of my mind, feeling as small and helpless as a rodent scurrying through a garbage truck, about to be crushed. I wanted to stop, to bolt and hide, but I forced myself forward, deeper into the shadows, searching for the memories of a killer.

Chapter 31

TYRONE'S MEN SHOVED Ryder back into the elevator cage and lowered him back into the darkness. Thankfully, they didn't lower him completely—a thin sliver of light ate into the black at the gap between the cage's roof and the rock wall.

Ryder hunkered down at the front of the cage, easing his makeshift shim from his coat sleeve carefully. He couldn't afford to drop the tiny box cutter and lose it through the gaps in the mesh steel floor.

As he worked, he caught snippets of Grey and Tyrone's conversation. "One place large enough to hold the cohort and their families..." Grey said. "If we surround it...choke points...trapped."

"We have the...C-4...hospital would make an excellent diversion." Tyrone's voice was much easier to hear, even if his words were more frightening.

Ryder squirmed as pain lanced through his hand and a sticky tendril of blood streamed from a cut. Using the tiny box cutter blade as a shim wasn't as easy as he'd hoped. He repositioned himself, braced the blade, and held it in place, sliding it in front of the toothed jaw of the cuff. Then he ratcheted the cuff tighter, the metal pinching his wrist. One click, two...there! The teeth slid against the metal of the box cutter's blade without finding purchase. He yanked back in the opposite direction, and the cuff opened.

Score one for the good guys. He pocketed the box cutter while he shook the feeling back into his hands and massaged his sore wrist. Then he tackled the second cuff.

Above him, Grey and Tyrone shouted out orders to their men. There was the noise of equipment being moved and a few words making it down to where Ryder waited. Sounded like Grey and Tyrone had decided on a plan of action and were moving out.

Finally free of the handcuffs, Ryder readied himself for escape. He didn't want to show his hand too early, so he waited until the noise had died down. Then he forced himself to wait some more, hating every second he counted down, knowing that it could mean lives lost.

After a full five minutes had passed without any signs of movement in the cavern above him, he secured the box cutter in his pocket and swung up to the front support beam, following the route Grey had taken earlier. At least Ryder had the light coming from above to aid him—although he still avoided looking down the shaft. The impenetrable blackness was a surefire route to vertigo.

As quietly as possible, he pulled his legs up through the gap between the top of the wall and the metal ceiling then reached for the chain support and shimmied up. There was one gut-wrenching moment when his leg slipped and he hung over the abyss, but he quickly regained his footing. The elevator cage swung with his motion as he clung to the chain, feet planted on the corrugated metal roof.

Next, a leap of faith onto the gate above him, then up and over to firm ground. He landed with a louder thud than he'd intended. Scurried into a dark corner behind the crates he'd seen earlier and waited. No one came. Surely they hadn't left him unattended?

He searched the crates for weapons. Nothing. Even more worrisome was that there were several C-4 containers that were also empty. He edged over to the table. Gone were the maps, leaving no easy way to know exactly what they were targeting. Also gone were the Good Samaritan ID badges.

No sign of any means of communication, at least not in this back section. He edged into the front cavern, skirting the shadows alongside the old hospital building, and craned his head around the corner to the entrance. Only a few lanterns remained. The tables had been swept clean, and the stockpiles of weapons were missing.

Still...it couldn't be this easy. There had to be a guard. Where? Despite his coat, Ryder shivered. Remembered long, lonely nights of guard duty when he was in the Army. He scanned the area—too many blind spots between the cavern's natural contours, abandoned equipment, and the rock falls. Then he heard a small scraping noise.

It came from behind the plywood wall he stood beside. Of course, the hospital building—shelter from the wind and cold, probably where they'd set up their kitchen and maybe a heater as well.

He considered sneaking past the dilapidated lean-to of a building and escaping on foot, but there was no time: He needed a vehicle, a phone, a weapon, and, if possible, some answers. All as quickly as possible. Which meant confronting the opposition.

Strategy would depend on their numbers. Ryder slipped around to the front of the building, edging a glance through the window closest to him. Lantern light cast a white-blue glow on the old-fashioned rippled glass. Inside, past gingham curtains rotted by time, was a room containing the rusty metal frames of three narrow cots, a few upended crates, a desk, a kerosene heater, and a man bent over a camp stove, coffeepot in hand.

He didn't move as if he had training. His MAC-10 machine pistol was slung carelessly across his back. The only other weapon Ryder spotted was a semiautomatic in a holster strapped to the man's thigh. He was younger than Ryder and taller, bulkier, but Ryder had the edge of surprise, not to mention experience.

At least that's what he told himself as he skirted the window and crept to the doorway missing a door. En route he scanned the area for other weapons but found nothing that suited his needs as well as the tiny box cutter. Hell, if hijackers could bring down entire airplanes armed only with box cutters, he could take out one guy.

Not giving the pessimist inside him time for a rebuttal, he sprang through the door and pounced on the other man. Ryder didn't waste time or energy on any of the silly fair-fight tactics they used in the movies. This was real life with real lives on the line.

He grabbed the man in a chokehold and drove the box cutter as deep as it would go into the space between the man's skull and the top of his spinal cord. Then he wrenched the blade back and forth until the man went limp.

The whole thing took less than three seconds—it was over before the other man even had time to mount a defense. Hell, it was over before the guy's brain had time to register that he'd lost control of his body. The guy crumpled to the ground, a whoosh emerging from his lungs with the movement, eyes wide open. If Rossi was here, she'd tell him he wouldn't truly be dead for another few minutes, until his brain ran out of oxygen, but Rossi wasn't here.

Ryder was glad of that. Never wanted her to see him like this—methodically taking a life as if it was nothing. Logic and ethics and even the law were on his side, but he'd just erased a person, someone unique who'd never lived before and who would never be created again, an entire existence banished forever from the universe because of Ryder's actions. He'd considered trying to take the man alive, restraining him and questioning him, but there simply was no time and it was much too risky. If Ryder didn't make it out of here alive, there was no one who could warn Rossi and the others.

He stripped the man of everything useful: his ballistic vest, weapons, parka—not his boots, they were too small—and a cell phone connected to a private VoIP server. First call he made was to Rossi, but it went straight to voice mail.

"They're coming for you. Tell Price and get out of there. There's at least eleven men, highly armed, including explosives, and I'm not sure how many more. ETA thirty to forty minutes if you're lucky. I'm on my way to help. Love you. Be safe." Then, just in case she missed it the first time or thought he didn't really mean it, he added, "I do love you."

Next, he called Devon Price. Thankfully, the other man answered. Ryder gave him a quick rundown, keeping his words as vague as possible using the unsecured phone. "I'm not sure exactly what they have planned, but if you stay, you're sitting ducks."

"Maybe they want us to leave? Easier to catch us when we're vulnerable."

Ryder appreciated Price's dilemma. Wrangling all those kids and their families, all civilians and unaccustomed to stealth or able to defend themselves, it was a tough call to make: stay where they had some security behind the locked doors of the tunnel bunkers but also then could be trapped? Or try to sneak past Grey and Tyrone's men, make it to another location where they might end up facing the exact same problem?

"Your call. You don't have much time, so sheltering in place might be the answer—all those civilians, next to impossible to move them on such short notice." As they spoke, Ryder was scouting the entrance to the mine—no signs of any other guards. A single pickup sat unattended a few yards away.

"They might not even find us—it's a maze down here. You could wander lost for days."

Ryder thought about that. Along with other Gestapo tactics. Despite the fact that there was a man dead, maybe this escape had been a bit too easy? "Get your people organized, but don't do anything until I get there."

"But—"

"Have your father's security expert," Ryder cut him off, "meet me where we first met—where the dog played with the kids and we had ice cream. I'm on my way." He hung up, hoping Price figured out his cryptic message. They'd first met at Good Sam's where Ozzie had been keeping the kids at the Advocacy Center company. He hoped the ER was busy—he needed the cover.

No sense delaying up here any longer. If it was a trap, he'd done his best to warn Rossi and Price. If not, he'd be there soon to help.

Chapter 32

IN MY OTHER fugues, all of my attention had been focused outward as my senses became hyperacute. Being able to hear, smell, feel things beyond my normal perception had saved my life and others', including Ryder's, making my fugues both a blessing and a curse.

But now, with nothing to stimulate my senses, all my energy focused inward. Sensations of past events swirled around me as I was caught in a maelstrom of memories. Not just from my life, but the lives of all of the people whose memories I'd collected. The impressions, captured moments important and trivial, of six lives in addition to my own, now including Daniel's. I did the math. It was two hundred and eighty-nine years' worth of memories.

Caught in the vortex of time, it felt as if every moment of those two hundred and eighty-nine years whipped through me, slicing into my consciousness, fighting for attention. How had Daniel done it? Reached into my mind and grabbed what he'd wanted without being suffocated by the weight of all those myriad fragments?

Somehow he'd lasered right in on Leo's data...and my own memory of my father's death. I tumbled through the void, sights and sounds and smells bombarding me, no gravity to orient me, no sense of time to guide me. Vertigo tossed me about like a leaf caught in a hurricane; if I'd been in control of my body, I would have been seasick by now.

Focus. I knew what I wanted: Leo and Tommaso. When did they first meet? What had they been working on besides the PXA formulations? I concentrated, and slowly a world built itself around me.

At last there was solid ground beneath my feet. I watched two men talk over coffee as they sat at an outdoor cafe, sunshine warm against my back although I cast no shadow, their voices clear despite the fact that I was several feet away. It was Leo's memory. I wasn't inside his head, but not quite outside it either. Instead, I faced the direction he faced, the air around me wavery as his focus and gaze shifted.

The man he was with was Tommaso Lazaretto. The scenery wasn't anywhere in Cambria City. Somehow, it felt more like the memories Daniel had shared of his time in Italy. I listened to the ambient noises: traffic horns a little sharper, higher pitched than I was used to, and a foreign language murmuring around the two men. Definitely Italian. Either Leo or Daniel must have spoken it, because the more I listened, the more I understood. Just as I understood they were in Florence.

I turned my attention back to Leo and Tommaso. "I analyzed the compound you brought me," Leo was saying. "Very interesting. You say your family originally developed it from venoms?"

Tommaso nodded. "Insect and viper venom. The formulation evolved over the centuries. We created several variations, including some using psychedelic mushrooms and herbs, others that required more exotic venoms...my family has made quite the study of useful organic compounds."

"Your family? Who are they, the Borgias?"

"Actually, we trained Cesare and Lucrezia Borgia. But we aren't interested in killing—"

"No, I can see that by this chemical structure. This compound has the potential to bind with neuroreceptors that control pain, sensation, and pleasure. With the right formulation, you could turn this into a drug to brainwash someone, control their mind, torture them—or provide them with ecstasy beyond imagining, so much so that they'd become catatonic and die from sheer pleasure while their body wasted away. The possibilities and commercial potential are outstanding."

Tommaso smiled indulgently at Leo's excitement. Leo wasn't stupid. He detected the other man's condescension but considered it a small price to pay to be able to work with the compound he'd already begun to think of as his own.

"Yes, we know," Tommaso said. "Which is why we want to hire you to create a family of easily replicated artificial variations to suit our many requirements. We want it to be efficient, fast-acting, with reproducible and predictable effects. And we need an easy-to-administer reversal agent."

Leo leaned back and made a show of his skepticism. "Tall order. It will take time, research subjects, money..."

"All of which are no problem. But we require a trustworthy researcher who can tackle the problem discreetly. Given our families' historical alliance, we of course came to you first."

"Then you've found your man." They shook hands. "It will help me to focus my research if you can explain exactly what you want to use the end result for."

"I can do better than that." Tommaso stood, throwing some euros onto the table. "Let me show you."

The scene dissolved to flickering black and white. It took me a few moments to realize that Leo and Tommaso were now in a darkened room, watching old movie footage on a widescreen

TV. An old man appeared to be sleeping as the camera approached him. The date at the lower corner read June 3, 1989.

"Is that—" Leo asked, leaning forward to scrutinize the man.

"Ayatollah Khomeini, yes. He was poised to break Iran's cease-fire with Iraq, which would have cost our family billions. We needed to stop him, but we also needed vital information on where he had hidden assets pilfered from the Iranian government's coffers."

A young girl appeared at the edge of the frame. The camera shook as an adult's hand guided her to the Ayatollah's sleeping form. She couldn't have been more than nine or ten years old. Even more interesting—she looked exactly like pictures of me at that age. A cousin? Maybe a half-sibling? If my biological mother wasn't really Patsy—a fact that still made my brain stutter—but rather Francesca Lazaretto, then anything could be true.

The girl knelt beside the man, turning her head and opening her mouth as the adult holding the camera placed a drop from a small glass bottle beneath her tongue. A few moments later, her face went slack. The girl placed her hand on the Ayatollah's just as her body froze. She was in a fugue.

"I don't understand," Leo said. "How did you get past security?"

"Please. We've been doing this for over six hundred years. Our family has infiltrated every major government, religious dynasty, and financial organization on the planet."

"And this girl, she took the compound—did it produce her catatonia?"

"No. That comes from the Scourge. A rare genetic disease caused by prions. Usually, it leads only to a horrific death in the victim's third or fourth decade. But occasionally a child will be born with a special gift. They are what we call Vessels."

"Vessels?"

"When they enter a fugue—enhanced by the compound as you saw here—they are able to touch the minds of others in similar fugues and access their memories."

"Wait. So you poisoned the Ayatollah, put him in one of these—"

"Fugues. In people not of our family, the compound creates more than a fugue. It's a coma that becomes fatal. The Ayatollah will never awake again. But the girl will retrieve his memories and recite them to us before she herself dies in a few days."

I could feel Leo's excitement at the myriad possibilities of both the compound and the prion disease Tommaso's family had inherited. "You people, your family—if you've been doing this for centuries, then you must..."

"Be privy to wealth and power beyond imagining? Yes. Unfortunately, our family is threatened. Recent global upheavals have placed us in a precarious position, and this girl was the last Vessel produced. We are masters of genetic manipulation but have been unable to reproduce her gift."

"No drug will re-create it either," Leo cautioned.

"What we want isn't just a drug that can create the fugue states needed to facilitate their gift, but we are also working on perfecting a prion disease that can infect others outside our bloodline."

"You want to produce more of these children, these Vessels." Leo didn't sound horrified. Rather, fascinated. "How many memories can they hold? Does it matter how old the other person is?"

"No correlation with age, but most Vessels die soon after their first memory retrieval. Vessels show symptoms of fatal insomnia before puberty and die young, even if they never use their gift."

"Not only rare but short-lived. Yes, I can see your problem. Very interesting. I think I can help. Perhaps with both the pharmaceutical compound as well as the prion disease and a delivery system. Have you considered creating a form of vaccination? Only, instead of introducing immunity, it will introduce the prions, start the abnormal proteins forming?"

Tommaso smiled at Leo's insight. "Yes, exactly. There is a breakthrough in genetic editing we developed several decades ago that is beginning to show promise."

"You mentioned wanting to establish a lab in my hometown. Is that because Kingston Enterprises is based there?"

"Your father suggested Cambria City as a testing center. We are in the process of establishing cohorts located around the world, trialing different combinations of our prion DNA. But Cambria City is of particular interest to me because there's someone there I've always wanted to meet."

"Who?"

"My sister. My father stole her from the family, abandoned my mother as well as generations of tradition."

Anticipation surged through Leo as he parsed Tommaso's words and expression. "You're not looking for a happy family reunion, are you?"

Tommaso's smile was half grin and half grimace, but his eyes were filled with hunger for vengeance. "Family first. Family always."

"*Omnes nominis defendere.* Above all, defend the family," Leo recited the family motto Daniel had hammered into him all his life.

"Exactly, my friend. Exactly. Her father is no longer around to pay for his crimes, but Dr. Angela Rossi is. And pay she will, with her very blood."

Chapter 33

DEVON HUNG UP from updating Flynn with Ryder's intel only to glance up and see that Randolph's mother, Veronica, had approached along with several other mothers, all with frightened expressions clouding their faces. Two of the mothers were in their early twenties, the youngest of the group, but they also appeared to be the least cowed by their experiences.

It was clear they'd overheard his conversation. Louise, sensing something was going on, emerged from Randolph's room and joined them.

"They're coming here?" one of the mothers demanded. "I thought you said we'd be safe. Isn't that why we left the Tower?"

"Who's coming? How many?" the other asked. "Are we leaving?"

Devon made his decision. "No. We're staying. Standing our ground."

Beside him, Louise stirred. "Are you certain that's the safest course of action? Perhaps—"

"Do you think we can safely move the children in less than ten minutes, Dr. Mehta?"

She glanced across the hall at Randolph. "No. Not all of them."

"And I'm not leaving anyone behind. So we stay."

He led the group of women into the larger dormitory. Best to have this out once and for all so they could stop wasting time and start preparing for war. "Attention, everyone. The men behind your children's illness are on their way here. Now, we're not sure that they know our exact location, and we're taking steps to defend our position here—"

"What's to keep them from sabotaging the water or shutting off our air?" a middle-aged man, his eyes cloudy with cataracts, shouted.

"I chose this section because it has access to the bunker's power station. It also operates the air filtration systems. We control the power. That gives us an edge."

Another woman, one of the grandmothers, flung another question at him. "How long do we have to live down here like rats in a maze?"

"As long as it takes. We have food, water. Maybe not the comforts of home, but we can protect ourselves. Which is why we're staying put, sheltering here."

"That's easy for you. If things go south, you can always buy your freedom, take your precious daughter and your precious doctor friends, and fly away on your private jet. What about the rest of us? We can't buy our way out of this, and we sure as hell can't fight our way out. How do we save our children?"

Louise stepped forward. "Devon didn't have to risk everything to bring you here and rescue you in the first place. He could have left with Esme any time he wanted. But he stayed to fight for all of you. Just like Angie did. Just like I am. Save your anger for the men who deserve it, the men who gave your children this disease. We've no hope at all if we can't focus on what's important and pull together."

Her calm, British accent added weight to her words. The parents nodded, slowly coming around to what Devon had already decided: They had no choice but to stay and fight.

Could he trust them with weapons? What assurance did he have that one of them wouldn't break ranks, try to negotiate their own truce, betray the rest? He controlled access to the tunnels beyond their bunker, but if the enemy breached their walls...

He sighed. If the enemy got that close, then it would be the same as any war: every man for himself.

☽ ✹ ☾

MY MIND SPUN in the silent void, and I yearned for my music to help me make sense of the chaos. Being inside Leo's memories, like Daniel's, there was no music—it was as if they were more than tone deaf. They simply refused to register any sensory stimulation not necessary to complete their goal. No wonder both had been able to also amputate their sense of empathy.

I needed more from Leo's memories, but I was already overwhelmed. It had finally sunk in: Tommaso, the man who killed himself rather than let me touch him was my brother.

Were we all products of Francesca's genetic manipulations and artificial inseminations? Had any of us ever been cherished as anything other than test subjects? Wanted for who we were, not simply the vagaries of our DNA?

Slowly, music leached into the darkness, surrounding me like a warm cocoon as I floated. Not just any music: my dad's concertina.

The song began, low and sad. I didn't understand the words—when I'd heard them, I'd been too young, only a baby, to realize they were another language. He sang, and I stopped crying. I'd never experienced this memory before. We were riding in a boat. The waves were choppy, and diesel stank up the air. I was sweaty and seasick and scared.

All that vanished with his music. When he finished, he cradled me in his arms, so close I could smell that he was frightened as well. But his arms were so strong around me, holding me so tight, I knew everything would be okay. And I slept.

When I woke, we were far away. We were safe, Daddy promised. We were on our way home.

I blinked, the fugue releasing me. Had Patsy known the truth? I'd sent her and the rest of my family—her side of the family, the only family I'd ever known aside from my father—away for their safety. What if the Lazarettos found them? Or found Ryder? Or Louise and her family or the children...my litany of worst-case scenarios seemed never-ending.

Suddenly, the warm darkness of the isolation chamber was no longer a comfort but a threat. Claustrophobia choked me as I scrambled my palms against the walls, searching for light, for the exit.

The hatch opened, but not by my hand. A slit of light shattered the darkness, and Flynn craned her head inside.

"They got Ryder. He escaped, he's fine," she added before I could ask. "But they're coming. I'm going after Ryder. Will you be all right here alone? I'll be back in a short while, but I need you to stay here."

Her voice softened at the last as if she was speaking to a child. Given that I was naked, shivering, hyperventilating, still wide-eyed with terror from my panic attack, and my brain was basically functioning at a primitive, reptilian level, it was a good thing.

I nodded.

She held my gaze, didn't move. "You will stay here?"

It took me a moment to find words. "Yes. I'll be fine. Go."

Finally, she saw what she wanted in me and left. My time in

the tank hadn't invigorated me. Instead, I felt as if I'd finished a twelve-hour shift in the ER. Guess that made sense. My mind had certainly been working overtime. Slowly, I climbed out of the tank, the thick, salty water sluicing from my body, and walked naked to the shower stall, hoping I'd feel better once I was clean again.

It didn't work. As I stood beneath the streaming water, all I could see was that little girl who looked like me, so trusting as she opened her mouth as if taking Communion. Did she know they had led her to her death? That they'd turned her sweet innocence into a murder weapon? For what? Power and profit.

That was my family, my real family. And their unholy legacy.

Now they wanted me. Daniel said I was the key to spreading the prions. Clearly, I was also one of these Vessels—only a new, improved mutation who could handle more than one set of memories trapped inside her brain.

What if I'd also passed that ability to the children, along with my prions? Any family who sacrificed their own young so callously would not think twice about using a stranger's child.

I sank down to the tiled floor of the shower, not caring that it was gritty with the salt I'd washed off. Cupping my face in my palms, I let the water pummel me, drowning out the sounds of my sobs.

I had no answers, only more questions. No. That wasn't true. There was one answer I could think of, one way to prevent the family from using me. My tears morphed into a strange laughter as I remembered my silly fantasy of flying to Tahiti and ending it all before the fatal insomnia turned me into a driveling, mindless, living corpse.

My last-ditch way out was still my best option. I just had to find a way to trade my death for the children's lives.

Chapter 34

RYDER FINISHED MAKING his final phone call as he pulled into Good Sam's parking garage. It was almost two in the morning, and he'd just left not-so-nice belated Christmas presents for the FBI, ATF, Homeland Security, police, and fire departments in the form of bomb threats directed at Good Samaritan. He hoped they wouldn't have to disrupt patient care too much, but he needed the diversion, and given what he'd seen up at the mine, he couldn't rule out an actual attack on the hospital.

After parking the truck diagonally across three spaces near the elevator, where it couldn't be missed by the authorities when they came to investigate, he left the cell phone on but abandoned it along with everything he'd taken from the man he killed. Except the pistol, a Taurus 92. That he kept, hidden beneath his suit jacket at the small of his back. Shivering without his overcoat, he glanced around in the yellow-tinged light of the garage. No signs of anyone following him, but that's what vehicle trackers were for.

He was more curious about how Tyrone and Grey intended to track him now that he was on foot. The phone was the obvious choice—too obvious.

Pretending he was on a single-minded mission for the sake

of the security cameras, he strode to the elevator and pressed the button. The doors opened. A dark-skinned woman in a nursing uniform was already inside, along with a cart stacked with scrubs and lab coats. She didn't seem to notice Ryder, caught up in her cell phone, head bobbing in time with music piped through her earbuds.

He pressed the button for the top floor. As soon as the doors slid shut behind them, he turned to the woman with a smile. "You got my message. Thought you'd be waiting in the ER."

Flynn reached past him, using an elevator key to stop the car between floors without the alarm sounding. Then she turned to Ryder. "I spotted a bunch of cops out of uniform up there. Figured they were looking for you."

"I may have phoned in a few bomb threats," he said as she moved her phone over his body, scanning for tracking devices.

"Didn't look like they were worried about bombs. They were the same cops watching Louise's house last night."

Exactly what he'd feared. Whoever Grey and Tyrone worked for, they'd totally compromised the police department.

Flynn ran her cell phone up and down Ryder's body, listening intently. She suddenly alerted, pressing her hand against Ryder's back. She removed the Taurus, throwing it onto the cart, then slid her fingers along his left leg down to his pants cuff. Flynn spun him around to face her, holding a small black circle the size of her fingertip and smiling in triumph.

She finished her scan and nodded in satisfaction, then turned the elevator key and hit the button for the next floor. They exited the elevator. A janitor was running a floor waxer back and forth along the hall. Flynn pushed her cart past him, casually brushing his shoulder and leaving the microtracker stuck to his navy work shirt.

Ryder followed her past the patient rooms, around the corner to where she turned into a supply closet. Once inside, she handed him a pistol—a nine-millimeter Beretta, along with two magazines and a holster. She also had a patrolman's jacket, ballistic vest, and cap for each of them as well as a new cell phone.

"Let's go, partner," she said, grinning as she adjusted her cap to a rakish angle. Didn't matter that they were being chased by a force that had them outgunned and outnumbered, or that they had no good plan to defeat the enemy and even less chance of success, nothing was going to stop Flynn from enjoying the moment. Ryder couldn't help but grin back at the girl's carpe diem attitude.

Flynn led the way down the back stairs. They made it to the basement without encountering anyone.

"What's the plan?" he asked as he followed her through the basement corridors to the tunnel entrance.

"We gear up, take the high ground, and pick off as many as we can to buy Devon time. If we can keep them in this section of the tunnels, they'll be trapped between Good Sam's and St. Tim's."

"The section of tunnels that the Royales used to stash their drugs." He nodded. "I'm guessing you didn't remove all of their booby traps."

"Exactly. Plus, I added a few surprises. The only path clear is via the overhead catwalk or the path you and Angie originally took when you found Esme down here last month. I'm texting you a map now."

They kept moving at a brisk pace down the dimly lit section of tunnels. Seemed like he was doomed to spend more of the night underground. At least this time he was the one holding the weapon. "So you and me, we're it?"

She stopped to unlock a heavy bulkhead door. The corridor beyond was lit, the doors lining it painted green. Ryder stepped inside, and Flynn closed the door behind him. He began down the hall. A door at the other end opened.

Out stepped Rossi. He couldn't help himself. Approaching enemy be damned, he ran to her. He knew of no words that could convey what he felt, so he settled for gathering her into his arms and holding her so tight he felt her heart pounding against his chest.

Chapter 35

SEEING RYDER WAS like being ambushed by a sudden bolt of lightning created of pure joy. It felt so good, being in his arms again. I could almost remember what life felt like back before I got sick, back when I was normal, living a normal life, sleeping normal sleep, envisioning a normal, long-lived future.

Ryder made me question every decision I'd made. Worse, he made me hope. I hungered for faith like his, the simple belief that somehow, someway *we* were possible. God forgive me, I surrendered to the feeling, to the hope, and let him hold me. The pendant he'd given me grew warm, pressed between our flesh as he framed my face in his hands and kissed me soundly.

"Missed you at dinner," he whispered with a wink. He knew I'd been dreading meeting his family at Christmas dinner—after all, I was the one who'd gotten him shot last month. "Don't worry. Mom's making pork and sauerkraut for New Year's, said you're invited, and she won't take no for an answer because it'd mean bad luck all year long."

I flushed, the thought of making it past tonight, much less surviving a week, shattering the fantasy. He relaxed his grip on me, giving me the room I needed without asking and without making me feel guilty for needing it. Which, of course, only made me want to flee back into his arms.

Flynn pushed between us, heading down the hall to another door. "Gear up," she said, waving us inside.

Ryder whistled at the sight of racks of rifles and machine guns and shotguns. "Nice. We'll be up top?" he asked as he selected one of the rifles and looked through its sights as if aiming into the distance. "About twenty feet, right? And the corridors are what, eighteen feet wide?" He put down the first gun and picked up another, then sorted through magazines of ammunition, making his selections. "We don't want overkill—can't risk a stray round going through any walls."

"The tunnel walls are steel reinforced concrete, eighteen inches wide. Interior walls the same but half as thick. Don't forget these." She handed him a set of night vision goggles that strapped over his head. They were shaped rather like a rhinoceros' horn: regular goggles at the base to cover both eyes, but one central receptacle to see through. I couldn't help but smile. He looked so strangely fierce yet comic.

"What are Grey and Tyrone's men armed with?" Flynn asked.

"MAC-10's, M-4's, and semiautomatics," he answered. "A few Remington 870s. Plus, I spotted cases of C-4."

I wasn't sure what that meant, except I knew the Remington was a shotgun, the same that law enforcement used. And C-4, I knew that from the movies. Plastic explosives. Not good.

Flynn turned to frown at me.

I shook my head. "No guns for me." What if I froze up with a fugue, pulled the trigger with a muscle spasm? "But you're not leaving me here to wait, so don't even suggest it."

"Wasn't going to—you're our secret weapon, remember? We can't risk you getting caught."

No one mentioned that I was also the main reason why

Grey and Tyrone were coming after us. I knew better than to suggest that I surrender—Flynn might see the strategic value if I could convince her it was the best way to save Esme, but Ryder would never agree.

"Why don't you take Rossi to shelter with Devon and the kids?" Ryder suggested to Flynn. "I can hold down the fort, cover your back."

Flynn hesitated as if she was seriously considering the idea, so I immediately jumped in.

"No. We all go together." They both gave me the "silly civilian has no idea what she's talking about" look, but I stared them down. "What are you going to do? Hog-tie me and carry me out of here?"

"Don't tempt me," Ryder said, his voice dropping ominously. "If it wouldn't slow us down—"

"Here," Flynn said, plopping a bulletproof vest into my arms. "Put this on." She turned to Ryder. "We don't have time to argue."

I slid the vest on. Ryder spun me, tightening the straps and making sure it fit properly. From the way he yanked at the Velcro, he was most definitely not happy. Made two of us, since I wished he was anywhere but here—after all, keeping him safe was the whole reason why I'd left him in the first place.

As he spun me around, I spotted a box with slotted compartments like what Patsy stored her Christmas ornaments in. Only this box was filled with brown balls that even I recognized. Hand grenades. When Ryder turned to finish settling his own gear, I reached for one. It fit perfectly in the palm of my hand, and my fingers curled naturally around it. The pin had a loop made of wire—just like in the movies. It was lighter than I thought it'd be, and I wondered if that made it harder to throw very far. Maybe it would be best to roll it or toss it underhand?

Ryder stopped adjusting his night vision gear long enough to frown. He took the grenade and returned it to the box. "Not in these confined spaces, too risky. Here. You can act as our spotter," he said, handing me a pair of binoculars. "Click there for thermal, there for infrared. And here's your zoom and focus."

Reluctantly, I tried out the binoculars. Then, while he and Flynn finished stuffing their vests with ammo and strapped handguns to their thighs, I slipped a grenade into my pocket.

There was one thing I was certain would bring our enemies out into the open. Me. If I had to go that route, I was sure as hell taking them down with me. End this once and for all.

"Angie," Flynn said. I startled, wasn't sure if she'd spotted me pocketing the grenade. If she had, she said nothing. As usual, her face was unreadable. "Check your phone. I've mapped out a safe corridor from Good Sam's to St. Tim's—same one you've traveled before. The side corridors are all booby-trapped, so avoid them. And I've marked safe places to climb up onto the catwalk. If we're lucky, we can stop them at Good Sam's. If not, we fall back, follow the catwalk, and keep sniping, take as many out as we can."

"Where are Devon and the kids?" Ryder asked, peering over my shoulder at the map on my phone.

"The area in orange on the other side of St. Tim's. If they get past us—"

"They'll run right into them."

"Devon has the section sealed off with locked hatches."

"Yeah, but easy enough for these guys to bring in a thermal lance, cut right through."

Flynn hefted the machine gun in her hands. "Exactly why we're not going to let them get past us."

FROM HIS PREVIOUS excursions into the tunnels, Ryder wasn't surprised by the stockpile of weapons—last month during their search for Leo, they'd found a ton of cheap, street-level arms left behind by the drug dealers who'd hidden their stash down here.

But these weapons were anything but cheap—or street-level. Belgian, made by FN Herstal. All military grade, state of the art.

Too bad Daniel Kingston hadn't also stockpiled more men to use them. Because, despite Flynn's optimism and sound military tactics, they were outnumbered at least five to one. Odds he didn't mind facing, as long as he could ensure Rossi's safety. He wished he could convince Flynn to take her, let him deal with Grey and Tyrone, but he knew neither woman would agree, and there was no more time to argue.

Flynn took the lead heading back out into the tunnels, Rossi the more protected position in the middle, while Ryder covered their backs.

"You said there were only eleven, right?" Flynn asked, pausing to glance at her phone. They were at the bottom of one of the retractable ladders leading up to the catwalk. She gestured for Rossi to climb while Ryder held the narrow lengths of chain and metal cross braces steady.

"Eleven, right," he murmured back. "Why?"

She held her phone up to him. "All eleven are coming through the Good Sam entrance."

Damn. He'd hoped his bomb threats would send enough law enforcement there to slow them down. Then he realized the problem. "All of them? Why aren't they trying to outflank us?"

Price had the other tunnel entrances secured, but Grey and Tyrone wouldn't know that.

"Exactly. I don't think they're trying to ambush us."

"No. They want to herd us. They'll have more men waiting—"

"If Devon tries to lead the children out, they're toast. And if they wait inside, they're sitting ducks once the bad guys find them."

Ryder grimaced at her blunt assessment. But she was right. "Let's make sure they don't find them. We neutralize these guys, and then whoever they bought off as backup won't stick around." At least he hoped not. Last thing he wanted was to end up in a shooting battle against other cops—men and women he knew.

The ladder stopped shimmying—Rossi had made it to the fixed section. He pointed to Flynn's phone screen now that he could free a hand.

The Lazaretto men were all dressed in firefighting gear. His bomb threat might have actually given them cover, damn it. Security wouldn't have challenged responding firefighters—and Flynn had said the cops she saw at Good Sam's were the ones they knew the Lazarettos had bought off.

He pointed to the screen. "Those two, Grey and Tyrone, they're the leaders. Said they were brothers."

"Angie said the entire Lazaretto family was involved. How many of them are there?"

"I don't know, but they mentioned at least two more by name. The other men with them didn't talk much, but they seemed loyal, followed orders without hesitation. Not sure if they're family or hired muscle."

"What's that on their backs? I don't think they're air tanks. Packs of additional weapons? Ammo?" Flynn squinted, but the men weren't positioned for the camera to get a good view. All of the men carried assault rifles and pistols, plus five of them had backpacks.

"Let's get into position." Ryder held the ladder for her—

she climbed it fast, barely touching the metal slats that served as rungs, instead using the chains like an acrobat ascending a rope would. As soon as she'd cleared the retractable section of ladder, he swung his own weight on it. It swayed in protest, but he only had to climb about twelve feet before he reached the more sturdy fixed ladder bolted into the concrete wall of the tunnel.

Ryder pulled the collapsible length of ladder up behind him, anchoring it to a hook on the wall, then scrambled up the main ladder the rest of the way, passing the foil-lined ductwork and myriad lengths of pipe to the catwalk that ran immediately above them. He'd expected the ducts and pipes to obstruct his vision, had been worried about how he'd be able to find a good angle to shoot from, but the designers had cleverly routed the catwalk so it didn't run parallel to the pipes but crossed over them at an angle. Made sense, as it allowed maintenance workers access to the vital areas but without needing to follow the twisting labyrinth of corridors below that the pipes did. Instead, the catwalk provided excellent straight-line shortcuts to the main sections of the bunker.

From below, the catwalk was invisible, hidden in the dark recesses of the tunnel's roof. But from up here, he had a direct sight line down to the corridors. He quickened his gait to catch up with Flynn and Rossi, who'd gone forward to the section above the route Grey and Tyrone would take from Good Sam.

"I'm going to have Devon kill the lights," Flynn said as soon as he arrived. "I didn't see any night vision gear on them, so it should give us an advantage."

Ryder nodded his agreement as he lowered his own NVG. The tunnels went black, losing even the low-level emergency illumination. Flynn sidled down a few paces, Rossi between them, all focused on the tunnel below.

Now came the hard part. The waiting.

Chapter 36

DESPITE THE FACT that people often call the ER a war zone, I'd never experienced anything like a true battle. Not even last month, when I'd faced Leo Kingston and killed him with my own hands. Nothing in my life had prepared me for this.

We sat on the metal mesh catwalk floor in the dark. Silent. Waiting. The binoculars were heavy, and all they revealed when I played with the settings were different colors reflecting the temperature of whatever the pipes running below us carried. When I looked at Flynn and Ryder through them, they turned into ghastly pale green-gray specters. Their features were surprisingly clear, but that only made it seem more surreal. Not only the strangely shaped night vision equipment, although that was weird enough. Rather, the expressions on their faces: more than calm, relaxed. Ready.

Same look I liked to see on my trauma team before the ambulance arrived. But here it felt like a cruel parody.

To be so calmly prepared to not save lives but take them.

To be facing others who felt the same way, who had no qualms about targeting innocent children to get what they wanted. As if killing was no different than buying stock, all in a day's work.

The hardest thing was seeing that calm readiness on the face of the man I loved.

Ryder must have sensed something, because he stretched his hand toward me far enough to reach my foot and squeeze it. Then he was back in position, on alert, scanning the corridor, searching for targets.

I lowered my binoculars. Ryder had told me my job was to scan the area beyond the corridor, to make sure we weren't ambushed or outflanked. In other words, to look anywhere except where he and Flynn would be killing people. I didn't feel calm or prepared. Not anxious or frightened, either. I felt saddened. Resigned.

The logic was impeccable: kill them before they could kill us or the children. A story as old as mankind. I think that was the problem. Knowing that whatever happened here tonight, it wouldn't end the bloodshed or solve anything.

Cautiously, I felt the grenade sagging heavy in my coat pocket. Could *I* end things? Was it even worth trying?

Leo's memories still flitted through my mind, pages of a textbook rustling back and forth as I searched for a solution. He'd been privy to Tommaso's research developing different formulations of the PXA. Tommaso had divulged a lot of his thinking about prions—my prions in particular—and why he thought Patient Zero's disease—my disease—was unique. He'd also mentioned that he'd used up all of his original sample—wherever the hell he'd gotten that from—developing his prion-transfer injection.

If no one had more of Patient Zero's tissue to work with, then maybe it could all end here. With me. It wouldn't save the children, but it could save more lives in the future.

I'd been willing to take my own life to spare my own suffering—did I have the courage to do the same to spare the lives of people I hadn't even met? And to take the lives of the Lazaretto brothers—part of my own family, no matter how disgusted that thought made me feel—along with mine?

Foul thoughts, considering cold-blooded murder. I felt as if my mind was polluted. But why had I taken the grenade in the first place if somewhere deep inside me I hadn't thought it was the best option?

Even without the binoculars, I felt both Flynn and Ryder alert. Then the sound of their guns firing. It was loud, especially up here so close to the concrete roof, but not as booming as I'd expected. More like a popping. Firecrackers going off too close.

Then the bullets began to come at us, pinging off metal and cracking against concrete. I clutched the binoculars tight, fighting the impulse to cover my head and hide. There wasn't anything to take cover behind, not up here on the catwalk. Ryder and Flynn shot a few more rounds, but nothing compared to the volume coming our way.

"One down," Ryder said in a calm voice barely raised above his usual tone.

"And one for me," Flynn replied. She had her phone's earpiece on and was giving someone a running report—Devon, I assumed. "That's two down. Nine left. They're taking cover, scattering."

Ryder duck-walked past me to take up a new position on the other side of Flynn. "What are they doing? Look, two o'clock."

Flynn craned her neck, and I raised the binoculars. They flared with sudden color. I focused them and saw two men waving what looked like wands at the stacks of supplies on the shelves lining the corridor beside them.

Ryder shot at the men, trying to drive them back into the open.

"Flamethrowers. Those backpacks," Ryder said, reloading his gun. "They've got flamethrowers."

"Not very big. Must be the kind gardeners use." Flynn aimed at the men and fired. They ducked back, taking cover. But the damage was done, flames spreading deeper into the shelves. With them came smoke.

"That's why they're dressed as firefighters," I said.

"All these pipes and none of them are sprinklers?" Ryder asked.

Flynn climbed to her feet. "No. They are. The valve must be turned off. Cover me while I go check."

She eased past Ryder as he knelt and fired into the smoke and flames.

"One more," he muttered. But the men below had zeroed in on his position and returned fire with a vengeance. I couldn't help myself. Bullets zipping around us, I ducked down and covered my head. Ryder kept firing back, inching his way over to me. Then he was covering me with his body, pulling me back the way we came.

My ears rang as the bullets finally stopped coming. We were back near the ladder before Ryder finally let me go. He rolled off me, fingers fumbling slightly as he reloaded, his breaths coming short and fast.

"Ryder, are you hit?" I crowded close, my vision useless, running my hands over his body.

"I'm all right," he gasped. "The vest caught it."

"Them," I corrected as I found two warm, metallic, flattened shapes with my fingers. "You sure that's all? No blood?"

The stink of the smoke from below made me cough as I traced my hands up to his neck, felt his pulse—barely elevated, steady and strong. Then I felt his arms and legs. No blood.

"Just need a moment. What are they doing? They'll use the smoke as cover to regroup, but you'll be able to see them with the binoculars."

I leaned over him and looked below—from our new position, the pipes partially obstructed the view, but I could make out the two leaders, Grey and Tyrone. "Nothing. They're just standing there. Like they're waiting."

My eyes watered from the smoke, and I had to lower the binoculars to wipe them. Ryder coughed, then grabbed his chest. "You probably cracked a rib."

"I'm fine," he insisted. "If we can't get the sprinklers going, we need to leave."

"No. That's what they're waiting for. They want to force our hand, make us move to where they can shoot us."

He pushed his night vision goggles up and rubbed his face on his sleeve. "I know. It's what I'd do. I'll cover you, and you follow the catwalk. Catch up with Flynn and keep going until you reach Devon and the others."

"No. I'm not leaving you."

"Don't worry about me. I'll pin them down, and they'll either have to retreat or risk getting caught in their own fire—those firefighter suits only buy them time, can't protect them forever."

"No," I insisted. "You'll be a sitting duck."

"Duh. That's why they call it a diversion." He shifted position, pain tightening his eyes. "Are they moving?"

I looked. "No. Still waiting." As I turned back to him, the grenade shifted in my pocket. I glanced past him to the ladder leading down. "I have a plan."

"Really? What?" He looked half serious and half ready to laugh.

"We give them what they came here for," I said. I held the grenade up for him to see. "And then I kill them all."

Chapter 37

DEVON KNEW BETTER than to disappear lest he cause an uproar among the parents, so he kept to himself in a corner of the dormitory as he listened to the battle unfold over his earbud. Flynn's play-by-play kept him oriented, but the news was definitely not good for the home team.

"Ryder and I are holding the high ground," Flynn reported. "But, Devon, they've got flamethrowers. The sprinkler system isn't working."

That explained the stench in the air. When he'd been prioritizing repairs, he'd never dreamed he'd need to move the sprinkler system to the top of the list. Not like he'd invited any fire marshals down to his secret underground lair to do a safety inspection.

"Can you reach the cutoff valve?" he asked.

"I'm there already. It's not working."

"Lefty-loosey..."

"Ha-hah. It's not that kind of valve. More like a lever with a big green arrow pointing to on and a red one pointing to off."

He held his phone, flipping through the maps he'd created of the tunnel sections. "The drug dealers must have shut off the main valve to keep their stash from getting wet."

"Where is it?"

"Hang on, I'm looking." He paced in a circle, turning his back to the parents watching him. "Got it. In the yellow section, near St. Tim's."

"I'm halfway there, but Rossi and Ryder are pinned down, taking heavy fire."

"I'm not far. Go, back them up. When the sprinklers turn on, use the diversion and get out of there."

"On it."

Devon memorized the fastest, safest route to the water valve and moved toward the door.

"Where are you going?" one of the young mothers asked, her voice loud enough that everyone turned to stare. "Not running out on us, are you?"

Anger lanced through him. He didn't have time for this shit. "Three people are fighting for their lives out there, trying to save your children, and they need my help." The woman's jaw dropped. Before she could say anything, he jerked his chin at Louise. "Dr. Mehta, while I'm gone, you're in charge."

He left, stalking down the hall, hoping to burn off some of his anger. He hated when emotions took control. That was the sure path to making stupid mistakes.

He'd made it through the locked doors and to the yellow section when the other line on his phone rang. He answered without looking—only a handful of people had this number.

"Is this Mr. Devon Price?" a man's voice came over the line, startling him.

He glanced at the screen. Ryder's number—at least it had been before his phone had been taken from him. He hauled in a breath, trying to force his voice to a normal register. "Yes, Mr. Lazaretto. What can I do for you?"

The man chuckled. "Very good. This is Tyrone Lazaretto. I like that you're quick on the uptake. As for what you can do for us, I believe you have several properties we wish to acquire. In exchange for the life of your daughter and the others."

So. They'd discovered Esme was related to him. He shouldn't be surprised. Given the resources the Lazaretto family controlled, a simple birth certificate database search was child's play. Devon kept moving. The water valve should be—there it was. A big red metal box labeled Fire Control.

"Which properties are we talking about? Seems as if you and your men are currently permanently damaging the value of one of my primary holdings. Not the best grounds for negotiation."

"Simply a means to get your attention. You have my word. You and your people can leave in safety once we get what we came for."

"I have sick children here." He opened the box and found the main valve for the sprinklers. Flynn was right. It was turned off. He tried to flip it, but it was frozen in place. Damn.

"Yes. I'm aware."

"I understand you might be able to offer them a chance at a treatment. Under my and my physician's supervision, of course. These are our children, not lab rats for you to experiment on." Devon allowed his anger to flow through to his muscles, slipping the phone into his pocket and using both hands on the valve. He tried not to grunt as he bent with his knees and pushed on the lever.

It moved. At first grudgingly, but once he got it past the halfway mark, it slid the rest of the way until it rested against the helpful green arrow.

He grabbed his phone, checked to see that he hadn't lost the call. No, still connected. He waited, refusing to be the first to break. There was a long pause, long enough for sweat to gather at the base of Devon's back.

Finally, the voice returned. "Very well, Mr. Price. You have a deal."

"You'll treat the children in exchange for—"

"I think you know already, Mr. Price."

"You want Tommaso's research. I have it." The thumb drive was still in his pocket. He didn't mention that he also had copies and so wouldn't be losing much by making the bargain. "Where shall we meet?"

"Come now. The lives of all those children, surely they're worth more than that?"

Devon clenched his fists, not answering despite the fact that he knew exactly what Lazaretto wanted.

"We are tired of these games, Mr. Price. Angela Rossi. Bring her to us."

꒰ 🌿 ꒱

I WAS GLAD I was too far away from Ryder for him to reach me. The look on his face—I'd never seen such a mixture of horror and regret.

"Give me that." He barked the words as an order.

I stood, gripping the thin railing, and edged across the metal grating of the catwalk closer to the ladder and farther from him.

"Rossi, stop. Don't go."

I hesitated, then turned back.

"Don't do it."

"It's the only way."

"No. It's not." Ryder used the railing to haul himself to his feet, pain lancing through the small, muffled noise that escaped him. I held up a hand as if to keep him at bay. Not him. His pain. Worse, his disappointment. In me.

"Don't you understand?" I pleaded my case. "They're targeting children. You're not saying that those men deserve any iota of compassion, of human regard, are you?"

"No. I agree with you. There is evil in this world. You and I, we've both seen it. I'm not saying these men don't deserve to die. I've already killed three tonight."

"Right. Self-defense. Isn't that the same as what I want to do?"

"I'm saying—" His brow creased with frustration. "I'm saying don't let it, them, doing what you're talking about...I can't lose you to that."

I swung my face heavenward, resisted the temptation to laugh. "You're missing the point, Ryder. I'm already lost."

Without looking at him, I turned to the ladder. The stench from the fire filled my nostrils even though I couldn't see any flames. With the smell came smoke, but even that was invisible up here in the shadows.

"Stop!"

I froze. Ryder had never raised his voice to me before. Not like that.

He grimaced and came close, settling both palms on my shoulders, leaning in. Blocking out the rest of the world, hidden by the maze of pipes and conduits, it was just me and him.

"I get that you're dying. I really do. But that's not the problem."

"Really? Then what is?"

"It's the choices you're making. It's as if you don't care anymore."

"How can you say that? Everything I do is to protect you, to save those children—"

"What about saving you, Rossi?"

I shrugged his hands off my body, turned away, head

down. "I'm beyond saving. We both know that."

"No. You're not." He coughed, muffled it with his hand. "Look at me. Please."

Reluctantly, I faced him.

"You might think you know when you're going to die, how you're going to die. But it's not true. It's all a lie. A delusion."

"Now who's being delusional? You've talked to Louise. You know how little time I have—" I stopped as he shook his head, denying my words. So typical of Ryder. Despite everything he'd seen and done, he was still at heart a man of faith. Foolish enough to have faith in me.

"Who cares?" he retorted. "You're dying, I'm dying, we're all dying. That's my point. Maybe the fatal insomnia will kill you—or maybe it will be something else. It doesn't matter. We're all facing a death sentence. Each and every one of us from the moment we are born into this world."

He reached for me once more, this time resting his hands on my hips, drawing me close. Tears streamed down his cheeks, but I knew they were from the smoke, not for me. At least that's what I told myself, blamed my own tears on.

"It's not the dying that matters. It's the living." His voice dropped, low and hoarse, almost a whisper.

"Are you saying I shouldn't fight back with the only weapon left to me? I should just let those kids die?"

"No. No. I'm saying you're not fighting alone. I'm saying you matter. Not just what's going on with your body and mind, but your soul. Who you really are. Don't let that part of you, the woman I fell in love with, die before the rest of you."

I flinched. "I'm sorry if you don't approve of my methods."

"Methods? You're talking about killing yourself and taking as many people as you can along with you!"

"Better me doing the dirty work than someone who has a future. After all, what do I have to lose?"

The look on his face as his hands fell away from me gave me my answer. He shook his head sorrowfully. "You have so much to lose, Rossi. So very much. I wish I knew how to make you see that."

Somewhere deep inside me, I felt a twist of pain, sharp enough to bring tears to my eyes. Not from smoke. Real tears. And yet my eyes were suddenly dry.

He was right. I was no longer the woman he had fallen in love with. I was broken, contaminated by memories not my own, my brain filled with so many lifetimes, too many lives, and yet I felt so empty, so very empty.

I left him there. Scrambled down the ladder to the tunnel floor. Better for everyone. Safer. Less painful.

These were the lies I told myself. Only, even I no longer believed them.

Chapter 38

RYDER LUNGED FOR Rossi, but she moved too fast, and the ladder would support only one person at a time. A hand landed on his arm, hauling him back. Flynn.

"What the hell?" she asked.

"Rossi has a grenade. She's going to kill herself and try to take as many of them with her."

Flynn simply nodded. "Not a bad plan. Except for the part where the doc dies. Come on."

She began moving down the catwalk away from the Good Sam corridor and the men below. And Rossi. Ryder glanced down, but couldn't spot Rossi through the pipes. He followed Flynn if only to get a better line of sight. "Where are you going?"

"Devon's going to turn the sprinklers on at the main valve." As if in answer to her words, a loud gurgling shook several of the thinner pipes. A moment later, there was the sound of water falling. The smoke increased, but it clung to the ground.

Flynn rubbed her hands together as if she'd performed a magic trick. "There. That will take care of the fire."

"Who cares about the fire? We need to stop Rossi."

The look Flynn gave him was pitying. "She's not an idiot. The doc won't use that grenade here where it would cause more harm than good. We're too close to the hospital, and she knows you're nearby. She'd never risk hurting you."

Too damn late for that.

Flynn kept moving. He rushed to catch up, his ribs stabbing with each step, but his breathing grew easier as they moved past the smoke. "Where are we going?"

"She'll want a contained area so she can be sure she's only risking bad guys, right? Someplace isolated, away from any innocents. I know where she's going."

"Where?" How bad had things deteriorated that he was taking tactical advice from a kid? How the hell had he let things get so out of control?

"The bell tower at St. Tim's. We can beat her there, set up an ambush."

❄

DEFINITELY NOT ONE of my better ideas, I couldn't help but think as I stepped off the ladder in time to get drenched by the sprinklers. It made for a nice diversion, though. The Lazarettos were scrambling, dropping their now-useless flamethrowers, fighting through smoke made thicker by the water squelching the flames.

I waited a safe distance from them. Close enough that when they aimed a light in my direction they could see who I was, far enough that they couldn't easily reach me.

As soon as their light hit me and one of them called my name, I turned and ran. They followed. A few shucked their fire gear to move faster, but as soon as they outpaced the others and threatened to close the distance, shots rang out from above. One more down, then another one left hobbling, grasping his knee with both hands.

I glanced heavenward, giving Ryder and Flynn a nod of

thanks before resuming my flight. From eleven down to five, not bad. Maybe I wouldn't need to follow through with my plan after all.

As I kept racing down the corridor, holding the binoculars up to my eyes to keep my bearings, the covering fire from above ended. I risked taking a quick look at the map Flynn had sent to my phone and realized that I'd come to the point where the catwalk she and Ryder were on diverged from the path my corridor took.

Men's footsteps pounded behind me. I thought furiously about where to lead them. The catwalk and tunnels didn't converge again until past St. Tim's. But that meant Ryder and Flynn would reach the cathedral before I did. I hoped they'd planned some kind of ambush. If not, I'd have no choice but to lead the Lazarettos safely away to where no one could get hurt if I detonated the grenade: the bell tower.

Chapter 39

AN EMPTY CATHEDRAL at four in the morning the day after Christmas. As he and Flynn took positions in the cathedral's antechamber at the top of the steps leading up from the tunnels, Ryder tried to decide if it was the best place to die or the worst. Good place for an ambush, but also no cover, so every time they took aim, they'd be exposing themselves to the enemy. At least they had the high ground.

Flynn was on her belly, making herself the smallest possible target. "I can cover everything except the far left corner. The way the stairs curve, there's a blind spot there."

He stood, sighting his weapon, shuffling back and forth until he had the area covered. "Got it."

"Yeah, why don't you paint a bull's-eye on you while you're at it."

The clatter of footsteps came from below. "It's me," Rossi called. "Me, me, me. No bad guys."

"We got you," Ryder shouted back. "Get up here." He tried to keep the fury from his voice, but seeing her made his adrenaline spike. "Are you okay?" he asked when she reached the top of the stairs.

Rossi stepped over Flynn, who looked up only long enough to flash a wink. "I'm fine."

He glanced away from his position to see for himself. "That was either the stupidest or the craziest thing I've ever—"

"Gave you the chance to take three more of them down," she retorted.

"How far back are they?"

"About thirty yards. But they aren't moving fast. I think they know it's a trap."

"No duh," Flynn snorted.

"Get out of here," Ryder told Rossi. "We've got this. Go hide in the rectory, tell Father Vance not to trust the city cops. He'll protect you."

"Like I'm going to get a priest killed? Do you not get it? They cannot take me alive. Period."

What the hell? He didn't move anything except his eyes, sliding his gaze away from his sights for a precious second. "No one's going to take you anywhere."

She blew out her breath in a huff and shook her head. He knew he'd missed something, something she'd been trying to tell him back up on the catwalk before she'd fled with her idiotic idea of a diversion—at least she hadn't used the damn grenade. Speaking of... "Go. But give me the grenade first."

"No way." She backed away from him. "I'm going up to the bell tower." She grabbed a clutch of hymnals from a stack on a table near the entrance to the church's nave. Threw down one after another as if leaving a trail of breadcrumbs.

"Rossi, what the hell?" He couldn't find the words to say anything more, not with his attention divided between her and his mission.

Flynn sighed. "She's right. Go with her. Protect her—more fun for me down here."

Rossi vanished through the arch into the cavernous main space of the cathedral. Ryder glanced back at Flynn. "There's five of them, I can't leave you."

"Don't you get it? They want Angie's DNA to experiment on."

Again, Ryder had no words. "Experiment?" he echoed. "Like hell."

"That's why they need her alive. If I can stop them, great. If not, then you take care of the rest, and she won't need that grenade. Then maybe Louise can figure all this genetic bullshit out and save the kids. If not," she shrugged, "been good knowing you."

More footsteps approached. These were slow and thoughtful. Determined men moving into tactical positions.

"Go," Flynn repeated. "I got this."

Echoes of Rossi's steps pounding up the stairs to the choir loft thudded through the church. A blind man with a deaf guide dog could follow her trail. She wasn't leaving anything to chance.

Neither was Ryder. "Thanks, Flynn."

He turned and ran after Rossi. She'd just reached the door at the top of the bell tower when he caught up with her.

"No." She shook her head at him. "You need to help Flynn."

Before he could answer, the sound of gunfire reverberated through the ancient space, echoing from the cathedral's stone walls like ricochets. Flynn taking fire.

Ryder reached past Rossi to push the heavy wooden door open, glancing around the bell tower to assess its tactical properties. Cover: none. Lines of sight: three hundred and sixty degrees for the area outside, only the doorway for the interior. Only thing the place had going for it were the thick stone walls and the almost as thick wooden door. Enough to stop a bullet or shotgun slug.

"Get out there." He pushed Rossi through the door, then

changed his mind and leaned into her for a quick kiss. As soon as they parted, her eyes wide and stunned, he closed the door between them, holding it shut with one hand, leaving her trapped on the outside.

She tried to yank the door open, pounded her fists against the wood, but he barely heard it as he focused all his senses on the spiral stone steps leading down. Last line of defense, he had to hold strong.

Unfortunately, as far as tactical advantages, the narrow landing at the top of the steps where he stood had even less going for it than the tower outside.

The gunfire below stuttered to a stop. Ryder waited. At the sight of the first muzzle inching around the curve of the steps, he fired. Was rewarded with the heavy thud of a man falling. But then the bullets came flying toward him. The first few caught him in his vest.

The next felt as if it exploded in his head. He almost dropped his weapon, slumped to the ground just as the door behind him opened. He wanted to shout at Rossi to stop, to close it, to stay safe. The words floated through his brain like intangible wisps, and even though his mouth was moving, no sound escaped.

❄

DEVON HEARD GUNFIRE coming from the tunnel leading to St. Tim's. He drew his pistol and raced in that direction, but by the time he reached the exit to the cathedral, the sound had died. Cautiously, he climbed the steps to the church basement, then up to the main floor. There he found two dead men in firemen's suits lying on the stairs. At the top of the steps, Flynn sat in blood, struggling to use a windbreaker as a tourniquet, blood gushing from a wound in her thigh.

"There's still three more," she said through clenched teeth as Devon knelt to wrap his belt around her leg. A thin scream emerged from her when he wrenched it tight, but the blood slowed to a trickle. "One's wounded, not sure about the other two. Would've had them but ran out of ammo."

"Angela?"

"She and Ryder went up to the bell tower. She won't let them take her alive. Has a grenade." Her voice was going blurry, and her eyes fluttered as she fell back, limp.

"What's going on here?" Father Vance bellowed as he approached from the cathedral, carrying a heavy candlestick as a weapon.

"Shhh, they're still here."

"Where? I didn't see anyone. Who?"

"Can you call an ambulance? Take her out the back alley?" The bell tower faced the front entrance, and the last thing Devon wanted was to get any paramedics shot. But Flynn couldn't wait for help much longer.

"Yes, of course." Vance knelt and gathered Flynn in his arms. He was a former bodybuilder, her thin frame no match for his strength.

Knowing Flynn was in good hands, Devon kept moving through the cathedral, pistol at the ready. More gunfire came from the front of the church, above him. The choir loft. He sprinted toward it.

A man's body lay at the foot of the steps leading up. Carefully, he stepped over it and climbed, sighting his pistol. A second flight of steps kept going up to the bell tower above. Before he could make the turn and continue up, a man stepped out from behind the massive organ and aimed a semiautomatic at him.

At first, he thought the man was going to shoot. He was a few inches shorter than Devon, with dark, Mediterranean looks. Devon took a chance. "Lazaretto? I'm Devon Price."

"Mr. Price. Tell me why I shouldn't kill you now. Seeing as how you've reneged on our deal."

"You need me alive if you want Angela Rossi."

"I think not. My brother has her cornered in the bell tower above us."

"Then there's no time to argue. She's got a grenade, and she won't be taken alive."

Chapter 40

I'D BARELY HAULED Ryder through the doorway when another man—Grey, Ryder had called him—appeared, aiming a pistol at us. "Let him go, Angela."

Grey spoke as if he knew me. Given his dark hair and eyes, maybe he did. If he was a Lazaretto, then we were probably related.

I ignored him and tugged against Ryder's weight, trying to get his body clear of the door in time to slam it shut, protect us both. His scalp was bleeding. It looked like only a graze, but even a graze could result in a skull fracture and hemorrhage. Ryder muttered something and tried to focus on me, all good signs, but then he went limp once more.

Grey began moving up the steps before I could get the door closed. Using the grenade was out of the question. Not with Ryder there with me. Instead, I bent and grabbed his pistol.

"Stop!" I screamed, raising the gun with shaking hands. But Grey didn't. He kept coming at us, his own pistol aimed not at me, but at Ryder. "Please," I begged. "Stop."

"You're not going to shoot anyone. Put the gun down, Angela," he said, his tone absolutely calm and certain as he reached the doorway. "Now. Or I shoot Detective Ryder." He knew I would do anything to protect Ryder. Including give myself up.

He was right. I would do anything to protect Ryder.

But Grey was wrong about me not shooting him. I was shaking so badly I might have missed if he hadn't been walking toward us. The boom of the gun made my entire body jerk. I felt the vibration as my finger kept squeezing the trigger over and over—but the top part of the gun had slid open, and I realized that one shot was my last and only chance.

Grey took another step toward us. I tried to cover Ryder's body, knowing that whether I surrendered or not, this man would leave no witnesses behind. Grey used both hands to steady his aim, but as he reached the doorway, he sank to one knee. His expression turned to one of shock.

I stood between him and Ryder—there was no way Grey could shoot without hitting me. I waited, wondering what it would feel like when the bullet struck.

He sank back, leaning against the wall to his left, still holding the gun with both hands, now aimed at the floor. He kept trying to raise it, but it was as if gravity simply refused to cooperate. His mouth formed words I couldn't hear, and flecks of blood flew free with them.

There was no wound that I could see, not until his body sagged to one side and his coat flapped open. A small ring of blood and charred fabric at his upper-right abdomen, just below the edge of his bulletproof vest. Little bleeding externally, which was a bad thing—for him.

I couldn't simply let him die. Not only because I was a doctor—and definitely not because I'm any kind of good person. But Grey knew things, had information that could help save the children. If I could first save him.

Cautious of the pistol he still gripped, I crawled toward him. He didn't seem to remember that he even held a weapon.

His face filled with terror, and he cringed back against the wall, as far away from me as he could get.

Suddenly, he was my father, all those years ago. "No." His plea was choked with blood. "No."

"I'm a doctor. Let me help."

Words gone, he shook his head. His color had gone gray, and sweat coated him. Shock. He didn't have much time left.

"Please," I coaxed him. "I can—"

A spray of pink mist and the shockwave of another gun firing from the doorway seemed to come simultaneously. In slow motion, I watched Grey's head snap backward, most of his brain emerging from the shattered remnants of the back of his skull.

Adrenaline cut through my shock, and I whirled to face the new threat. Another man stood in the doorway, a satisfied smile on his face as he turned his aim on Ryder, now exposed. Tyrone, Grey's accomplice. And brother, if what they'd told Ryder was true. Lazarettos, like me. The thought filled my mouth with bile.

"What did you do?" I asked, not caring that this was not the time for either conversation or recrimination. I staggered to my feet, stepping in front of Ryder, putting myself between him and Tyrone. "I was trying to help him. Why—"

"He would have rather died than let you touch him, dear Angela. I did my duty, as did he. Besides, only one can return triumphant, bringing the prize home."

"Prize? What prize?"

"You, Angela. You are the prize." Tyrone tried to step to where he'd have a clear shot at Ryder, but I moved to block him once more.

This do-si-do was getting us nowhere. I lunged for the ledge, where I had a view of the entire city, including the more than lethal drop to the stone steps below. Maybe I didn't need the grenade. "Stop. I'll jump—and I'm guessing you want me alive."

His jaw tightened with dissatisfaction, but he nodded and holstered his weapon. "Come with me, and Detective Ryder lives."

"No. You leave now." I swung a leg over the parapet. Stalemate.

Tyrone sighed, gestured with his hand. Devon appeared from behind him.

He approached me, both hands out, palms empty. "It's over, Angela. Give me the grenade, and I'll get an ambulance for Ryder."

I shook my head in disbelief. "No..." But even the single syllable emerged uncertain. "No," I tried again, but the second try wasn't any better.

Devon kept coming closer, finally stepping past Ryder to reach me. He took my arms and guided me down, then slid one hand into my pocket and took the grenade.

"I'm sorry," he whispered. "They promised a cure for the children. Hold them to that. Will you do that? For Esme?"

I nodded, my entire body numb as he escorted me down the steps, Tyrone holding his pistol on us, leaving Ryder behind. He was alive. That much I'd accomplished, at least.

But how many more lives had my cowardice condemned?

☽ ✹ ☾

RYDER FELT PEOPLE moving around him. Above him. Then a frigid breeze. Sirens in the distance. He opened his eyes, surprised that they were closed and that he was lying on his back—hadn't he been standing?

"Rossi?" He looked around—not that there was much to look at. An open door, its wood splintered and pocked by bullets.

An empty bell tower. Except for the corpse across from him. Grey. Dead. Had Ryder done that? Streaks of blood on the stone surrounding Ryder—his, he assumed from the blood streaming down his face.

He clawed his way to a sitting position, then to his knees where he could look out over the parapet to the street below. Ambulance lights in the distance, but what grabbed his attention was the black Town Car sliding to a stop at the curb.

Two men escorted a woman down the steps from the cathedral.

"Rossi!" he cried out, but the wind swept his voice back into his face like a slap. She never looked up. "Rossi," he tried again but could barely choke the word clear.

Ryder called her name long after she vanished from his sight, the men bundling her into the Town Car just as the ambulance arrived. He slumped against the rough stone ledge, leaning his head on it, looking out over the city.

The moon, that gorgeous plump, overripe moon that had filled the sky earlier when he'd first spotted Rossi up here had long since set. In its wake was a smudge of blood red, far away on the eastern horizon. Too dull to provide any helpful light yet bright enough to cloak the stars and erase them from sight.

Ryder's blood turned sticky as it clouded his vision and choked one eye closed. Yet, even as his mind dazed and grew dim, the world around him going deaf and dark, still he whispered her name.

Chapter 41

AFTER DEVON AND Tyrone escorted me to Tyrone's car, we left Devon behind and drove out of the city. Tyrone radiated furious energy—I could see it in his white-knuckled fists, in the tight line of his lips. He'd said he needed me alive, but I knew he wanted to kill me.

Something stopped him—presumably the person on the other end of a muttered phone conversation he had. Thanks to Daniel's and Leo's memories, I could understand Italian somewhat, but not when it galloped past so fast that the words ran together. Finally, he hung up and settled back, reduced to simply glaring at me.

Me, I had so many questions, so many second thoughts, so many regrets... I curled up in the corner of the seat, my back to Tyrone, my face pressed against the cold glass of the window, my eyes closed, although sleep was not an option.

We finally arrived at an airstrip hidden somewhere among the fields of a farm. No one was in sight except for a pilot and two more anonymous men who came and opened my door. Tyrone left me, walking to the rear ramp of what appeared to be a small cargo plane. I didn't recognize the logo, some airfreight service. For the first time, I became frightened—they could be taking me anywhere.

Then I saw the crate. Plastic, three feet square on each side, solid, except for four rows of air holes along the top wall. The kind of cage you'd transport an animal in. I planted my feet and shook my head, trying to escape back into the rear seat. The two men laughed, pulled me out of the car, and held me dangling in the air, shouting to Tyrone in Italian.

"Because of her, Michael and Tommaso are dead," he called back. "As long as she is alive when I bring her to Mother, she can travel like the animal she is."

I fought back, kicking and twisting, using my knees, elbows, anything I could, but they grabbed my shoes and stripped them off, along with my jacket. Then they handcuffed my wrists behind my back, carried me to the crate, and lowered me inside, pinioning my feet against the door when I tried to kick it out. They slammed it shut and locked it.

"Where are you taking me?" I screamed in frustration.

No answer except their laughter.

The space was too tiny to sit up. I folded my body and curled up on one side. Ryder would find me, I thought. Hell, Flynn was probably hanging on to the plane's undercarriage right this second, a bowie knife clamped between her teeth.

The image made me smile and brought fresh tears. Flynn wasn't under the plane. I wasn't even sure if she was still alive. Ryder... No, with that head injury, all I could do was hope he was okay. Besides, this was my family, and I'd seen their power, knew what they could do. Last thing I wanted was for Ryder to get himself killed. I prayed that he wasn't looking, that he never found me. Because that would mean his death, I was certain.

The plane took off, rumbling and jolting down the runway before wallowing its way into the air. The crate was held by cargo ties—orange straps that I could see beyond the air holes in the top. But they weren't tight enough to keep it from sliding back and forth with any slight movement from the plane. They had me restrained; there was no reason to treat me like an animal. Why were they so frightened of me?

I remembered the way Tommaso and Michael Grey had looked at me before they died. They had been scared. Of me. Maybe I could use that.

At the very least, I could make their trip as hellish as mine. I banged and kicked against the solid walls of the crate, shrieking in frustration. The only response came when one of the men draped a quilted cargo blanket over the crate, blocking any view I had left through the air holes.

The cargo hold stank of aviation fuel and machine oil and rotten fruit. Either we were flying into a storm, or the pilot was avoiding detection by not climbing high enough to avoid turbulence, I wasn't sure, but the ride grew so rough that the crate bounced off the metal floor, straining against the cargo ties holding it in place.

Finally, my motion sickness overwhelmed me, and I vomited. The rank fluid covered me, the stench making me even more miserable.

The unseen men exclaimed as the smell leaked past the blanket and filled the cargo hold. The turbulence eased off finally. The blanket was removed, and one of the men appeared above me. He yelled at me in Italian, then jammed water bottles into the air holes, dousing me with the liquid, diluting the vomit until the smell was bearable. Then he vanished once more. Leaving me soaking wet, freezing cold, and sloshing in bilious water trapped at the bottom of the crate.

Miserable. Frightened. Powerless. Exactly what they wanted.

I was tired of giving them what they wanted. At least I could make myself more comfortable. Maybe even give me a chance to fight back when we arrived at our destination. Show them I hadn't broken. Not yet.

I tucked my knees up to my chest as tight as they would go and leaned back, stretching my handcuffed wrists down over my butt. Once I got them past my hipbones, I was stuck—not enough room to stretch forward, so no choice but to lay my head down into the foul water polluting the bottom of the cage. Every muscle screamed as I twisted and folded and inched my wrists up while pulling my legs down. Several times I thought I'd never fight free, not with the walls of the crate blocking every movement, but I refused to give up and finally my hands slid just far enough for me to edge my wrists past my heels.

I lay curled up, panting, the exertion filling me with a momentary sense of relief, my motion sickness and sodden shivering forgotten. I raised my hands before my face, grinning at them as if they were small miracles. Of course, I was still handcuffed, trapped, but I felt in control, no longer subject to the random whimsy of gravity.

With my hands in front of me, I could reach for Ryder's pendant. My touchstone. I pressed it to my flesh, closed my eyes, and imagined his arms around me. A calm settled over me, my breathing steadied, and I was able to enter a fugue, casting my senses out beyond the crate.

The men were across from me, sleeping. I could hear their rhythmic breathing. We'd already been flying for several hours, but in what direction? Italy? Or some far-flung hidden lab? The only light inside the plane came from dim red and green lights along the floor and ceiling. Nothing more to be learned.

Which left me with nothing more to do except wait. But that didn't mean I had to waste the time. Gingerly, but with more confidence than I'd had before in the isolation tank, I reached for Leo's memories of his work with Tommaso. I needed to know everything I could before I faced my family.

By the time we finally landed, I'd thrown up until my stomach was emptied and had also peed myself along the way. Sometime during the long flight, the blanket had slid free from the crate. Tyrone and the men had slept through it all.

As soon as the plane stopped, I saw Tyrone pass my crate on his way off the plane. The other men sprang to their feet and removed the cargo straps.

Through the open doors of the cargo bay, I caught a glimpse of sunshine, blue sky, no clouds, the scent of salt water and the sound of seagulls mixed in with the roar of jet engines. A quick transfer to the back of a van—no windows, no light, more nausea, but I was able to down the bottle of electrolyte solution they threw in to me. Proof that despite my discomfort, they still needed me alive.

Another few hours' drive before the doors opened once more, then the crate lurching as the men grunted to push it onto a boat.

Not a cargo ship, a motorboat, not very large from the little I could see as they secured the crate to the deck. A tarp was thrown over top, blocking both my vision and my air. The ride was rocky, my body slamming from one wall to the other as if the driver was trying to ensure that I arrived at our destination with the maximum amount of bruises. I lost track of the time, but it felt as if I lost another night to the journey.

I retched and dry-heaved but had nothing left to vomit. And little energy to fight. My muscles were cramped and locked into place from the confinement, and my vertigo was overwhelming. All I could do was clench Ryder's tree of life pendant, holding on to my one last tie to him.

Finally, we stopped. The tarp was thrown off, and I hauled in gulps of fresh sea air. The bright sunshine of the noonday sun made me blink. The crate was raised, then slid forward, then dropped onto solid ground, although my stomach still felt as if we were bouncing along the waves. I braced myself, wanting to fight, to kick, to show them I hadn't broken.

"Open it," an unseen woman's voice came.

The door to the crate opened. Before I could launch any attack, the men grabbed my ankles and dragged me out into the sunshine. My legs were so numb I couldn't stand, couldn't do more than twist my torso so that I could get a good look at my destination.

I was on a concrete jetty, the motorboat tied up to the piling behind me. In front of me was a large, ornate, wrought-iron gate. It had lethal-appearing spikes jabbing up from its top edge and also equally deadly horizontal spikes protruding out. No one was getting up and over it alive, it seemed to proclaim. It was obviously ancient, hundreds of years old, standing a good twelve feet high and at least that wide.

The wall it was set into was brick, covered with cement or stucco. Higher than the gate by two feet or more, also with spikes lining its top edge. The wall extended in both directions as far as I could see, the seawater lapping against its base, green algae smeared at the high-tide line. At the far reaches of my vision, the wall curved—an island. This was an island.

The men grabbed an elbow each and hauled me to my feet. I couldn't stand, my legs sagging uselessly beneath me.

"Welcome to your new home," the woman said from behind me, her voice anything but welcoming.

I twisted my head, fighting free of the curtain of wet hair that clung to my face, until I could see her. She was a little taller than I am, same dark hair, same dark eyes, a wrinkle-free face, yet I'd still peg her age in her fifties. Something about those eyes...they were...without mercy.

The woman met my gaze with an unreadable expression then strode past me, forcing me to turn once more to keep her in sight. She was the leader, the one in command, the one I had to focus on. Another boat arrived, this one a sleek, old-fashioned wooden motorboat. I'd seen ones like it in old movies set in Italy.

Tyrone emerged, hopping onto the jetty with a jaunty grace, ignoring me entirely as he strode over to the woman and kissed her on both cheeks. "Mother. What do you think of the present I brought you? Your long-lost daughter has returned to save us all."

Chapter 42

FRANCESCA WALKED AWAY from the dock, schooling her expression until she was safely out of view of both Angela and Tyrone. Angela, her child who should have died in infancy, to see her not only alive but healthy, whole...it was beyond Francesca's wildest hopes.

Poor Angelo, so innocent and guileless. Dear, sweet boy. When she'd realized that the child she created with her egg and his sperm carried a lethal defect above and beyond the Scourge, she'd thought it a kindness to let him take the child, to have someone to love her before she died.

Yet, here she was. Not dead but gifted far more than any Lazaretto in recorded history. The daughter she'd abandoned had returned to save them all.

If Francesca could convince her to help. She nodded in passing to a group of health aides shuffling along with their patients then continued up to her office. At first she'd been furious at Tyrone for his treatment of Angela—crating her like a wild animal. But she understood his fury. Because of Angela, his brothers were dead.

Worse, because of Angela, the brothers had failed. An unforgivable sin for a Lazaretto.

As she paced her office, she came to a decision. They had

only a few days to persuade Angela to join them. Otherwise, she would need to take what she needed by force—which would leave Angela dead or comatose, unable to use her gift.

Better that than to risk the girl turning on them, joining forces with Marco.

Perhaps Tyrone's instincts had been correct. Angela had never had to endure the deprivations the rest of Francesca's people had been subjected to. Perhaps by experiencing that, the girl would be more sympathetic, malleable.

Francesca nodded to herself. Her hand trembled as she reached for her phone, and her mind blazed with a kaleidoscope of stabbing, diamond-sharp colors. She slumped into her chair, barely reaching it before the fugue devoured her, imprisoning her body and mind.

RYDER WOKE TO bright lights stabbing his eyes. He tried to wave them off with a hand but couldn't. An IV was taped to his arm. "What happened? Rossi?"

Alarms beeped, echoing the pounding in his head. His entire body felt bruised, but mostly his head. He couldn't raise it. It hurt even to move his eyes.

A man wearing surgical scrubs appeared at Ryder's side, hovering over him. "You're at Good Samaritan Medical Center, Detective Ryder." He reached across Ryder to turn off the damn alarms. "You're quite a lucky man. Some thoracic contusions, but no permanent damage. Your vest took the brunt of the impact. Nurses counted five bullets."

He leaned away, disappearing from Ryder's vision but continued his litany of Ryder's injuries. "Which left me free to address your head injury. Again, lucky man. If I were you, I'd go buy a lottery ticket. The bullet impacted your skull at an upward trajectory."

Ryder blinked, his vision filling with the image of a muzzle flash below him, the darkened stairway, his back to a door.

"That created a minor depressed skull fracture with minimal parenchymal bleeding. We surgically elevated the fracture, extracted a small blood clot, and have been monitoring you. So far, no signs of excessive intracranial pressure or swelling. And, I'm glad to report, your post-op scan is clear of any further hemorrhage or cerebral contusion. Like I said, lucky man." The surgeon bounced back into view, beaming as if he was the one responsible for Ryder's luck instead of Ryder's tactical position.

"What day?" Ryder choked out the words. His mouth was dry, tasted of sour lemon that made him even more thirsty.

"Day? December twenty-eighth. You've been here two days."

Two days? Ryder struggled to sit up. Rossi could be anywhere in the world by now. How was he going to find her?

"Whoa there, cowboy." The surgeon effortlessly restrained Ryder with a single palm against his shoulder. "You just got out of the ICU. You're not going anywhere."

"When?"

"When can you leave?" The surgeon considered. "If we can get you eating and on your feet today, I'll repeat the scan tomorrow. If not, the next day. If the scan looks good, you can go."

Two more days? No. Not going to happen. Ryder knew better than to plead his case with the surgeon—he'd learned that the hard way during his last hospital stay after he'd been shot.

The surgeon began to leave, then turned back as if sensing his patient might not be among the most compliant. "No matter what, you'll need to take it easy for several weeks, maybe even months. No strenuous activity, no work. Even TV is out. I'm serious. You were incredibly lucky. Don't push that luck. Not if you don't want to risk complications like a re-bleed or post-concussive syndrome."

With those grim words, condemning Ryder to basically sitting on his thumbs while Rossi was out there facing Lord only knew what and while some crazy Italian family unleashed an epidemic of lethal prions on the world, the surgeon left.

As soon as he vanished, Ryder scanned the room and planned his escape.

❂

MY FIRST DAY on the island passed in a blur. At first, no one spoke to me, no one looked me in the eye. They were all so frightened of me. As if I were a feral beast, untamed and dangerous.

Francesca's people—I was not sure how to label them. More than servants, they were all part of the Lazaretto family, yet there was a definite hierarchy, some kind of caste system. Anyway, that first morning on the dock, Francesca stalked off, leaving Tyrone to shuffle me through the massive gates.

We stood in a large courtyard, a distinctive modern building to my right, all metal and steel. It was a sharp contrast to the ancient stone monastery that stood across from it, its length hugging the shoreline. Tyrone led me into the monastery, his two men holding my arms as I stumbled, still not steady on my legs.

Daniel's memory overlaid my vision as I passed through the arched corridor with its stone walls. Parts of the monastery dated back to the years when the Black Death threatened Venice, but I could see that it had been updated with all the modern conveniences, such as security cameras in every room and hallway.

The room they ushered me to would have been called opulent and given five stars by any hotel reviewer: a crystal chandelier suspended above a large bed, thick wool carpets in rich colors under my feet, wide windows framed by expensive silk drapes that swung open to a view of Venice with its towers and domed buildings filling the horizon in that direction. Of course, any review would need to overlook the restraints attached to the bed frame, the dressing table filled with medications and lab equipment, and the monitors tastefully hidden behind a screen.

Two women waited for me. Neither was older than I was, but they both had the hardened expressions of prison guards. Tyrone and his men left me with them. Wordless, they undressed me, scrubbed me clean in the adjoining bathroom—a bathroom as large as my apartment with its toilet, bidet, sunken tub with jets and gold fixtures, walk-in shower area large enough to accommodate a patient on a stretcher, and its own isolation tank.

That's when I realized the truth of this place: It was where the Lazarettos came to die.

Daniel's and Leo's memories filled in the gaps. The Lazarettos had many facilities scattered around the world, but this island was special. During the plague years, the family's founding father, himself a physician, realized that members of his family were strangely immune to the pestilence, and yet half of them were still dying young, devastated by their own strange plague, what he termed the Scourge.

When the Black Death struck, the Venetians were the first to use quarantine measures to slow its progression. Their doctors established island sanctuaries where the sick could be cared for away from the main population. This island was one of those, its monastery converted to a hospital.

By the time the Black Death passed and Venetian society

returned to normal, the Lazarettos had conceived a plan to use the special gifts their family Scourge provided them and began their climb to power.

Now the island housed family members with the Scourge. They acted as servants, trained as researchers, cared for other family members too sick to care for themselves, and, like me, played the role of laboratory rats to Francesca's Dr. Frankenstein.

Second in power to her younger brother, Marco, who, since he did not carry the fatal insomnia genes and therefore was not at risk to develop the psychosis, dementia, and early death that went along with prion disease, ran the family business elsewhere in the world.

But not here. This island and everyone on it were ruled by Francesca.

All this passed through my mind quickly—thanks to my enforced confinement on the plane for all those hours, I was becoming more adept at accessing the knowledge I wanted without falling into a full-blown fugue. Knowing that I could exert some control over my body—for the first time in a month—helped me to remain calm.

Even when they toweled me dry, wrapped me in a plush robe, and sat me in a chair where they cut off my hair and shaved my head.

I sat in silence, knowing my words were useless, and simply let them do it. My priorities were to get the cure for the children, to stop Francesca from releasing the prions. But still, it took everything I had not to cry when the first long lock of hair fell to my lap.

Save the children, I thought as the razor buzzed and more hair flew. *Stop Francesca*. It became my mantra. Along with one more, less charitable thought: *Make them pay*.

Chapter 43

AFTER SHAVING MY head, the two women secured a wireless EEG cap—just like the one Louise had had me wear earlier—to my scalp and stood back as if admiring their work. One leaned forward to reach for Ryder's pendant, the last memory from my old life. Whiplash fast, I grabbed her wrist and twisted it hard, bringing her to her knees.

"No." It was the first word I'd spoken since I arrived.

They exchanged glances, and she nodded without meeting my gaze. I was expecting a struggle, some reprisal for my rebellion, but when I released her, she scurried away, fear filling her face.

My triumph was short-lived. They dressed me in silk pajamas, a robe, and slippers before leading me, without actually touching me, from the room and along stone corridors that twisted in a maze. Thankfully, Daniel and Francesca had explored the island together, searching for hidden corners away from her family's prying eyes where they could find some privacy.

As we walked, I overlaid a rough map from Daniel's memories, pleased to see how accurate his observations had been. It made sense. After all, Daniel had been an architectural engineer before he devoted himself to finance.

Leo had also been here with Tommaso, but he'd had little

regard for his surroundings, had been more obsessed with the lab and the research opportunities. Also helpful. During my time on the plane, I'd developed a theory about Tommaso's research. Now, as I sorted through Leo's and Daniel's memories, a plan began to form and, with it, a glimmer of hope.

All I had to do was learn everything I could about Francesca's cure, elude the guards and the security cameras, escape the fifteen-foot-high walls, and cross miles of open water until I reached Venice.

As a plan, it was definitely lacking substance, but it distracted me from why I was really here: for Francesca to experiment on.

Her office was on the top floor of a tower twice as tall and twice as wide as the bell tower I'd left behind at St. Tim's. The walls were just as thick and even more ancient—it served as a watchtower to defend the island. The views through the new, modern windows were amazing. In addition to stunning views of Venice to the south, I could also make out the outlines of several islands nearby, each with its own distinctive towers jutting up from sea level. Murano and San Michele, Daniel's memory informed me.

The height gave me some perspective on the Lazarettos' island itself. It was small, maybe ten city blocks in total area, with this monastery as its largest building running the width of the island. I glanced down at the roof of the modern building across the courtyard from the dock. Serious HVAC and ventilation systems—obviously their lab. The rest of the island was taken up with gardens and cottages, giving it the lush appeal of a retreat.

Appearances, deceptions—if the Lazarettos had a family motto, it should include those two words, I thought as I turned back to face the woman who'd brought me here.

She stood across the room, looking elegant in a wool dress

and silk scarf. Thick wool rugs covered the stone floor and in the center of the room stood an octagonal, centuries-old slanted desk that had once been used by monks to illuminate manuscripts. Everything appeared serene, welcoming even.

Except for the very modern examination chair with thick restraints—a chair that eerily resembled the dental chair Tommaso had been strapped to when he took his own life. Tyrone stood beside it, grinning. Guess it was only fitting, a bit of a karma boomerang.

I decided to shake things up a bit—and hopefully convince them I was here to cooperate and wouldn't need the restraints. First small step in my plan: lull the enemy into complacence.

Before my guards could escort me to the exam chair, I strode over to it and settled myself in, wrapping my robe around my legs so it wouldn't trail on the floor. Best part: It put Tyrone out of sight behind me, making it easier to avoid his narrow-eyed glower. At least until he moved to stand beside Francesca at the desk in the center of the room.

From Leo's memories of his discussions with Tommaso, I knew Francesca's research needed two things from me: my stem cells to replicate the artificial prion disease and my eggs to inseminate and create a new generation of children who carried my unique mutation.

Both of which required time to prepare my body with special hormone injections—giving me a window of opportunity to escape. After the children received the cure.

That part still had me worried. Francesca had shown no hesitation in killing innocents. Were Tommaso's research and my DNA enough to convince her to keep her word and save the children back home?

The only way for her plan to save her family to work would be if she kept the cure secret, a precious commodity to be doled out to the highest bidder. I could almost imagine Daniel's nod of approval that I was finally shedding my sentimental view of the world and instead seeing human lives in terms of the commerce and power they could be bargained for.

Francesca took a tablet from the standing desk and arched an eyebrow at me. Maybe her appearance was colored by Daniel's memories filtering through my mind, but although I knew she had to be in her late fifties, she appeared much younger. Her face was creaseless, her hair even darker than mine without a hint of gray. Only her eyes, piercing and merciless, revealed her age.

"Your Mr. Price won't release Tommaso's research until he has confirmation that you arrived here unharmed." She turned the tablet, and Devon's face appeared.

From the equipment behind him, I realized he was at Good Sam's, sitting in one of the ugly visitor chairs. The view shifted the slightest bit, revealing Flynn beside him in a hospital bed. She winked at me, letting me know more than Devon couldn't mention or show: Ryder was okay, the children were okay, everyone was okay.

"Angela, are you all right?" he asked, shifting the screen to focus on his face, which revealed no emotion, appropriate for negotiations. Any stranger viewing the feed would be hard-pressed to interpret that quick glimpse of Flynn in the background.

"I'm fine. As soon as Louise verifies the cure, you can release the research." I waited, hoping he got my message to stall. I wanted the children to get the treatment they needed, but I also wanted to make sure they got the right treatment. After all, the Lazarettos were masters at the art of poison.

Without missing a beat, he nodded. "Of course. Let me know when—"

"That was not our agreement," Tyrone interrupted.

"Of course it was. Angela's cooperation in exchange for the cure. I'm not a physician. I'll need to confirm the treatment before we use it on children. Then I'll send you the research."

Once I knew the treatment worked and the children were safe, all I needed to do was ensure that Francesca would never again be able to infect anyone with the prion disease that the children and I carried. That was the gaping void in my nebulous plan, but I'd only just arrived. Hopefully, a little time spent with Francesca and her research facilities would provide a solution.

Francesca ended the video call and waved my attendants away. They drifted down the stairs. Tyrone lingered despite Francesca's pointed glance. "Mother, surely you're not going to negotiate with these outsiders?"

"Leave us." Francesca settled into the only other chair in the room, a leather armchair suitable for a CEO.

He glared in my direction and left.

We were alone. Mother and daughter.

Blood enemies.

Her gaze was one of appraisal. "I could take what I need from you."

"You could try. But you'd also risk damaging the only…what do you call people like me? Vessel. I understand we're quite rare. And valuable." I felt like I was playing a role in a movie, repeating lines fed to me by another woman, someone much calmer, more in control than I was. I have no idea who I was channeling, maybe Sister Patrice with her serene refusal to accept defeat, no matter how overwhelming the odds.

Whoever I was pretending to be as I settled back and raised an eyebrow at Francesca, she bought it.

"Maybe I don't need to give Mr. Price the treatment," she countered. "After all, if Tommaso was able to create a transmissible form of the Scourge with access to only a sample of your blood, think what I and my team can do with an unlimited supply of your stem cells?"

Tommaso had had a sample of my blood? The image of a blood bank bag of plasma floated across my vision. I thought back, remembered the Good Sam blood drive from last year. Nice to have at least one mystery solved. But it wasn't helpful as far as the current crisis.

"It took Tommaso over a year—do you have that long?" I nodded to her hands, both shaking with tremors. It could have just as easily been me unable to control my muscle spasms, but I'd take whatever luck threw my way.

She clamped one hand over the other, pressing them against the arm of her chair. "There are other ways to force you to cooperate. Your adopted family, I imagine you're quite close to them."

"My *real* family. The family my father chose. Instead of staying with you."

Her hands tightened into fists, and the muscles around her mouth tightened. I knew that look, had seen it often enough in the ER when things didn't go the way people wanted them to. She wanted to hit me. Good, I'd struck a chord.

I relaxed in my chair as if it was a chaise lounge instead of an instrument of torture. Waved a hand toward the windows with their exquisite views. "Does everyone here have fatal insomnia?"

She blinked at the change of topic. "Yes. No one comes here who doesn't suffer from the Scourge. This is our sanctuary."

"Actually, I think the word you're looking for is cemetery. How convenient it must be for the rest of the family, the healthy ones, to exile the people who actually contribute the most. They take the credit, enjoy the riches and power you—"

"*We*," she said pointedly.

I shrugged away her correction, refusing to associate myself with this band of cutthroats. "The riches you create and share with them. That's why you're doing this, isn't it? If you have control of the prions, a way to spread them, as well as the cure, then you have all the power."

"Maybe you are a Lazaretto after all. What do you really want?"

"Only what we asked for. The cure for the children and myself. Along with an end to this nonsense about spreading prions into the population. You're a scientist, you must see the danger in that."

"Danger we're immune to," she countered. "Why do you think it's nonsense?"

"I know that, until you found me, your other cohorts were failures."

Her hands relaxed, and I knew I'd made a serious mistake. She shook her head at me as she smiled. Despite the sunlight streaming through the windows, the room felt chilly. "You think the other cohorts were failures?"

"Isn't that why you had Tyrone and his brother kill them?"

"No. My dear, we didn't destroy the other cohorts because we failed to infect them with the Scourge. We destroyed the evidence of how successful we were. Too successful by far—the Scourge we created killed everyone, burned out of control. They were dead before any of them could ever have been useful as a Vessel. Dead before we could even begin to attempt a treatment."

My playacting failed me, and I sat up, alarmed as I glimpsed the full extent of what she'd done. "How many cohorts were there? How many types of prion disease were you playing with?"

"I created new mutations in each of my children. Those formed the basis of my clinical trials," she replied with the smile of a proud mother. "Twenty-seven in total, including you."

Twenty-seven new strains of deadly prions? All transmissible, able to infect anyone in the world? I couldn't speak, couldn't even begin to form the words, much less get them past my lips clamped tight against the horror.

Then I realized one other thing. The final proof of just how terribly I'd miscalculated. "You don't have a cure, do you?"

"I never used the word 'cure.' That was Mr. Price."

"You've destroyed the other prions, right?" Desperation colored my voice.

Her eyes crinkled in delight as she realized she'd found the price of my cooperation. "Our family has protected the Venetian Republic for centuries. We saved them from the Black Death by inventing the concept of quarantine with island sanctuaries such as this one."

I frowned at her answer—or lack of one.

"Do you know what they call quarantine islands, the Italian name?"

I shook my head, still reeling from the realization that one woman had control of twenty-seven different plagues that would make the Black Death seem like the common cold if any one of them ever escaped into the world at large.

"Lazaretto," she answered her own question. "They named them in our honor. Our family has a long tradition of quarantining the dangers that threaten the world. I'm merely continuing that tradition."

It took me a moment to translate. "You didn't destroy the prions."

"Of course not," she answered. "They're all stored here, safe and sound. Ready for when I need them. The perfect weapons. To protect my family. Maybe even someday to save our world. After all, we are immune."

I leapt from my chair, wanting to run, wanting to throttle

her, wanting to do...something. And immediately realized how helpless I was against the threat she wielded. How could I have been so naïve? Thinking all I needed to do was save the children and prevent any further use of the prions we carried? "We, this family, are a few hundred people in a world of seven billion innocents who are at risk."

"Exactly. A world run amok, filled with despots and needless suffering. But you, my dear, lost daughter, are going to help me save first our family, and then the world."

Chapter 44

RYDER FOUND FRESH clothing hanging in the closet of his hospital room: a T-shirt and jeans, clean socks and underwear, a pair of sneakers. His sister's work, most likely. He'd asked the nurses to send all visitors away—he had enough on his hands trying to ignore the drumming in his head and pain spiking his chest with each breath, not to mention his worries about Rossi. Was she okay? Where had they taken her?

A thousand visions of exactly what they could be doing to her gave him the strength he needed to make it from his bed and across the room. It took him the better part of an hour, and he felt like he might throw up, but he'd made it.

The simple act of dressing took even longer. He glanced in the mirror attached to the closet as he opened the door. The surgeon had shaved his head, and a horseshoe of staples surrounded an area above his ear that was stained brown-red with bruising. The two black eyes surprised him. Although most of the swelling had gone down, they were dark indigo and purple with a green-yellow tint to the skin below.

He took a breath, regretted it. Shrugged free of the patient gown and spotted the matching bruises along his rib cage. Sent a prayer heavenward, in thanks to whoever had invented ballistic vests. Slowly, with agonizing movements, he managed to dress himself. Only had to fall back against the bed four times when the room threatened to turn turtle.

Tying his shoes turned out to be the most logistically difficult maneuver. Bending over was out of the question, not without his crap balance sending him to the floor, and pulling each leg up to his chest made breathing impossible as pain exploded in his chest. He ended up tying the laces loosely, just enough so they wouldn't drag and trip him, dropping his shoes to the floor, then sliding each foot in.

Mission accomplished.

He shuffled out the door and down the hall. A quick glance at the board behind the nurses' station gave him Flynn's room number, three doors down. He tried to force himself not to lean against the wall, but without a hand to guide him, his dizzy, off-balance brain kept sending him off course. The buzzing in his head wasn't helping either.

Finally, he reached the door. Flynn lay in bed, her leg swathed in bandages, an IV snaking out of her arm. Beside her, working on a tablet, Devon Price sat in one of the two visitor's chairs.

At the sight of Price sitting there, unharmed, not even a damn wrinkle in his damn designer suit, rage flashed over Ryder. His head thundered in time with his heartbeat as he bounded across the room. Price looked up, just in time for Ryder's fist to land squarely on his jaw, knocking him sideways, out of his chair.

Ryder stood there, panting, the room swimming around him, head still pounding. Price scrambled to his feet, hands up, ready to defend himself. Ryder heaved in a breath and stepped back until his legs hit the edge of the other visitor's chair, then he sank into it before he fell down and made a real fool of himself.

"You son of a bitch," he snarled as Price straightened his jacket and regained his seat. "I saw you. You gave her to them.

You gave Rossi up. To those, those bastards—"

Price rubbed his jaw as he considered his answer. "I did it to save her. And she did it to save you."

Flynn watched from the bed, her expression half amused and half disdain—in other words, typical Flynn.

"What the hell's that supposed to mean?" Ryder demanded, hands fisting with the urge to hit him again. His bruised knuckles protested the movement, and he flexed his fingers to make sure he hadn't broken anything. "For all we know, those animals are dissecting her, experimenting on her..."

He trailed off, unable to put into words the horror he felt. Even Flynn seemed aghast at the idea of Rossi in the hands of the Lazarettos. She shifted her weight to sit up straighter and said, "No. They need her alive. Isn't that what Louise said?"

Price nodded. "While you were napping the past two days," he told Ryder, "Louise went through Tommaso's research that I recovered." He said the last in a tone of aggrievement as if Ryder hadn't given credit where credit was due. What the hell did Price think that sock in the jaw was about? "She says Tommaso was on to something. Angela has a unique mutation. One that not only allowed him to create an artificial prion disease he injected into the children, but one that he thought would also provide a potential cure if he had more of Angela's stem cells to work with."

"See? They're cutting her up, and for what? To make more sick kids? While they keep the cure for themselves. We have to stop them. Which," he knifed a glare at Price, "would have been a helluva lot easier if someone hadn't betrayed her and sacrificed her to start with."

"It was her decision." Price met his glare effortlessly. "She was going to jump, Ryder. Splash herself all over the steps of the cathedral. That's how desperate she was. But I made a deal."

"Oh, great. Like father, like son. Another Kingston wheeling and dealing. How many innocent lives is it going to cost this time?"

"Rossi and Tommaso's research in exchange for the cure for the children."

"You know that will never happen. They'll figure it out without Tommaso's research, and then they still have Rossi. Or they give us a so-called cure that ends up making the kids better one day and killing them the next. These people cannot be trusted."

Flynn smiled at that. Her toothy, predator smile that was usually a prelude to bullets flying and blood flowing. "That's why Devon is planning to go get her. He tracked her as far as Venice."

"Italy?" It made sense. "I've no jurisdiction there, and no way can we get the Feds on board, not in the time frame we have. The State Department will never allow it, and you can bet the Italian authorities will be hopelessly compromised."

Price rose to his feet. "Guess that's one of the perks of being a private citizen. I don't have to worry about rules and regulations."

Despite his throbbing head and blurry vision, not to mention the weird buzzing rattling through his brain, Ryder pushed himself upright. "No way in hell am I letting you go alone."

"What about your rules, your chain of command, Detective?"

"Hell with that. Even cops get to take a vacation every once in a while."

"I'll take care of the children and their families. You two take care of Angie. And yourselves," Flynn said from the bed, regret that she couldn't join them clear in her tone. "Bring her home."

"We will," Ryder promised. Price nodded his agreement. Together, they left, for once moving in perfect accord.

Chapter 45

FRANCESCA'S SMILE WAS indulgent. "You were an emergency physician. Saw firsthand the chaos that engulfs this world. Surely you would agree that someone must take charge. Our family has proven itself uniquely qualified, so why not us?"

I didn't bother to hide my disdain. "Right. Because using children as assassins, stealing secrets and power, and engineering a disease that could wipe out mankind are all unique leadership qualifications."

She merely shrugged, somehow made even that small movement seem elegant. "Do you want to leave? You're free to go."

I gestured at the chair with its thick straps. "All evidence to the contrary."

"You think that chair is meant for you?" Her laugh was musical, designed to make songbirds jealous. "My dear child. You have so very much to learn. The chair is for me."

I frowned my confusion. She crossed the room and sat down in the chair I'd abandoned. "You've experienced the *almanaccare*, yes? The fugues that are our blessing and our curse?"

It took me a moment to parse her Italian pronunciation. Almanac Care. The name of the fake company Tommaso had used.

"The waking dreams," she translated as I heard Daniel's voice simultaneously echo her words. "They take many forms. From your medical records, I see that yours are accompanied by catatonia—so were mine when I was your age. But now, like so many of our brothers and sisters, they inflict me with a wandering, a mindless need to walk, that is quite dangerous. I cannot control where my body takes me, cannot see the dangers. In my mind, I'm living the perfect life, strolling in a garden or dancing with a loved one. So when I feel the onset of a waking dream, an *almanaccare*, I come here and sit."

She raised one of the straps and flipped it over. Velcro. "No locks or chains. A simple safety measure. That is all."

That explained the restraints on the bed I'd noticed, as well as the cameras everywhere. Monitoring patients, not preventing prisoners from escaping.

Still, I was leery. Francesca noted my hesitation and stood, her skirt swirling with the motion. "Come, let me show you your legacy. Then you make your choice."

She was lying. There was no way she'd give up her plans if I chose to leave. But that gave me an edge: She needed me alive.

I followed her as she led the way out of the tower and down into the heart of the monastery, rubbing my palm against the ancient stones of the stairwell, wishing I could magically release the secrets these walls had witnessed.

The monastery was a long and narrow building, three stories tall, with all the arches, gargoyles, and other embellishments you'd expect. The watchtower that housed Francesca's office anchored the end closest to the dock. At the opposite end, the linear construction gave way to a gorgeous domed basilica. Francesca led me down the main corridor, her pace slow enough that I could look inside the rooms on each side—it seemed that other than my suite, no one here kept doors closed.

"We protect each other," she told me as we passed a room where a man and woman, barely out of their teens and both with shaven heads and wearing EEG caps, were helping another man in an EEG cap, maybe my age, into a wheelchair. "Those still healthy watch over the ones who are unable to care for themselves. This is not a prison but rather a sanctuary where our suffering is eased."

I stared at her. "You mean euthanasia?"

"I mean whatever a person requests. Many of the ones stricken at a young age request to have their suffering ended quickly. Interestingly, the older ones—myself included—have learned to embrace both the blessings and the pain the Scourge brings us."

"Blessings? Like stealing memories?"

"For those with that gift. But even those of us who aren't Vessels receive special guidance from our fugues. Yours take the form of hypersensory awareness, yes?"

I nodded, reluctant to let her know about my enhanced memory and knowledge processing that also came during a fugue.

"Your uncle's included a heightened insight about patterns forming in the economy and geopolitics. He used them to foresee coming trends, counseling my father, the family leader, to position us to take advantage of them. Mine allow me to process complex genetic sequences and DNA patterns. They formed the basis of my research and allowed me to define the mutations that will allow us to turn our Scourge into a weapon to protect the family."

"A weapon that has already left dozens of innocents dead," I reminded her. She shrugged as if growing weary of my idealistic arguments. "So you control your fugues? I mean, after all this time—"

"No. I can stimulate what my mind works on during a fugue by immersing myself in a topic, using various medications and the sensory-deprivation chamber, but I can't force them. I must wait for that master stroke of inspiration." She turned to me, her expression eager, a hawk pouncing on a young rabbit. "Have you learned how to control yours?"

"I wish." I met her gaze, hoping she couldn't sense my lie. Last thing I needed was to give her more reason to want to use me as part of her scheme. "I'm just starting to be able to sense when they'll strike. I get an aura, like patients with epilepsy or migraines sometimes do."

"I'll have our neurologists start you on a regimen of pharmaceuticals that should stimulate more fugues so that we can record your EEG patterns. You'll spend tonight in the isolation tank—it will help you regain your strength as well as give us a baseline. We want to predict and measure your physiological responses before we attempt to activate your gift as a Vessel."

Her tone was nonchalant, as if we weren't talking about events that had nearly killed me or about stealing another person's memory and leaving them dead. It hit me: It wasn't just my DNA that Francesca would use as a weapon against innocents. It was my mind.

No. I would not let that happen.

She sensed my agitation and rested her hand on my arm as if we truly were family. We arrived at the end of the hallway at a large room with windows on three sides. The amazing views over the water weren't what caught my eye. It was the room's occupants. Children. Running, playing, studying, laughing, smiling. At least two dozen of them.

I watched them without smiling. Because each of them, like me, had been shaven bald and wore an EEG cap. "They all have fatal insomnia?"

She nodded. "You spoke of saving children. What about saving your own family? With your help, these could be the last to die from the Scourge."

"Why haven't you developed a gene therapy for the family?"

"We tried. Too many spontaneous mutations. Like the ones that gave us you." She frowned, her gaze distant, as if she remembered something from long ago. "I made a mistake with you. I see that now. Your mutation is more stable than I had anticipated."

"You mean we can cure my fatal insomnia? And the children infected with it?"

"In time. Yes."

A blessing and a curse. A weapon that could destroy the world or save a family. My family. I glanced at her, working hard to mask my emotions. She was mad, of course, quite insane. And yet, in her own way, brilliant.

She took me by the arm once more. "Let me show you our laboratory facilities. I think you'll be excited to see how far ahead of the rest of the world we are."

Right. Cutting-edge research designed to kill millions rather than save lives. As if that would get me excited enough to cooperate with her.

I drew upon what little reserves of patience and acting skills I had left and nodded. She led me across the courtyard to the smaller modern building that lay in the monastery's shadow. Here, the cameras were definitely designed for security rather than patient monitoring, swiveling to follow our every step as we approached the entrance.

A guard stood beside the door. He wasn't bald and didn't have an EEG cap, although he appeared extremely uncomfortable, fidgeting with the weapon strapped across his chest and not looking me in the face. I seemed to have that effect on most of the islanders once they realized who I was.

Standing beside the guard was Tyrone, favoring me with his usual glower. "Mother, I don't think this is a good idea."

"Nonsense," she said, sweeping me through the entrance, leaving Tyrone behind. The research building was steel and glass within a sweeping diagonal steel framework, giving it a futuristic appearance, a distinct contrast to the well-loved, well-worn stone monastery across the courtyard.

"You need to understand that we take our mission to protect the world seriously," she said as we strolled past a variety of labs with a dozen or more scientists working, all with EEG monitors. The family resemblance was clear—and during the short walk, I saw two of them glance at their watches as if getting an alarm then slump into the nearest chair before freezing with the unmistakable vacant visage of a fugue state. Not only studying fatal insomnia, living with it.

We circled past the outer labs to an inner glass-walled space that boasted additional security. Inside it were more glass-walled cubicles: self-contained isolation laboratories designed to handle high-risk contaminants like prions. The Lazarettos may have been immune to the mutant prions they worked with, but I was glad to see they still took precautions against releasing the disease into the environment.

Of course they were. Best way to protect their profit. There were only two workers here, cataloging specimens before placing them into special freezers. The door nearest us boasted state-of-the-art biometric security—the kind I'd seen before only in movies.

Francesca nodded to the security console. "No one gains access without proper authorization. Every sample is accounted for and secured." The workers finished sealing the freezer and left the isolation area. Then they vanished through a door on the far side of the lab. "Even though our family is immune, we use every precaution."

She seemed disappointed when I didn't immediately voice my approval. She took my arm in hers and bent her head to mine as if imparting essential maternal knowledge. "The prions are our weapons, but they are also our defense. Just as in the past century when ensuring peace required the threat of a world-ending nuclear holocaust, we now have the means to save the future."

The family's future, a future controlled by Lazarettos like Francesca, Tommaso, and Tyrone. A future I wanted no part of.

Francesca sensed my horror at her vision. "I understand this is overwhelming. But we're running out of time. You see, my brother, Marco, he has only given us until the New Year."

I frowned, her words surprising me. "I don't understand."

"Marco has decided that the family no longer requires the Scourge to prosper. That the best way to end it is to end us." She gestured with her hands. "Everyone on this island. In three days, he'll send his men to take the prions and do with them as he likes."

"Is he a scientist as well?" Maybe the prions would be better off with this Marco. Maybe he'd destroy them once and for all, protect the world.

"Marco? No, my dear. He's not a scientist. He's a businessman. Profit rules his world. And we, everyone here, we are no longer profitable. He'll sell the prions to the highest bidder, let them loose on the world without regard to the consequences, secure in the fact that he is immune."

"And exactly how is that different than what you plan?" I challenged her, irritated by being played as a pawn in their quest for dominance.

"I'll protect not only our people but the world from the

prions because I won't make a move until I have a cure. That is why I was forced to sacrifice the first cohorts—as well as my own children who carried those mutations. But it's all come down to us. You and I, Angela. Together we can save the world." She paused, her lips pursing in a frown. "Or together we can fail and let Marco destroy it."

Chapter 46

PRICE DROVE THEM to Ryder's house first. Ryder grabbed his go-bag and added a few extras, including clothing for Rossi. "Weapons?" he asked. "Can we take them on the plane? I'm not sure about the laws in Italy."

To his surprise, Price gave a nervous shrug. "Best not to risk anything that would get us stopped or draw attention."

"Right. Worst comes to worst you can buy the Beretta factory or something."

Devon controlled all of Kingston Enterprises and the family fortune. Ryder removed his pistol and ammunition from the ruck. He found his passport with its virgin pages on his bureau. Since leaving the Army, he hadn't had a chance to travel anywhere exotic—had been hoping all that would change with Rossi in his life. He looked around his bedroom, the empty feeling pressing down on him like a weight. Everything had already changed because of Rossi.

He hoisted the ruck. "Let's go."

They drove directly to the airport. "You don't have to stop at your mansion, change into a designer travel outfit?" Price said nothing, simply shifted in his seat. "You do have your passport, right?"

"Yes. Got it a few years ago. Saw a Nat Geo special on

Belize and thought I'd check out their beaches, hunt for Mayan ruins, but a job came up, and I never got to use it." Price parked the car outside a hangar in the general aviation section. A sleek Gulfstream awaited them. "I'm not sure how this works, haven't used the jet myself."

Ryder was focused on the mission. "The crew will know."

He grabbed his bag and walked toward the jet. Price popped the trunk on the Town Car and hauled a small valise from it. At least Price traveled light, wouldn't be slowing Ryder down. A man in his forties popped out from the hangar and strode over to them.

"Mr. Price, welcome. I'm James. I'll be your steward for your flight. The pilots are doing their preflight checks, and we'll be ready to leave shortly." He escorted them up the narrow set of steps into the jet's cabin. "We've a fully stocked bar and kitchen. There's a stateroom in the rear if you want to lie down, or all of the seats fully recline."

The man kept droning on, taking their coats and bags, but Ryder tuned him out. All he needed was someplace to sit—one thing the Army had taught him was how to sleep anywhere. Given his subpar physical shape, his head pounding, balance still off, every breath and step lancing pain through his ribs, last thing he wanted was to add exhaustion to the mix.

He took a seat. Price sat opposite, a small table in between that he set up his laptop on. It was strange the way Price kept squirming, twisting in his seat to look around. For the first time, Ryder remembered that Price was a decade younger than he was. Usually, Price was so confident and self-assured that he forgot about the difference in their ages.

Finally, they took off, Price's grip on his armrests knuckle-white.

"Don't like flying?" Ryder asked. Given that he was aching

head to toe and it was Price who'd gotten them into this mess by sending Rossi off with the Lazarettos, he was not unhappy to see the other man suffering.

"Not sure. This is my first time." Price gave a self-deprecating shrug. "Where would a kid from the Tower ever need to fly? Philly's the farthest away I've ever made it." The plane leveled off, but his grip didn't ease up.

Ryder took pity on the man. "Relax. Greatest risk of a crash comes at takeoff and landing. Get some rest; you're going to need it."

With that, he stretched out on the leather seat, folded an arm over his eyes, and went to sleep. Best way to make the time go faster. Plus, the only way he could be with Rossi right now was in his dreams.

☽ ⚹ ☾

IT TOOK ALL my acting skills to convince Francesca that I was considering helping her. She went to great lengths to prove to me that I wasn't a prisoner, that I actually had a choice, giving me free rein of the island and the non-critical areas of the research lab. I took full advantage of her good-will, fake as it was, even persuading her to give Louise their best treatment—not a cure, but a regimen to help decrease fugues and other symptoms.

"I don't understand," I asked Francesca on that first day, after we left the lab. "If your brother is threatening your people and your work, why don't you just leave?"

She seemed puzzled by the idea. "Leave? We can't do that. This is our home. This is our family. We could never abandon them."

"But your family wants to steal the prions—there are millions of lives at risk. Why not destroy your research before

Marco gets here?"

Another shake of her head as if we were each speaking an alien language. "I cannot destroy the prions. That work will save our family. The family comes first. Always and forever. I may not agree with Marco, and I'll fight him until the end, but I would never betray the family."

After that, I gave up on trying to find any rational common ground and focused on finding the cure.

We spent the next two days together, poring over Tommaso's research. Francesca was truly brilliant. And truly insane. I was tempted to stay long enough to create a cure, hoping I could somehow steal it and destroy the prions before Francesca went through with her plan and released them, but once I realized that, like Tommaso's, her research was also a dead end, I knew I had to escape.

Knowing there was no cure made my decision to leave easier, although I wished there was a way I could destroy the prion research before I left. Although the lab was equipped with a fail-safe system that would unleash caustic lye and eradicate the prions, I couldn't break through the security to trigger it. If Francesca couldn't move forward with her plan to create a cure and release the prions without my stem cells, then better to leave now before she could harvest them. And before her brother came to steal them and unleash them on the world.

During my few days here, I'd noticed that the island had its own rhythm, especially during the predawn hours when even the worst of the insomniacs were quiet. There was a predictable traffic pattern of boats coming and going: fresh food came, trash left; clean linens shipped in, dirty laundry shipped out; wine and liquor arrived, recyclables departed.

Each morning, I'd watched the boats dock at the landing outside the gates, saw their clever use of small cranes to transfer prepackaged bundles to and from the dock, noted when and where the boats were left unattended, if even for a few seconds.

The boat operators weren't especially security conscious, not like the guards who never left the gates to the dock unsupervised. But if I could make it to a boat from the water, the view from the dock would be blocked by the cargo and the boat's hull.

All I had to do was find a way past the walls and bars and into the water.

It was Daniel who gave me my answer. During my exploration of the island, I'd happened upon an alcove on the first floor of the ancient monastery building with a display of very old glass bottles and vials. There were droppers, calibrated measuring tools, sealed jars of all shapes and sizes, even distillation vessels. Apothecary tools. Hand blown, some exquisitely delicate.

A memory from Daniel filtered through my vision: Francesca showing him this same display, explaining how for centuries the family had their own glass factory, creating the special equipment they needed to distill their venoms, creating both poisons and cures. She'd led him down a set of worn, stone steps, deep into a subterranean grotto carved out of the heart of the island. It was cool and damp, a constant stream of water circling in and out via a pristine tidal pond filled with crystal-clear water. Beside it were the ancient stone ovens used to forge the molten glass before it was blown, manipulated, and cooled in the water.

At the time, thirty-some years ago, the abandoned glass forge was their secret rendezvous site. Now, it was the start of my escape.

I waited until even with the irregular sleep-wake cycle of my fellow fatal insomniacs, the monastery had gone silent. It was just past four in the morning on the thirty-first. As I'd done on previous nights, I tossed and turned and finally left my bed to go into the bathroom and use the isolation tank—the one place where I'd be free of the EEG monitor and the ubiquitous surveillance cameras. I turned the lights off in the room, climbed into the tank for a few minutes, then with the lights off in the tank, climbed back out and redressed in the dark.

Knowing that I'd be going for a swim, I sealed a set of pajamas—the only clothing Francesca had allowed me—into a plastic bag stolen from the packaging of one of the EEG caps and slipped out of my room. The lights in the corridor were dimmed, and no one was around.

I hugged the wall and followed a path of what I hoped were blind spots from the cameras. It seemed they'd been designed and positioned more for patient safety—to make sure no one wandered into danger while disoriented from a fugue— than for security. Made sense. As Francesca had said, no one visited the island except family members suffering from fatal insomnia. Other than the lab, there was no need for any security. And it was pretty obvious that they'd never kept anyone prisoner here before. The only guards I'd seen during my time here were the men stationed at the main gate and the entrance to the lab.

I liked the idea of using their hubris against them and especially enjoyed the fact that Francesca's youthful indiscretions with Daniel Kingston were the path to my salvation. I followed the ancient stone steps down to the grotto where the glass-blowing furnaces sat empty, my footsteps disguised by the lapping of water in the tidal pool. It was the end of December, making hypothermia a definite risk, but I didn't have to swim very far. If I'd timed it right, I wouldn't be in the water for long.

I waded through the pool, shivering. The water was maybe fifty degrees at most. At the grotto's entrance, the water became deep enough for me to swim. I tied the plastic bag to my waist with a spare bathrobe belt, dived in, sputtered against the cold, and swam.

The dark water closed over my head, and I realized the one thing I'd forgotten to factor into my plan: the current.

Chapter 47

AT FIRST I panicked, allowing the greedy sea to smother me with its freezing embrace. The currents tugged at me, pulling me out to sea, no matter how hard I thrashed. Ryder's pendant bobbed up, but noticing it brought me the calm I needed to focus. That and a memory of my father teaching me and my baby sister to swim, coaxing us through our fear of the water.

I forced myself to relax, kicking only enough to keep my head above water. As I floated, I realized the current was doing the work for me—it flowed naturally around the island and was taking me toward the side where the dock was. Soon, I was treading water out of sight of the guards inside the gates, waiting for the first boat to arrive.

It was the laundry man. Perfect. As his crane clattered and squeaked, hoisting bales of fresh linen onto the dock, I swam to the side and pulled myself up over the gunwale. I lay on a bale of uniforms that stank of dead fish, hauling in my breath, shuddering with the cold. Finally, I pushed two bales apart, leaving just enough room for me to hide between them, and rolled down into the space, the laundry on either side hiding me from everyone except the occasional seagull flying directly overhead.

The boat pulled away without any sign of an alert from the

island. We chugged out onto the rollicking open water. I was surrounded by dirty linen, which hopefully meant no reason for anyone to come near my part of the boat. It was a tight fit for changing into my dry clothing, but I managed it before the boat docked at its next stop.

I waited past the island stops until the laundry boat docked at one of the hotels on the Grand Canal in Venice proper. Once we came to a stop, I raised my head up far enough to watch the boatman.

He must have been friends with the staff here at the Europa, because instead of immediately unloading his baskets of fresh linens, he waved a hearty greeting to someone out of sight on the dock and hopped off, disappearing through the staff entrance. I edged past the bales of laundry until I reached the side of the boat. Grabbing on to a cleat on the dock, I hoisted myself up and over, then duck-walked through the puddles covering the dock to the guest side of the terrace where only a knee-high ledge with planters of flowers separated the working dock from a dining area.

Two steps later and I was on the guest side of the wall and heading through the vacant dining room, out a set of double doors, through an empty ballroom, and into a large marble-floored hallway leading past the concierge desk into the main hotel lobby. A phone. I needed a phone and a place to hide—I was much too obvious in my silk pajamas and bare feet.

I found both behind the chest-high concierge desk. The clock on the phone said twenty after six—the Lazarettos would know I was gone by now and would be tracing the laundry boat's route. I hoped I hadn't gotten the boatman into too much trouble.

Behind the desk was a cloakroom and in the corner of that what appeared to be a lost and found. I stretched the phone cord as far into the cloakroom as possible and dialed Ryder. Had to hang up and do it twice until I got the country code correct. Not just one. Zero-zero-one.

By now I was shaking with fatigue and fear. I wrapped an abandoned pink and yellow flowered raincoat around me. It was two sizes too large, but I didn't mind—it was warm. I added a wool scarf to complete my disguise and hide my shaven head. No one had left any shoes behind, unfortunately.

Finally, Ryder answered. "It's me. Is it safe to talk?" I asked, not sure if his phone might be monitored. After what I'd seen of the Lazarettos' operations, I wouldn't put it past them.

"Rossi." His voice flooded with relief, as did my entire body. I sagged against the doorjamb, sliding to sit on the ground when my legs gave out. "Are you all right? Where are you?"

"I'm okay, but they're looking for me. I'm at a hotel called the Europa on the Grand Canal. That's Venice. Italy." How the hell was he going to get anyone here in time to help me? I was wasting precious time calling him—but I couldn't help myself. I needed to hear his voice. And warn him not to trust any deal they made with Francesca.

"We're not far," he replied.

"What? How?"

"Price. He tracked you to Venice, but after that, we lost you."

Men's voices came from the corridor. They sounded loud, angry—or maybe just Italian boisterous. It was hard to tell. They weren't close enough for me to understand anything they were saying.

I muted the phone but left the speaker on so Ryder could still hear. The footsteps grew louder, the marble floor making them sound like gunshots. Two men came into view: the boatman, talking very fast and gesticulating wildly, and Tyrone, who did not look happy, not at all.

"Tyrone's here," I whispered before sliding the phone back onto the ledge beneath the desk. Then I scuttled back into the cloakroom to hide behind the door, pressing my eye to the tiny opening between the hinges. I hated that I was essentially backed into a corner here—Ryder would have scoffed at my tactical position, but I didn't have much choice in the matter.

Tyrone and the boatman stopped in front of the desk, arguing, their voices raised until a man in a hotel uniform approached from the lobby, clearly asking them to lower their voices. The boatman shut up and sidled away as Tyrone spoke to the concierge, showing him something on his phone—a photo of me, I was certain since he ran his hand over his head as if to show the man I now had no hair.

The concierge shook his head vehemently. They leaned against the desk, not four feet away from me. I tried not to stare directly at Tyrone for fear that he would sense my presence, but when I looked away, I saw imprints of my wet, bare feet clearly visible on the marble floor behind the desk. I cringed and glanced around the small room for anything I could use as a weapon.

Ryder was on his way, I told myself. But that only made things worse, because then Tyrone would know he was here and might hurt him. I grabbed the nearest object as a weapon: a small, foldable pocket umbrella from the lost-and-found carton.

When I looked back through the slit between the hinges, I swallowed a gasp. Tyrone was leaning over the desk, fumbling on the ledge for something. If he turned his head, he would see that the phone's speaker indicator was lit.

The concierge took umbrage over Tyrone's trespass and practically slapped him away from his territory. He took a half step around the desk, grabbed a bowl of matchbooks, and offered it to Tyrone. When Tyrone took out his pack of cigarettes, the concierge shook his head and pointed to the door to the terrace, back the way Tyrone had come.

Tyrone grumbled and frowned, but the concierge held his ground, and he finally left. Probably to question the staff in charge of the dock.

My relief was short-lived as the concierge rounded the desk and seemed ready to start work. Where was Ryder? How long would it take him to reach me?

A man's voice called out from the main lobby. My heart sped. It was Devon. He was chatting up the desk clerks, playing the loud, ignorant tourist, and they were waving the concierge over to help.

I edged past the door as soon as the concierge disappeared into the lobby, using the desk to hide me as I scanned both directions. I looked up to see Ryder beckoning to me from a corridor on the other side of the lobby.

I fought not to stare at him. Not because of how bad he looked—he had a ball cap on, but nothing could disguise his black eyes, and he was much too pale.

All I wanted to do was spend the rest of eternity looking at him.

First, I had to focus on the job at hand. Cross the lobby without being spotted. Okay. Act natural. That was the best way not to draw attention. I drew my scarf up over my missing hair—slim disguise, but it was all I had—and strolled across the opulent lobby as if I belonged there.

Ryder backed up behind two swinging doors, watching me as he held one open. I crossed into the hallway, out of sight of the main lobby desk, through the doorway, and fell into his arms.

Chapter 48

RYDER BUNDLED ROSSI into his arms. He squeezed her tighter than he needed to, as if she was a wisp of a dream that a strong breeze would steal away. They needed to move, move now, now, now, before Tyrone returned with more men, but he couldn't help himself. He needed this. Just this moment. Not of passion or romance, but of relief. As if, finally, his heart was healed.

Too soon, he set her on her feet and took her hand. "Move quickly but with confidence. Two tourists out for a morning stroll."

She nodded, wrapped the scarf tighter around her head—Christ, what had they done to her?—and gamely kept pace with him despite her lack of shoes. He led her down the carpeted hallway to the steps, then down and out the fire exit that was hidden down a short corridor. Price had disarmed the alarm when they came in, so no worries there, but still, he went first and scouted the narrow, cobblestoned alley beyond.

No movement except a man pushing a cart away from them. Ryder beckoned to her, and they hurried down the alley. It was barely seven, the city just waking. He wished he could do something about her bare feet, but the best thing was to get her to safety, and they didn't have far to go.

"We're working from a flat Price rented under a dummy

name," he whispered as they skirted puddles and hurried along the cobblestones. He had to admit, Price and the Kingston fortune were coming in handy. "It's over near the opera house, just a few blocks away. Can you make it that far?"

She nodded, her eyes wide as they crossed the main thoroughfare and headed down a side street populated by restaurants and jewelry shops. A small bridge crossed over a canal, another short walk to the plaza where the stately opera house stood, then a right turn down an anonymous alley so narrow they could barely walk side by side.

Twelve seconds later, he'd unlocked a door with a polished lion's head doorknocker, and they were inside, safe and sound. Finally, he did what he'd been desperate to do since the last time he'd seen her.

He pulled her into his arms and kissed her. She reached her arms up to encircle his neck, and his ball cap tumbled to the ground. He slid his hands beneath the bulky raincoat she wore, exploring her body as if assuring himself that she truly was unharmed. Her scarf slid free as they finally parted.

"My God. What did they do to you?" he asked, tracing his lips over her shaven scalp. Leave it to Rossi to look even more beautiful without hair—although he would miss it. He loved how it fell, so silken against his chest when they made love, the way it cascaded and shimmered when she played her fiddle.

"I could ask you the same thing." She stretched a finger but didn't touch the surgical horseshoe of staples along his scalp.

"Not as good a job as when you stapled me together last month."

"Seriously, Ryder." Her tone grew stern. He loved it when she played doctor. "You shouldn't even be out of bed—"

"I'm fine." If fine included thundering headaches, vertigo, nausea, and ribs that tried to stab him with every breath. "Now that you're here."

She shook her head, but couldn't hide her smile. She kissed him again, gently. "I missed you."

"Easy fix for that." He wrapped his arms around her once again.

A key rattled in the lock. Ryder spun, reaching for the Beretta at his back. He pushed Rossi behind him.

"Don't mind me," Price said as he opened the door. Ryder cursed his lousy timing.

"Any sign of them?" Ryder asked, forcing himself to concentrate on the fact that they were still in enemy territory. Difficult to do with Rossi's body pressed against him in the narrow hallway.

"Yes, but nowhere near here. And before you ask, no, they didn't follow me." Devon shoved past Ryder to greet Rossi with open arms. "Angela." His tone started out triumphant but twisted into regret. He gave her a long hug, then pulled her down the hallway to the sitting room that overlooked the canal. "Guess you're one princess who doesn't need a Prince Charming to come to her rescue."

"Give her a break," Ryder said. "She's freezing. The bath is upstairs, and I brought clothing." He wanted to take her up himself, but he and Price needed to talk.

She curled up on an armchair big enough for only one, her coat wrapped around her as she shivered. "No. I need to tell you first."

"What?" Price asked, perching on the heavy coffee table in front of her.

Ryder hovered behind her, wanting to pluck her from the chair and take her upstairs, get her warm and in bed, but he shoved those protective instincts aside to focus on the mission. She was right. A debrief took priority over her comfort, as much as he hated to admit that.

By the time she finished telling her harrowing story, describing Francesca's plan, the containment lab where the lethal prions were stored, the island filled with dying family members, he couldn't help himself; he'd sat on the arm of the chair and curled his arm around her shoulders, refusing to let her go no matter how unprofessional it might be.

"We need to go back," she finished. "Destroy those prions."

"Major obstacles," Ryder delineated. "We can't let them grab Rossi again. That's numbers one through ten. Then we have getting past the guards and onto the island—"

"The grotto I escaped through."

"If they haven't tumbled onto the fact that you used it. Big if," Price put in, standing up and wandering around the room with its heavy antiques. He ended up at the other end, where a hall led past the kitchen to the front bedroom. Price held a hand up as if he'd just thought of an idea and vanished into the room.

"I'm actually not too worried about getting in," Ryder continued. "I have some ideas there. But once we're inside, we'll have the entire populace to deal with—"

"Most of them are sick, unarmed. We can't just go around shooting everyone."

"I understand. But that only gives the armed forces another advantage: human shields. Even beside that, our biggest obstacle—"

"The containment lab. The only person I saw able to access it was Francesca. The security system is keyed to her biometrics plus special codes on every control."

Price returned from the bedroom. "How'd you two like a late Christmas present?" he asked, pulling a phone from his pocket and waggling it before them.

"You have a program that can hack into the security and bypass it?" Ryder asked.

"Not quite that good, but almost. This phone was Tommaso's. I sent it to my Russian friends to break the encryption. They found a security app coded to his biometrics and aimed at one location."

"The containment lab."

"Bingo. They dug into the root code and retrieved the design's master override codes. And they reprogrammed it to my biometrics."

"Great." Rossi sat up, excited. "So you can destroy the lab?"

"Once I get my thumbprint onto one of the lab's scanners."

"Then we're in," Ryder said.

"We're in."

Chapter 49

I FELT WORLDS better after a hot shower and getting dressed in my own clothing. Ryder had left a tray with breakfast—heavy on the fruit and protein—along with my medication on a table in the bedroom. He'd arranged the blueberries and raspberries in the shape of a heart. The child-like innocence of the gesture in the midst of what we were facing made me laugh.

I was glad he hadn't waited for me to finish in the bathroom. As brittle as my emotions were, I would have cried instead of laughed if I'd had to face him. At the very least, we would have ended up on the massive four-poster bed with its thick, welcoming duvet and silk sheets. If that happened, I doubted if I'd have the strength to ever leave his arms.

Along with the breakfast tray was a tablet. I knew the time difference meant waking Louise, but I had to check on the children, so I took a chance that she was near her computer.

"Angie? You're all right." Louise's voice powered through the tablet's speakers once we were connected for a video chat. I lowered the volume. Her eyes grew wide. "Wow. Love the new look. Very Mad Max."

I rolled my eyes. Then sobered immediately. "I didn't get the cure—there isn't one. Not yet. Francesca said with my stem cells she could make one, but honestly, she's nuts. We're talking megalomaniac, I want to rule the world, James Bond villain level of wackadoo. And I looked at Tommaso's research—he was headed down a blind alley." I blew out my breath, hating to put into words my greatest fear. "Maybe there is no cure."

To my surprise, Louise actually grinned. She looked ghastly—her eyes were sunken with circles of exhaustion, and she looked like she'd lost weight in the short time since I'd seen her last. Add in her toothy grin and I almost had to look away from my friend.

"I wouldn't be so sure of that," she said. No trace of fatigue in her voice. In fact, she sounded downright jovial. "Francesca and the rest of your family might be round the twist, but they're also bloody genius when it comes to immunogenetics."

"Don't toy with me, Louise. What did you find?"

"It's not a cure. But," her voice upticked with excitement, "we have a definite treatment. Better than what Francesca shared with us."

"Really?" I hated the hint of desperation in my voice, but I was starving for some good news. "What is it?"

"Well...I can't take full credit. It's a combination of Francesca's and Tommaso's research, plus my clinical observations of your case progression, and Geoff, along with some of his geeky friends."

"Geoff? How did he help?" Louise's husband was a biostatistician, not a clinician. His work was in identifying epidemiologic trends, not treatments.

"Turned out fortuitous that Devon sent him and Tiff home to London. Because while Tiff and Grandmama have been burning through Geoff's inheritance, Geoff got a bit obsessed with Tommaso's research then shared it with some of his equally obsessive friends in the UK."

"Doctors?"

"Of a sort. Veterinarian immunogeneticists."

"Veterinarians?" Then it hit me. UK. Of course. "Studying mad cow disease."

"Exactly. They were fascinated by your particular mutation." She said it as if it was something to be proud of. "But realized that in addition to the prion genes, there's another genetic anomaly that you carry. Specifically, your genes that produce aquaporin are highly activated."

I blinked, trying to access memories about aquaporin but with no success. Tommaso must have never mentioned it to Leo. "ER doctor here. I don't speak gene-geek. Translation, please?"

"Aquaporin is the chemical in cerebrospinal fluid that washes away the detritus the brain's cells produce on a daily basis. It's most active during deep stages of sleep."

The brain's trash collector. "So it cleans up damaged proteins like prions? But in patients with fatal insomnia, not only are they making tons of prions, they're not sleeping, so their body never has the chance to flush the prions out?"

"Exactly. Given the severity of your genetic mutations, you should have been dead long ago. In infancy, from hydrocephalus caused by producing too much CSF, or killed by your fatal insomnia before you hit puberty."

She was still smiling, which freaked me out, but I knew that meant there was an upside coming. "But, because your body produces aquaporin both day and night, and it's not tied to the diurnal sleep cycle like in normal people, your fatal insomnia progressed more slowly and with less damage than expected. I suspect this is also why your symptoms improve after each of your fugues."

She was right. I hadn't thought of it before because the other side effects of the fugues were so unpleasant, but my actual fatal insomnia symptoms had improved—that had been how I'd been able to fight Leo last month. "My fugues are actually helping me?"

"Not as much as a good night's sleep or time in the isolation tank would, but yes. Now that you're controlling them, they're acting like a meditative state, which allows your aquaporin to work more efficiently. I need more EEG tracings to be certain, but that's my working theory."

I tried to wrap my head around the fact that my two potentially lethal genetic defects had not only canceled each other out but had combined to create a synergy that had brought me my unique gifts. "How does this translate into a treatment? I can't spend my days in the iso tank, and neither can the kids."

"We have drugs that can stimulate production of aquaporin. They're benign, little chance of side effects, and they should slow the progression. Again, not a cure. But I've begun the children on them, and we're already seeing improvement."

Finally, I allowed myself to relax and actually smiled at her. More than smile, I found myself blinking back tears. "The kids, they're going to be all right? At least until we can create a cure?"

"It's a short-term fix at best, and we still need to monitor them closely, but we bought ourselves some time." Typical Louise, the cautiously optimistic neurologist.

"Hang on, let me get Devon." I ran downstairs to the living room, where Devon and Ryder were huddled over Devon's laptop. "Devon, Louise needs to talk to you."

He leapt to his feet, almost knocking a coffee cup off the table, but Ryder caught it before it sloshed onto the computer. "Is it Esme? Is she okay?"

I handed him the tablet. "I'll let her tell you herself."

He hesitated before taking the tablet.

"It's good news," I assured him.

He took the tablet into the other room. A few moments later, a whoop of delight reverberated through the walls.

Ryder glanced up. He didn't say anything. He didn't need to—it was all in his face as he pulled me down to his lap and snugged his arms around me. "Told you to have faith."

"You did." I turned to him and kissed him. "Now all we need to worry about is stopping Francesca before she can unleash her prions on the rest of the world. And then get back home, find a real cure, and get it to the kids."

He froze. Just for an instant, but I felt it. "You don't want me to go. You want me to stay here, where it's safe, let you and Devon face them alone?"

"It is your DNA she needs," he replied in the reasonable tone of a general planning his strategy.

I jumped off his lap. "Neither of you have been there, know the layout. Plus, you don't have any medical knowledge. Not to mention the fact that I'm immune to the prions, and you aren't, so if anything, I should be going alone, leaving you behind."

Silence thudded between us. He took his time climbing to his feet, not looking at me, not looking anywhere as he gathered his ammunition.

Then he let loose with a barrage. "Just this once, will you listen to me? I mean, I know you have this grand idea that the only way to save the world is if you die. Right from the beginning, ever since that first night we met, seems like all you've done is run off to try to save everyone on your own, even if you might die trying. Well, that hasn't worked out so well, has it? You have to trust me. No one can do it all by themselves. Not even you. I know you want to protect me and everyone else; you think you're expendable, that you're dying anyway, so what's it matter? It does matter. You matter. And if you want to beat Francesca, if you want to stop this, then you have to stop trying to do everything yourself. You have to have faith. In you, in us. In a future."

He stole a breath, ready to argue over any protests I mounted.

I stood, unflinching. For once, I didn't duck for cover. I took it, listened, and examined each and every one of his arguments. Because I realized this was too important for me to let fear get in our way. Not my fear of dying—my fear of *him* dying, of losing him, of being left alone to live without him.

"This time, we do things my way," he continued. "This time, we do it together. I have a plan, and it's a damn good plan, but it won't work if all you do is rush in and kill yourself. What do you say? Are you in this with me, together?"

"Yes." As soon as the syllable escaped, a feeling of calm certainty came over me.

Not Ryder. His pacing stuttered—I'd caught him off guard. He spun to face me. "What? Just like that?"

"I was wrong. You were right." I smiled at his confusion, closed the distance between us, and reached a finger to his lips before he could protest. "I was wrong. I've screwed things up over and over because I keep trying to do them my way, alone. This is our last chance to get it right. So, what's the plan?"

Chapter 50

DEVON SPENT THE day putting the final polish on their plan while Angela rested and Ryder gathered their supplies. They were going to make their move on the island tonight. New Year's Eve.

As he sipped his coffee—no wine, not tonight—and looked out over the flat's rooftop terrace, Devon smiled as he remembered the look on Ryder's face when he learned that Venetians didn't usually celebrate the New Year with fireworks— a necessary part of his plan.

That was before Devon used the Kingston name and fortune to convince several cruise ships in port to host their own festivities and added a barge conveniently located near the Lazarettos' island, loaded with a generous supply of fireworks. A few lavish bribes took care of the rest.

Tonight was the last night that anyone would ever need to fear the Lazarettos. He, a bastard guttersnipe former gangbanger, was going to destroy them. The least they deserved after what they did to his Esme. And that bitch, Francesca? If he had the chance, he'd strangle her with his bare hands.

Devon savored the view of the opera house for another long moment before going back inside. Time to boogie-woogie, as Esme would say. Well, he'd never actually heard her say it, but it was the kind of thing he imagined a happy, healthy girl would say.

It was early afternoon back home. When he returned to his room, before changing into the wet suit Ryder had bought him, he called Flynn via video.

"Everything all right?" she asked by way of greeting.

"Yes, we'll be heading out in an hour. Just thought I'd say hi to Esme before I go."

Her smile was warm and genuine. Was she going soft on him?

"It snowed last night." She turned the phone around.

There was a moment of jostling, and he realized she was using a crutch to hobble over to the window. She'd moved the families from the tunnels to the Kingston brownstone—easier for Flynn while her leg was out of commission and less stressful on the parents. The tunnels had served their purpose, but as Flynn had argued when she called two days ago to inform him of her decision, kids need fresh air and sunshine.

"See her?" The view out the window was a winter wonderland. The children were laughing and tumbling through the snow. None of them freezing, no signs of the vacant stares he'd seen in them just a few days ago. "She's there, making a snow angel."

Devon couldn't label the feeling that washed over him. More than love or fatherly concern or joy...contentment? Was that what this warm glow centered in his chest was? Was this what normal people felt, watching their families while getting ready to leave for work, knowing that what they did would make their children proud, protect their loved ones?

He had no clue. He'd never felt it before.

Ozzie bounded into the camera's frame, rolling in the snow, destroying the carefully crafted snow angel as he toppled onto Esme. She laughed and hugged the dog, rubbing his belly.

"Want me to go get her?" Flynn's voice came through.

Devon swallowed hard. His grip on the phone tightened as if it was a lifeline.

"No." He choked on the word. "Let her play. Give her a kiss for me and tell her I said hi."

There was a pause. Flynn kept the phone aimed out the window at Esme. "Sure. No problem. Good luck tonight."

"Luck's got nothing to do with it." He ended the call before he could make a fool of himself, sagged down to sit on the bed. This was it. Tonight he saved his daughter—and all the other innocents Francesca Lazaretto threatened.

Tonight it ended.

🌙 ✳ 🌚

As we headed to the dock, the lights of dozens of boats crowded the Grand Canal. They came in all sizes and shapes, from sleek pleasure cruisers to yachts and sailboats, even several Chinese junks with distinctive square sails. All lit with colorful lights as they glided back and forth at the entrance to the city.

Despite the fact that it was still an hour before midnight, the intermittent pop of fireworks sounded throughout the city as celebrations for the New Year began. Tourists, no doubt, but every little bit helped our cause.

Devon guided us to the dock where the boat he'd rented was waiting—an old-fashioned teak-paneled pleasure craft common to Venice. Like Ryder and me, he wore a wet suit beneath his clothing. The main drawback to Ryder's plan was that we couldn't also wear bulletproof vests.

Ryder threw his gear bags onto the boat then helped me in. Devon took his place at the wheel, the engines roaring with eagerness. He turned to nod at Ryder, who threw off the lines then leapt on board. And we were off, moving slowly through the crowded waters of the lagoon.

We traveled in silence—there wasn't anything more to say. We'd spent all day going over our movements. While Devon steered the boat, I sat nestled in the warmth of Ryder's arms, reclining on the leather bench seat. The plan was simple: Devon and I would leave the boat near the grotto entrance, move into position, and wait for Ryder's diversion to draw the guards away from the lab to the dock.

Devon and I would enter the lab and trigger the security system's fail-safe that would destroy the prion samples. If that failed, Devon had brought plastic explosives and a detonator, but given the number of civilians on the island, that would be our last resort. We wanted to save lives, not take them.

Finally, the island with its distinctive watchtower came into sight. Like the others we'd passed, colorful holiday lights adorned its buildings and dock. The area near the grotto's entrance was on the far side, away from the dock, and lay in darkness.

Devon killed the engine, allowing the tide to drift us close to the inlet. Neither he nor I knew how to dive, so we wanted to keep our swim as short as possible. Ryder would take the boat out farther, out of range of any searchlights from the island, and anchor it before using his scuba gear to swim undetected to the dock.

"Be careful," he told us as he exchanged positions with Devon, taking the wheel. "They've had enough time to secure the grotto."

"If they figured out that's where Angela escaped from," Devon put in as he stripped off his clothing.

"Don't risk anything on ifs. You see someone, you assume they're armed and take them down." He was talking to Devon but staring at me. I was the weak link—unarmed, defenseless. I hated that, wished they'd let me go by myself, but only Devon could use Tommaso's phone with its reprogrammed biometrics.

Devon hoisted the dry bag with his pistol, ammunition, and cell phone secured inside and nodded to Ryder. We blended into the night with our black wet suits and hoods. I stood on my tiptoes, bracing my arms on Ryder's shoulders, and kissed him thoroughly.

"Just to remind you of what you'll be missing if you don't come back," I whispered, wishing I knew how to tell him what I felt. If I'd had my fiddle, I could have shown him with my music; words made for a poor substitution.

He had by far the most dangerous job, playing decoy with at least seven armed men, but he didn't seem worried at all. Instead, he smiled, his expression calm and confident.

"Have faith." He kissed me on the forehead, then winked. "See you soon."

Devon slipped over the side and into the water with a quiet splash. I followed. The water was cold but, thanks to the wet suit, nothing like my swim when I'd first escaped. We stroked toward the inlet leading to the grotto. Behind us came the low growl of the boat heading back out to sea.

The tide was at its peak—Ryder had timed it that way. It would turn while we were on the island and be headed out when we left. He'd been as meticulous in planning our escape as he was in preparing our arrival, including outfitting Devon with a pistol equipped with a suppressor.

Devon waved me to wait behind the rocks at the cavern's entrance while he scouted inside. He unpacked his pistol and cell phone in its waterproof case from the dry bag, slipped free of his fins, and silently waded through the tidal pool into the grotto. I watched anxiously, barely able to make out the deeper dark of the entrance from the shadows of the rock face surrounding it.

A sudden explosion followed by a series of booms startled me. The sky above me lit up—fireworks from the barge Devon had hired. Midnight. Ryder's diversion, right on schedule.

"Angela," Devon whispered urgently. "Come on."

The light from the fireworks helped me to see him. I waded through the water to join him. He reached a hand and helped me to step free from the pool onto the stone ledge where the old glass furnaces stood. Two bodies were crumpled against the wall of the nearest furnace, their blood dark against the stone. They weren't guards—at least not from the group I'd seen earlier—but they both had machine pistols.

"Francesca must have brought in reinforcements," I told Devon.

"More likely Tyrone. So much for the element of surprise."

I wished we could let Ryder know, but we'd decided against using radios or phones—Ryder hadn't been able to get encrypted, secure ones on such short notice, and given the Lazarettos' resources, he wasn't sure that even military equipment wouldn't be compromised. But, if everything went according to plan, we wouldn't need them.

Devon and I skirted the shadows, leaving the grotto by way of the ancient staircase carved into the island's bedrock. At the top, I waited while he used the security override on Tommaso's phone to cut the security cameras in the corridor leading to the courtyard. As soon as we reached the next safe area to take cover, he turned them back on, hopefully before anyone noticed the lapse.

"The civilians are all on the top floor, watching the fireworks," he whispered as he scrolled through the camera feeds on his phone. "We're clear down here."

We jogged down the hall, the only trace of our passing our wet footsteps. When we reached the courtyard entrance, we waited in the shadows behind the columns. Now it was up to Ryder.

Chapter 51

RYDER BRACED HIMSELF against an algae-slicked piling as he shrugged free of his dive tank and regulator. The fireworks made for an even better distraction than he'd anticipated.

He swung up to look over the edge of the dock. The nearest guards were the two sentries just inside the gate, both with their necks craned to watch the fireworks instead of the water. Perfect.

Bobbing back down, he skirted the dock along with the motorboat docked there and swam to the seawall, using its irregular surface and the high tide to buoy him so that he could reach the far inside corner of the concrete pier. Shaking off the water, he pushed his back against the wall, and weapon ready, he sidled until the gate was immediately to his right, the guards just beyond. He didn't need to get inside the gate that protected the compound. All he needed was to get their attention as well as the attention of the guards across the courtyard at the lab.

Which meant no suppressor on his MP5. With one final glance at his watch, right on schedule, he envisioned the position of the guard farthest from him—the one who would have a line of sight on Ryder first. Then he swung free of the shadows and opened fire.

RYDER'S ATTACK DREW the guards from the lab. Two ran out right away. Devon held me back as two more joined in the battle. When the coast was clear, we ran across the courtyard. I couldn't stop thinking of Ryder, outnumbered six to one.

Even more infuriating was knowing that he'd laugh at the odds. Men.

Tommaso's phone got us through the main doors. I led the way to the containment lab.

"You need to wait here," I told him at the heavy glass door. "I'm immune, you aren't."

He nodded and unlocked the door for me. I sprinted to the inner lab pod, cycling through another set of doors until I reached the freezer holding the prions. The plan was for me to remove the prions from the freezer so that they'd be directly exposed to the caustic lye sprinklers. Then Devon would activate the fail-safe to trigger them.

I yanked on the freezer door. Nothing. Then I noticed the biometric security pad beside it. Damn it. I waved to Devon to join me. To his credit, despite his lack of immunity, he didn't hesitate.

"I need your thumbprint," I told him, gesturing to the pad.

Before he could unlock the freezer, two guards entered the containment lab from the far end of the room, looking around. I ducked down behind the waist-high freezer, pulling Devon with me. We had a few seconds before they'd move to where they could spot us.

Devon reached a cautious hand up to place his thumb on the biometric lock. The click of the freezer opening sounded louder than the fireworks outside.

"Alto!" a man shouted.

"Hurry," Devon told me as he popped up to fire on the guards.

"I'm trying." Gingerly, I scooped racks of glass vials into my arms. They rattled together, the glass making a tinkling noise, and I froze, trying to steady my hands.

"Angela!"

A third guard had entered from behind us, attempting to sneak up on us. Glass flew around me as he shot through the pod's glass walls.

Devon launched his body to cover mine. We collided into a lab bench, broken glass scattering in our wake. He rolled me to the ground and shoved me beneath the steel bench as bullets pinged the metal surface.

All I could see was his back as I cringed against the sound of bullets ricocheting off of metal. How did people ever get used to this?

"Don't they care about unleashing the prions?" he shouted as he returned fire. The guard who tried to ambush us from behind slumped to the floor, motionless.

"They're immune."

Over his shoulder, I saw one of the first two men fall. The other cried out in pain. Devon kept shooting until the last man also dropped. Finally, Devon turned to me, giving me room to crawl free. His face was bleeding, and there were slivers of glass caught in the flesh of his scalp, arms, and hands, piercing the fabric of his wet suit.

"Devon," I exclaimed in dismay as I realized where the shards had originated. When he'd tackled me, he'd landed on top of the prion specimens. I plucked two glass splinters free from his arm before he shook me off.

"Yeah. Guess there's no immunity for friends of the family?"

All I could do was shake my head. "The treatment might work—"

"Go. Get out of here before more of them come." He replaced the magazine in his pistol.

"What about the prions?" I couldn't see a single intact container in view. The prions had been dispersed all over the lab. Not just mine, but the far more deadly ones from Francesca's earlier experiments. Now we had no choice but to use the caustic lye. But how to decontaminate Devon?

He stood and pulled me to my feet. "The self-destruct will take care of them. Just like it did at Tommaso's lab back home."

Hard to believe that was only a few nights ago. We made it to the thick glass door leading into the main corridor. He pulled it open for me, ever the gallant. As I passed through it, I spotted movement back the way the guards had come from, across the lab. "Look out!"

Devon shoved me through the door and whirled, leaning his back against the door, closing it. Shots rang out. I saw his body shudder, knew he was hit. I tried to open the door to get to him, but his weight pushed against it as he fired at the new threat: another guard.

"Lock it down," he called as he reloaded.

"No. Not with you inside." A bullet smashed against the glass. A star-shaped crack formed across its surface. Then another one. Devon dropped down, his back against the door. A smear of blood followed his movement. "Devon, come on. Get out of there."

I tried to push the door open, but his weight was still against it. The bullets kept coming, but he wasn't returning fire.

"Let me in," I shouted. "You need help."

He turned to face me, his expression grim. Now I saw what he was doing instead of firing back; he'd been dialing Francesca's code into the security app, the one that communicated with the fail-safe mechanism. I threw all my weight against the door, but he'd already locked it.

"Devon, no!" I cried, pressing my palm against the glass, pleading with him. "It's not too late. You don't have to do this."

"If I open that door, he could get out and spread the prions. Or, God forbid, now that they're in me, I could. I couldn't face that. I won't."

He pressed another button on the phone then reached up to place his thumb against the security pad. "Tell Esme—" Thick yellow liquid sprayed from above. "Hell, don't tell her anything. She's better off not knowing."

"Devon—" I was sobbing now as the caustic lye rained down, bringing with it clouds of destruction. His phone fell to the ground.

He shuddered in pain, a gasp escaping him. "Don't watch, Angela. Please, go—"

His wet suit smoldered where the lye ate away at the fabric. He covered his face, already red, the flesh slipping down in awful ribbons of blood, and turned his back to me.

"Devon," I choked on his name.

He raised his arm. A final gunshot impacted the glass, bringing with it blood mixed with brain tissue and bone.

I couldn't help it, I banged on the door, tears clouding my vision as much as the yellow haze of smoke filling the room beyond the glass. So typical. Leaving this world on his own terms. He'd died to save me, to save us all.

A man's hand grabbed my arm, yanking me to my feet. Tyrone. He circled his arm around my shoulder, jabbed a pistol to my neck.

"You're going to answer for this."

I struggled with him, not wanting to leave Devon. My mind

was clouded with emotions, and that final gunshot kept playing over and over. I spun toward Tyrone and slapped him as hard as I could.

It was stupid. Not an act of aggression—if I'd wanted to do serious harm, there were plenty of other places I could have hit him more effectively. At that moment, I simply needed to give voice to my rage, to my sorrow. If I'd still had the hand grenade from our fight in the tunnels a few nights ago, I surely would have used it instead.

I would have gone out on my own terms, finishing this once and for all. Like Devon had.

My slap barely rocked Tyrone. He actually laughed at me, then struck me backhanded, sending me reeling into the opposite wall.

We hadn't defeated Francesca, not while she still had access to one more source of a transmissible prion mutation: me.

Tyrone grabbed me, twisting my arm back and up until a yelp of pain escaped me as he dragged me down the hall to the stairs to the courtyard.

"Mother wants you alive," Tyrone muttered into my ear over the clatter of equipment falling and melting in the lab beside us. "But she doesn't *need* you alive. She can finish her work by harvesting DNA from your corpse."

I couldn't help my fear. Had Devon's sacrifice been in vain? It should have been me inside that lab with him. Then everyone else would be safe, the prions destroyed—including the ones inside me. Now I had to find another way. My fingers brushed against Ryder's pendant. I could do this. I had to.

I was out of choices, and the world was running out of time.

Chapter 52

THE NICE THING about providing a diversion was that Ryder didn't have to worry too much about his aim, although the professional in him still kept score as he downed the first guard at the gate. This job was about attracting attention to bring the enemy to him and away from Rossi and Price.

Once several more guards had arrived, he ducked back against the seawall, giving them no line of sight. Didn't stop them from shooting, which was fine by him. He reached into his dry bag for his flashbang grenades and lobbed two over the wall above him.

He'd also brought a few real grenades, just in case Price and Rossi failed and it came down to him to take care of the lab. No way in hell was anyone else going through what the Lazarettos had subjected Rossi and those kids to. Period.

He counted to four, the flashbangs went off, and he spun back to aim through the wrought-iron gates at the disoriented men on the other side. Three more down—wounded was better than dead because it took manpower to help them to safety. At least that's how it'd worked in every other battle Ryder had been in. But not here.

The Lazarettos ignored their fallen comrades, despite the fact that Rossi had said everyone here was family. They simply stepped over them and kept shooting. Ryder wished he'd gone for kill shots.

Despite Price's fancy tech, an alarm must have sounded at the lab, because two more men separated from the eight that Ryder had engaged and ran inside. He brought the enemy's numbers down to three—a feat easier than it sounded given that he had superior cover and the gate they defended limited their line of fire.

A mechanical whine made it through the booming in his ears as the gates opened. He cautiously edged forward around the wall, just enough to take a look to see what they had planned.

A woman stood in the center of the courtyard, totally exposed and totally unconcerned. She was taller than Rossi but with the same dark hair and regal cheekbones. This had to be Francesca Lazaretto.

She was unarmed and Rossi's mother, but still, Ryder raised his weapon, taking aim.

She beckoned to someone nearby. Tyrone Lazaretto dragged Rossi into view, holding her as a human shield.

"Game's over, Detective Ryder," he called out. "You lose. Again."

☽ ✺ ☾

I TUGGED AGAINST Tyrone's arm around my neck, enough to breathe and find my voice. "We did it," I shouted to Ryder, knowing he'd get the message. "We destroyed the lab."

Only the muzzle of his gun and a sliver of his face was visible from behind the stone pillar that anchored the gate into the seawall. He nodded his understanding, his expression grim.

We'd talked about this, that no matter what happened, the Lazarettos could not take me alive again. He raised his gun, aiming at me and Tyrone. But then, suddenly, Ryder froze. His face twisted in a look of anguish.

He stepped forward, his hands raised, his gun hanging uselessly across his chest. Another step and I could see the man behind him holding a pistol to Ryder's back. Two more men stepped inside the courtyard, one on either side of Ryder, followed by a fourth man. He carried no weapons and was dressed in an elegant designer suit. His black hair was slicked back, the fireworks overhead making it glisten with light.

"Marco," Francesca spat out her brother's name.

"Francesca." He gave her a nod. "I knew that if I forced a deadline on you, you'd finally reveal your hand. Hand the Vessel over to me. Now."

Tyrone tensed behind me and I realized that Ryder wasn't looking at me, but instead had made eye contact with him. Suddenly, Ryder dropped to the ground, kicking the legs out from the man behind him. Ryder came up shooting, taking out that man and the next closest one, while Tyrone finished off the third.

Marco appeared shocked. He turned back toward the dock where the rest of his men still waited. Tyrone let me go and trained his weapon on Marco, who froze. Ryder darted through the gates. More gunfire followed.

Marco flinched and stared at Tyrone, his mouth opening as if ready to bargain his way out of this. Before he could say anything, another shot sounded. Not from Tyrone. It was Francesca who fired.

I jumped, startled. Marco blew out his breath as if sighing, then fell to his knees. I ran toward him. He'd been shot in the left chest—almost directly over the heart.

"Stop," Francesca ordered me, her voice slicing through the sound of the fireworks overhead and the residual echo of gunfire. I ignored her, dropping to Marco's side. I reached out a hand to touch him, but Tyrone yanked me away and back onto my feet.

Francesca marched over to me, frowning at Tyrone as if disappointed in his inability to kill Ryder when he had the chance, and grabbed me. She held a small pistol to the back of my neck.

"Lower your weapons," she called out as she prodded me forward, toward the dock. All I could hope was that Ryder was the one left standing on the dock and not Marco's men. Tyrone took up position on one side of the gate, covering us as we crossed through it.

Ryder stood alone on the dock, the bodies of two more men at his feet. His eyes narrowed when he saw us, and I knew he wanted to shoot Tyrone.

"Put the gun down," Francesca commanded. "Now."

I shook my head at Ryder, despite Francesca digging the pistol into my spine. I wanted him to shoot me, dive into the sea, and swim to safety. He frowned in silent argument, unslung the machine gun, and set it on the ground.

He must have a plan, I told myself. Ryder would never give up. And he'd promised me that he'd never let Francesca use me to hurt anyone else. Last resort, he'd said. He'd do it, if it was the last resort.

"Very good." Francesca kept me moving.

I purposely chose a path that placed us between Tyrone and Ryder, hoping it would give Ryder time to make a move and keep Tyrone from shooting him.

Tyrone, of course, did not cooperate, joining his mother and me as we passed through the open gate and onto the dock. Now Ryder no longer had the cover of the wall for protection.

"Shoot him," Francesca ordered, shoving me toward the boat bobbing in the water.

"With pleasure, Mother."

I threw an elbow at Tyrone, but Ryder was already moving. He lunged at Tyrone, knocking him to the ground while I struggled to free myself from Francesca. She could have shot me, but she didn't. Instead, she slammed the pistol against the side of my head.

Reeling, I stumbled toward the edge of the dock. Fireworks boomed above us, competing with the ringing in my ears and the stars that exploded through my vision as I tried to shake my head clear again.

Francesca grabbed my arm, trying to haul me with her to the boat tied up at the dock. I pulled back, hard, lost my balance, and fell against the edge of the jetty, pain lancing through my arm as it hit the concrete.

I tumbled into the water, taking her with me, just as I heard another gunshot from the dock.

As the water swallowed us, I heard Ryder call my name. I was still disoriented from the blow to the head, but Francesca wasn't—she was clawing at me, trying to get her arm around my neck.

I couldn't tell if she was trying to drown me or save me, but instincts took over, and I fought back. The pain crashing through my arm was overwhelming, leaving me reeling with nausea. It was broken, useless.

We kept falling down, down into the dark depths. The water here was much deeper than on the other side of the island where the grotto was. I had no idea how far down it went, but the lights above had vanished, leaving us in complete darkness.

Francesca's hands slid down my body—she had sunk farther down, was now clutching at my waist, tumbling me backward, off-balance.

I kicked free of her, but before I could decide which way

was the surface, she bobbed up far enough to grab at my ankle. It was impossible with one arm for me to stroke hard enough to break her grip. I felt myself sliding down, stars bursting overhead—I wasn't sure if they were fireworks or the lightning strikes of dying brain cells coloring my vision.

Desperate, I bent over, my arm screaming in pain at the movement, and slid my fingers between my ankle and Francesca's hand. Her face turned up, but her eyes were not filled with panic or even fear. Instead, they met mine with imploring desperation.

When I heard her voice inside my head, I realized: She was dying. Was her last wish to see me dead as well?

No, she called to me as we tumbled together in the void that accompanied death. *You must live. You're their only hope. You must save our family. Save them all.*

Bubbles streamed from her mouth as her lips went slack. Still, her eyes stared at me, refusing to yield.

Her hope and yearning filled me as her memories rushed in with a shuddering force. With it came her hatred of her brother, of her father, and the other Lazarettos who had used her and her people, my people, the afflicted.

Her hate didn't burn. Rather, it was something insidious, oily as it clung and slithered and seeped into vulnerable crevices. I wanted no part of her life or the memories that had turned her into the monster she'd become. But, as with the others whose lives filled my mind, I had no choice.

Please, she begged as the darkness swept through her. *Save them. Then destroy the rest.*

The blackness tore at her, shredding her voice. She screamed in fury but finally surrendered to the void.

I tried to hold on to her, had some random hope of saving us both, but her body was too heavy, dragging me down with it. Finally, I released her to the depths, her gaze unseeing, filled with a lifeless stare, until the dark water consumed her body.

My chest was on fire, my mind black with the desperate need to breathe, my energy spent. I kicked halfheartedly up toward the stars blazing across the blackness above me. Thought of Ryder and kicked harder, trying to use my good arm. But it was no use. Gold, silver, blazing red rippled across the world over me, out of reach.

I felt a strange peace as my body sank.

Finally, after so many days of silence, music wove its magic, cloaking me in silken threads of joy. My father. Singing. For me and only me. A true memory. My memory. Not stolen or ripped from a dying mind.

Dance, Angela, he coaxed me. *Feel the music. Dance.*

I kicked my feet in time with his tune. It was one he'd created special just for me—a duet for the fiddle and concertina. He called it "The Wanderer's Jig." Suddenly, the pain left my body as I remembered the chords, felt my fingers press against my bow, my knees bouncing, toes tapping, entire body swaying alongside my father. I smelled his breath and sweat, that earthy masculine scent that meant home and safe haven.

And I danced. As I moved, Ryder's pendant broke free of my wet suit, floating before my eyes, its tree of life glowing in the darkness as if it had come alive.

Light shattered the blackness around me, a roaring thunder filling my ears, threatening to drown out our music. The stars were so close I could almost touch them, yet so far away. Too far.

My questing hand forgave the stars and settled on Ryder's pendant, clasping it with my last remaining strength.

A black streak rippled through the water, and a man's hands grabbed me by my waist as if to twirl me, join in on our jig. I turned and smiled. It was Ryder, of course.

Why did he look so frightened?

We crashed into the cold night air, the sky a spectacle of color, the crack and boom of the fireworks echoing across the water. I leaned back in Ryder's arms, let him do the work as I fought to simply breathe and he pulled us both to shore.

"Thank you, Papa," I whispered to the stars. I closed my eyes, Ryder's warmth thawing me, and felt certain that my father heard.

Chapter 53

THANKS TO DEVON'S boat and cash, they made a clean getaway.

Rossi didn't have her passport yet, but neither of them could face going back to Devon's flat to pack his things, so after a visit to the hospital, where they'd gotten her arm X-rayed—two bones, clean break—and a cast, Ryder booked them into a hotel on the Grand Canal. He was probably out of a job, so should have been watching his budget, but after what they'd just been through, he figured they deserved a treat. Still, he wasn't prepared for the opulence—he counted five different types of marble in the lobby alone, which was large enough to host a cotillion and had gold-leaf patterns swirling across the ceiling that appeared handcrafted.

Their room was equally stunning, including a terrace that faced the water. With the French doors open, a light breeze stirring the gauze curtains, their view from the bed was of a gorgeous domed basilica.

While Rossi contacted Louise, he called Flynn, broke the news about Devon's death.

"He was ready," she said in her usual heartless fashion. "After he left, I found his will. He named you the executor and COO of Kingston Enterprises. Rossi gets half, Esme the other half, and he named me her guardian."

Ryder shook his head in a silent chuckle. Flynn wasn't even old enough to vote. "He made the right choice. You'll do right by Esme."

She made a choking noise. Emotion? From Flynn? "Thanks." She hung up.

"Sure you don't need a doctor?" he asked Rossi after she'd finally finished talking with Louise, instructing her on her ideas for a new fatal insomnia cure she'd devised from the information she'd taken from Francesca's mind. "We can go back to the hospital."

She smiled wanly at him, her dark eyes so sunken they made her face appear bruised. "I am a doctor. No, I just need some rest."

"Is Louise sending her treatment? Because it will take you a while to actually make the cure, right?"

"She's sending it along with my passport. I can wait."

He disagreed but had learned the hard way not to argue.

"If it works on the kids, it will work on you, too, right?" Damn, he'd been trying not to ask, hated forcing her to answer, but he was tired of hidden truths. From here on out, it would be the two of them, together, facing whatever. To do that, he had to know everything.

"Yes, but it's not a cure—my brain has more areas of vacuolization than the children suffered. Even the cure can't fix the damage already done. It will just stop the disease from progressing." Vacuoles. Those freaky empty areas that made her MRI look like slices of Swiss cheese.

"So you'll still—"

"Have access to memories? Yes." She reached for his hand with her good one, taking care not to jostle her arm in the cast propped on a stack of pillows. She leaned back against him on the bed as the sunrise filled the sky with ribbons of ruby etched

318

against the indigo night.

"And I'll still have fugues. But now I'm in control." She raised her hand to the Pashtun pendant he'd given her. "Maybe we can use Devon's legacy to do some good with the Kingston money. Like hunt down the rest of my family. There are more of them out there. Who knows what they're plotting?"

"More prion diseases?" He fought a shudder.

She thought for a moment, her face going vacant, and he knew she was searching Francesca's memories. "No. Not prions. But they've been stealing secrets and treasures and fortunes for so long... It's not going to be easy."

"I'm up for it. If you are."

She yawned and patted his arm, snuggling up against him. "How about if we start with home? Clearing out the corruption and making it a safe place for Esme to grow up?"

"Now you're talking my language. There's so much waste—we could turn the Tower into a model of community cooperation, like Devon envisioned. And if we can clean up the mayor's office and city council, then the police and DA will be easy. Maybe we could—"

Her head nodded against his shoulder. "Ryder," she murmured, "would you do me one favor?"

"Sure, anything."

"Shut up so I can get some sleep."

Laughter rippled through him as he wrapped his arms around her and pulled her closer. She was asleep within seconds.

"We saved the world, you and I," he whispered as he lay there, wide awake, staring out the window at the stars surrendering to the light. "But for us, the best is yet to come." He kissed the top of her head. "Sweet dreams, Rossi."

ABOUT THE AUTHOR

Pediatric ER doctor turned *New York Times* bestselling thriller writer CJ Lyons has been a storyteller all her life—something that landed her in many time-outs as a kid. She writes her Thrillers with Heart for the same reason that she became a doctor: because she believes we all have the power to change our world.

In the ER she witnessed many acts of courage by her patients and their families, learning that heroes truly are born every day. When not writing, she can be found walking the beaches near her Lowcountry home, listening to the voices in her head and plotting new and devious ways to create mayhem for her characters.

CJ has been called a "master within the genre" (Pittsburgh Magazine) and her work has been praised as "breathtakingly fast-paced" and "riveting" (Publishers Weekly) with "characters with beating hearts and three dimensions" (Newsday).

Her novels have twice won the International Thriller Writers' prestigious Thriller Award, the RT Reviewers' Choice Award, the Readers' Choice Award, the RT Seal of Excellence, and the Daphne du Maurier Award for Excellence in Mystery and Suspense.

To learn more about CJ's Thrillers with Heart go to www.CJLyons.net

EDGY READS